The Flight of the *Silver Vixen*

THE FLIGHT
of the
SILVER VIXEN

By Annalinde Matichei

The Sun Daughter Press

Other books by
THE SUN DAUGHTER PRESS
(The Feminine Publishing Company)

The Gospel of Our Mother God
The Feminine Universe by Alice Lucy Trent
Sappho: One Hundred Lyrics ed. Sushuri Madonna-chei
Enter Amelia Bingham by Geneviève Falconer

The Flight of the Silver Vixen
Published by
THE SUN DAUGHTER PRESS

First edition MMXI

© MMXI Annalinde Matichei

Contents

Chapter 1

The Wide Black Yonder

SULALINDE SASHARA was the most gorgeous blonde on the base. At least many brunettes thought so. Fleetsoldier Anna Candret certainly thought so. She watched Sashara-chei leave every evening, past the checkpost and into her sleek red Sepharilla. How many blondes drive a Sepharilla? That girl was really something.

"Still crushin' on the Commodore's secretary?" asked Velenthe.

"Just watching her is all."

"She's worth watchin'. But she'd never go for an ordinary fleet-brunette like you."

"I was just watching her: that's *all*. And you're late."

"Not by my watch."

"You set your watch to any time that suits you."

Velenthe grinned. She was a tall fleet-brunette on exchange from Dendreline. She looked ridiculously dashing in the uniform and knew it. "It's my watch, ain't it?"

"You pulled the graveyard patrol again? Someone doesn't like you, Velenthe."

"Suits me fine. I like to stroll around the base in the crepuscular hours. I like the moonlight and the quiet and the long sultry nights. I like keepin' an eye on things when there's nothin' to keep an eye on. My kind of work. No work. I often wonder why we have to guard this place at all."

"The demon ever waits," quoted Fleetsoldier Candret sententiously.

"Well, it's been waitin' a good long time. For all its reprehensible qualities, that ol' demon sure ain't lackin' in patience. Reckon it'll still be waitin' when I'm dead an' gone."

"You ready to take the grand tour of the perimeter fence?"

"Lovely evenin' for it."

They headed out through the lightly wooded perimeter of Ushasti Fleet-Base. The sun was low in the sky now, and the air starting to cool a little from the intense heat of the southern day. The sensereli were chirping in the trees.

7

They had not been walking long before they came to a section of the wire perimeter fence that had been cut away.

"Now who do you reckon would'a done that?" asked Velenthe.

"So much for your quiet night," said Candret.

And as if to underscore her words in the most literal way, the quiet of the evening was broken by a mechanical hiss. The entry ramp of one of the ships was opening.

Running, the two fleetsoldiers followed the sound. It was Her Majesty's Aethyr-Ship *Silver Vixen*, a new experimental craft designed for maximum speed and striking power in a relatively small size and with minimal crew. This was the Aethyr-Vikhar's pet project.

The entry ramp was down. The fleetsoldiers drew their weapons and approached it cautiously. Suddenly there was the roar of a revving engine and a wild whoop. A hoverbike came speeding down the ramp, nearly bowling the guards over. It was ridden by a teenage brunette brandishing a streaming banner.

"Don't shoot, it's human!" commanded Candret. "It's some kid. She's taken the ship's pennant."

Pennant raids were not unknown. They usually took place between rival cadet ships. But stealing the pennant from an experimental super-ship was something new.

"Crazy biker kids. Let's get after her."

The fleetsoldiers rushed to the stand, mounted two of the guard hoverbikes, and set off after the thief, through the cut fence and onto the open and deserted roads of the lower Ushasti region. The hoverbikes issued to the Fleet Guard were military-tuned Chandras, faster than anything available on the open market. The thief had a custom-tuned bike that was pretty zippy, but not up to military standards. As the sky took on the violet hue of early evening, the gap between pursuers and pursued steadily closed. Finally they ran her off the road by the side of Lake Ushasti.

"Hand over the pennant," said Fleetsoldier Candret.

The teenage brunette gave it to her with a courteous flourish and a deep bow. She was wearing a black leather jacket and matching skirt, high, slender protective boots, and black leather gloves. She had no helmet, and her mid-length raven hair was wind-blown wild, but her burgundy lipstick and dark brown eyeliner were immaculate.

"Did you really think you could outrun the Royal Novaryan Aethyr Command, *khindi*?" asked Fs. Candret.

"No," replied the teen, smiling pleasantly. "I thought I could give you ten minutes' run for your money, but I only managed eight. You're good."

"Yeah, we'll do till good comes along," said Fs. Velenthe.

"Still, eight minutes does the trick," said the teen, grinning even more broadly.

"What trick?" asked Fs. Candret.

"Can't tell you just yet," said the teen.

"Get on the back of my bike," said Fs. Candret. "You're coming back to base. You'll talk to the Aethyr-Vikhar."

"What about my Chandra?"

"Lock her down. You won't be using her for a while."

The teenager made a few finger gestures on her hand-transceiver, and her hoverbike's systems locked down. A fine mist surrounded it, emanating from several tiny nozzles, and rapidly hardened into a weatherproof coating that cling-wrapped the bike and took on the coloring of the grass verge on which it was parked.

"And now," said Fs. Candret, "if you would care to———"

The air was filled with a strange and distinctive chirruping hum. It was a sound the fleet guards had heard before. The sound of the new experimental ship's hyperthrust engines. They turned back in the direction of the base to see the *Silver Vixen* rising slowly into the magenta sky.

"About that trick," said the teen brunette. "I can tell you now."

THE crew-concourse of the *Silver Vixen* was occupied by five teenagers: three elegant blondes and two brunettes in black hoverbike gear. One of the brunettes, tall, with Eastern features, clearly dominated the room with her energy and personality. Her lips were painted crimson, her almond eyes highlighted with jet black liquid liner. Her hair was swept in the dashing front quiff adopted by many bikers, with one strand calculatedly out of place. Her name was Antala FiaMartia, and very few people who heard it ever forgot it.

Just as raiAntala stood out among the brunettes as the clear leader and dominant force, so one figure stood out among the blondes; not by her energy or her overwhelming personality, but by a quiet yet absolute regality in her bearing. That bearing, it is true, was outwardly little different from that of any other member of an aristocratic teenage hoverbike gang. Nonetheless, it was firmly underpinned by the knowledge that the solar Blood Imperial flowed in her veins: a knowledge that was in all circumstances inseparable from effortless power, but by the same token was never more than a step from the heavy burden of fundamental responsibility.

The Princess Mela was also Estrenne in features, and, as with most Estrenne blondes, her hair was as stark white as raiAntala's was jet black. She wore a simple flare-skirted day-dress somehow as if it had been a robe of state. This unconscious regality was more marked today than usual, because, for all that this hijacking was no more than a prank, it was also the distant and playful echo of a State occasion.

RaiAntala made a military-style salute, touching her right arm to her left shoulder, and dropped gallantly onto one knee.

"The ship is yours, Your Highness," she announced.

"Splendid work, Captain Antala," she said. "As you claimed, you are a very clever strategist."

"Oh, I picked up a few tips at the Academy. That and one's native genius, of course."

"What now, Madam Captain?"

"We shall soon be over the Golden Sea, Your Highness. RaiChinchi is increasing our speed steadily as well as our altitude. In ten minutes or so we should reach escape velocity, and then off we go into the dear old aethyr."

"Any sign of pursuit?"

"Not so far, but I doubt if it will be long before they get after us, Your Highness. They have two ships at the Ushasti base. They will get them up shortly, but they are both big warships, faster than the *Vixen* at top speed, but much clumsier and less maneuverable. It will take them some time even to get off the ground. As far as I know, all ships at aethyr are quite a long way off. There are four other bases in Novarya which may have light craft on standby. They will probably scramble those and get them on our tail as quickly as they can. They, I fancy, will be our main concern."

"What should we do, Captain?"

"Our best bet, Your Highness, is to get off the planet as quickly as possible and lose ourselves in the wide black yonder before they have a chance to track us."

HEREDITARY Aethyr-Vikhar Ray' Shuratil Liante was immaculate in her white uniform with four gold rings on each sleeve, blue and gold epaulettes, two rows of gold buttons, and the Cross of Silvestrine at her neck. Her lipstick was the regulation shade, her hair pulled sternly from her face and hanging in a heavy braid behind her. She was calm, but it was the calm of a seasoned officer in time of emergency. She looked impassively at the teenage brunette flanked by two guards.

"Name?" she asked.

"Look, why the manacles?" asked the brunette. "I am not a wild dog or an alien. What do you think I am going to do?"

"I have no idea who you are, or what you may do," replied the Vikhar. "That is what we are here to establish. Name?"

"Alinda Maxentia, ma'am."

"Nationality?"

"Vintesque."

"Who are you working for?"

"I am not 'working' for anyone, ma'am. I just helped some friends play a joke."

"A joke? Is that what they told you?"

"Yes, ma'am."

"And you believed that? The defense of the Empire compromised for a joke?"

"Well, not quite a joke perhaps—a jink—a joyride—you know."

"I don't know, and I don't think you know either. These 'friends'—how long had you known them?"

"A few months——"

"A few months. But you are quite sure they are stealing vital defense craft for a joke?'

"They're just kids, ma'am. They aren't aliens or demons or

anything. Just kids from this country and Quirinelle that live kind of wild way up north."

"Way up north? Near the badlands?"

"Yes, ma'am, but———"

"Are you unaware that dark beings can disguise themselves? That some can possess people? That schizomorph aliens have a sex that is almost indistinguishable from maidenkind?"

"They are all from good families, ma'am."

"So they told you."

"Look, ma'am, I am not supposed to tell you this———"

"You'd better tell me everything you know, child."

"One of them is your daughter."

"Mela? Are you insane? She is a Princess of the Blood. She *can't* act against the Empire."

"That's what I am telling you, ma'am. They aren't acting against the Empire, just having a little fun."

"Listen, child, I don't know if you are lying or if some creature is masquerading as my daughter, but I intend to———"

A blue-and-gold-uniformed Flag Lieutenant entered without knocking.

"Chalwë," she said, saluting.

"Chalwë, Lieutenant. Have you gotten the *Vixen* yet?"

"Not yet, ma'am, but five Far-Darters have been dispatched from Tristillane. Our tracking station has the *Vixen's* bearings, and we are streaming them to the interception party's ordinators. The *Vixen* has a head start, of course, but the Darters should have her within the hour."

"Thank Sai Vikhë for that."

ANOTHER adolescent brunette rushed into the *Silver Vixen's* crew-concourse.

"Message from raiChinchi, raiAnters," she said breathlessly.

"Captain Antala when you are on official business," said the Captain.

"Chalwë, Skipsipops." She saluted. "RaiChinchi says we are approaching escape veloccers. So hold onto your pretty blue bonnets."

"Raya! All right, brunettes get the blondes to the safety chamber and strap them in. Strap yourselves in too, if you want to."

"What about you, Skips?"

"Don't worry about me."

"We'd quite like you conscious and functioning for the big chase scene."

"I said don't worry about me. *Gnati?*"

"All right. I *gnati.*"

Princess Mela was led to the safety chamber with the other blondes, while raiAntala wandered up to the control room to oversee raiChinchi.

"She's *vaht'he,*" said raiClaralin, the brunette who was fastening rairaiMela's safety harness, perhaps half-consciously choosing a word that commonly means 'mad' but has more ancient associations of 'inspired'. "It isn't just her own life she's playing with now. Can't you do something with her, rairaiMela?"

"You knew what she was like before you came," said the Princess. "You aren't turning chicken now, are you?"

"Of course not. But there's no need to be irresponsible."

RairaiMela laughed. "What's responsible about swoggling a navy ship and putting out to aethyr in it? Perhaps you should take up safer games like knitting or something."

"Very g'doinking funny," said raiClaralin giving a final tug to the safety harness. The blondes were all secured, and the brunettes were now strapping themselves in. Despite her dismissive manner, rairaiMela did worry a little about raiAnters. She remembered the first night she had ridden with her in a duel on her great chrome-glistening hoverbike. The wind blowing in her hair; the thrill of the 150 mph frictionless glide over the long grass at Chevendil; the crazy head-on collision course with another bike doing the same speed. RairaiMela's own nerve had cracked briefly that night.

"We'll hit at 300 miles an hour," she had screamed. "Merciful Dea, there'll be nothing left of us."

RaiAntala's steely-calm voice sounded in her wireless earbuds. "She knows that too. She'll chicken. Don't worry."

The other rider did chicken, of course. They always did. Riding against raiAntala, the only alternative was death. Riding *with* her meant taking one's life in one's hands. Sharing the thrills of a *vaht'he* daredevil who didn't seem to care much whether she lived or died.

But perhaps raiClaralin was right. Things were getting a bit more serious now. Their very irresponsibility had put them into a position where some degree of responsibility was called for.

After all, this was an important experimental ship. A Queen's ship: ultimately the Empress's ship. They had a duty at least to get it back intact after the jink.

Deep in thought, rairaiMela had hardly noticed the stress of leaving the planet's atmosphere. She was a very minor Novaryan and Imperial Princess who had run away from her finishing school in Upper Annashire and lived the life of a crazy Quirrie ton-up girl with a group of other wildly irresponsible young aristocrats.

Now they were playing the same crazy game at much higher speeds and for much higher stakes; and while the others played at deferring to her royalty and raiAnters played at captaining the ship —well, it didn't matter. They'd be rounded up in a while, and 'Nettie would have to get them off.

Unaccountably, she found herself half looking forward to being caught and to authority's re-asserting itself. One didn't like the feeling of having to *become* authority.

Anyway, for the present it was still the Great Game. The big chase scene. Keep out of their reach for as long as possible. That was the objective.

Chapter 2

A Crease in the Aethyr

"Good business, raiChinchi," said raiAntala in the control room. "We've made it free and clear; out of the atmosphere into the wide open aethyr."

"Did you think we mightn't?" asked raiChinchi.

"Well, you've never done it before, have you? Of course, I didn't doubt you, but sometimes a first time can be tricky, I imagine."

"Can't see why," said raiChinchi. "The physics is all perfectly clear. Just a question of putting theory into practice."

"What's that thing over there?" asked raiAntala, pointing ahead into the aethyr. "It looks like—I don't know what—like the aurora borealis in space."

"Oh, yes, that. You can't see it from planetside. You can't even see it from the aethyr all the time. Sometimes it's there, sometimes it isn't. They call it an aethyr-crease. As far as we understand it, the aethyr somehow turns in on itself."

"What does that mean?"

"Well, imagine a piece of paper, and suppose that paper was the whole of space. You might be at one edge, and the opposite edge would be an inconceivable distance away. But if the paper were folded in half, you would be right next to the opposite edge, even though, traveling on the surface of the paper, it would still be just as far. Of course, this would be pretty unimaginable to you because your universe would be in two dimensions, like the paper."

"You mean our three-dimensional universe might be 'folded' in another dimension that we can't even perceive?"

"That is the theory. No one is absolutely certain, though. There might be various folds at different times. It might fold into elaborate patterns and unfold again, just as many of Natura's works form patterns. We could not see any of this with our three-dimensional perception, except when we actually came upon a 'crease' like that one."

"What would happen if we flew into it? Has anyone ever tried?"

"Yes, two parties of explorers on two different occasions. Neither of them ever came back, so we are no wiser."

"How excessively fascinating."

"D'YOU think we'll get into awful trouble?" asked 'Lannie. "When they catch us, I mean."

"No, hon," replied Sharan. "In Novarya, a maid's duty is to do whatever her mistress tells her. If she don't do that she's breaking the law. But if she does, she's in the clear. Any misdemeanor is the responsibility of the mistress."

The two girls stood facing each other in the ship's galley in their short black dresses and starched white aprons. Sharan had been the best cocktail waitress in Annaton when Princess Mela had offered her triple the money and a life of adventure. After all, one could hardly take to the aethyr without decent cocktails.

"It's not like that back home in Quirinelle, is it, Sharrie?"

"No, hon. In Quirinelle individuals are equal in the eyes of the law, but in Novarya bonded maids are regarded in the light of their bond."

"But we did volunteer to come up here with Her Highness, didn't we?"

"That don't make no difference. A maid is supposed to serve her mistress at all times, and whether the mistress is doing wrong is entirely her responsibility—unless she's under age. Now Her Highness *is* under age—but so are we. So if anyone is punished it will still be her, so long as we're in Novarya, and since it's a Novaryan ship, any proceedings will be Novaryan, won't they?"

"Greenies! You ain't half well up in the law, Sharrie."

"You want to be when you get involved in this sort o' business."

"But what about Her Highness? Won't she get in trouble?"

"She thinks the old Vikhar will get her off of any bother. I don't know. But she says: 'Sharrie, are you game for the biggest jink in history? I promise you won't get into any trouble, but we might all get killed'. So I says: 'All right'. Then I says that to you, and you says 'all right' too. Well, you're only young once, ain't you? And if the mistresses ain't chicken, I don't see why we should be."

"That's how I see it too. Anyway, they'll look after their own skins, I reckon."

"I wouldn't reckon too hard on that, hon. That Miss Antala don't care about nothin'."

"It's Captain Antala now, Sharrie."

"Maybe it is; but she still don't care about nothin'. Come on, hurry up with them cocktails, or we won't even be obeying our mistress. Then we'll be offenders in Novarya too!"

They each took a tray of elaborate and brightly-colored cocktails and set out for the main concourse of the ship.

"The drinks at last!" shouted raiAntala, taking one from a tray. "I am now in a position to propose a toast to the biggest swoggle, the fastest joyride, and the most outlandish fun in history."

A cheer rose from the assembled company.

"Here's to the *Silver Vixen*," shouted raiClaralin Carshalton.

"And here's to the clean pair of heels we're about to show the Novaryan Navy!" shouted raiAntala. There was great hilarity as they drained their glasses. The maids moved about refilling them.

"Only one more cocktail for the brunettes," said raiAntala firmly. "We may have tricky business ahead, and I want a crew, not a party."

It perhaps sounded uncharacteristically responsible for raiAntala, but those who knew her best, raiChinchi and the Princess, knew it was not. Wild as she was, she never over-indulged in alcohol when riding hard or dueling. She kept her wits about her and expected those riding with her to do the same.

She cast her eye over the company. First in her eyes was raiChinchi Reteliyanhe: her first name was really Chirenchihara, but even her family called her Chinchi. She was an East Novaryan from a family of those scientists who had made the profoundly traditionalist nation of Novarya into the most technically advanced country in the West: not by abandoning its traditional character, but by applying the principles of traditional metaphysics to the new problems of technical development. RaiChinchi's mind dwelled almost exclusively upon the plane of theory. Practicalities to her were but a question of the proper application of ideas; and yet somehow, at the Aethyr Command Academy, she had found herself drawn to the fiery young officer cadet raiAntala, had advised her on her madcap schemes and even taken part in them; and when raiAntala had left the Academy under rather unfortunate circumstances, raiChinchi had decided to leave with her, because she felt raiAntala needed someone to look after her.

It was a curious bond between the two brunettes. RaiChinchi felt that in raiAntala she had found a person of supreme quality whom it was her duty to stay beside. RaiAntala found her friend's devotion inexplicable and felt somewhat guilty at involving this brilliant young technician in a life of cocktail parties and midnight rides. The thing had irritated raiAntala. She wanted to waste her life. Why must she be forced to feel that she was wasting raiChinchi's life as well? And then to worry about it? She often resolved to send her away, but then—well—raiChinchi was raiChinchi; faithful, serious raiChinchi. How could one send her away?

In a way this whole venture had started because of raiChinchi. She had read in the *Morning Letter* about the new experimental craft, the *Silver Vixen*. She had followed it up on the Ushasti Research Facility's ordinator system. She no longer had access to any academic ordinator systems, but, given the general principles of its data structure, she could break into just about anything in a matter of minutes. Lacking that information, the task could easily take her several hours, but she was very familiar with the main Novaryan University and military systems.

The *Silver Vixen* became something like an obsession with raiChinchi. She talked about its hyperthrust, its reverse-gravitar, and its weapons systems in much the way that raiAntala herself might discuss a coveted new model of hoverbike.

Oddly enough, it was rairaiMela who first suggested it. It was in the Hot Six espresso bar in Doriston. RaiAntala had been talking to her about raiChinchi and her new love—as always, feeling a little troubled about the waste of her brilliant scientific mind—and rairaiMela said: "Why don't we get it for her, then?"

"Get what?" asked raiAntala. The idea was so radical that for a moment she failed to grasp it.

"The *Silver Vixen*, of course. We could swoggle it."

"Swoggle *her*," corrected raiAntala. "Ships are blondes, like bikes."

18

"Well, swoggle *her* then. Why not? She'd be a ripping toy for raiChinchi and rather a jink for us."

"Swoggle the *Silver Vixen*? Are you *vaht'he* ?"

"Aren't you? Of course, 'Nettie will be furious but——"

"Yes, I forgot. Your brunette mater is Aethyr-Vikhar for that division, isn't she?"

"That's right. She's a darling, but somewhat irascible. Especially when someone puts the big snitch on her most important ship. Not that anyone ever *has* put the big snitch on her most important ship so far. But I can positively guarantee she'll be irascible when someone does. I mean, she gets irascible enough about overdone sausages at breakfast."

The fact that rairaiMela's brunette parent was the final custodian responsible for the *Silver Vixen* did not make any difference to the practicality of the swoggling thereof. They had no intention of using the relationship as part of the scheme. The very idea was dishonorable according to the curious code of these young tearaways. But in some indefinable way, the relationship made it all seem closer and more possible to rairaiMela, and now it was making it seem closer and more possible to raiAntala.

"You know, we *could* do it," she said. "It would take a bit of planning. We'd need to find a tactical approach. But we could do it."

"You having your second cocktail, raiAnters?" RaiAntala's reverie was broken by raiClaralin Carshalton. She took a bubbling Blonde Bombshell in its black-stemmed triangular Art-Neo glass from the silver tray borne by one of the maids. RaiClaralin raised her glass. RaiAntala noticed her perfectly varnished red nails, her matching lipstick, her dashing black-lined eyes. RaiClaralin was a daring rider, a hard drinker, and a potential rival for the place of lead-brunette of the pack. She hadn't quite the nerve to challenge the present Captain; but if raiAntala slipped—well, raiClaralin was a good brunette to have in one's crew provided one could keep on top of her.

RaiClaralin came over to raiAntala and raiChinchi, who were standing together, each immersed in her own thoughts.

"I say, you've done a wonderful job, swoggling the *Vixen* and then getting her clear of orbit, all clean as a whistle. I can't imagine why the Navy ever sacked you two."

"Gro-ohs misbehavior," chimed in raiCharmian, a blonde school friend of rairaiMela's from one of the older Quirinelle families. "On raiAnters's part, of course. RaiChinchi is far too sensible and serious, aren't you, raiChinchers?"

RaiAntala's eyes flashed. She did not like to see raiChinchi baited like this, but what could one do about blondes?

RaiChinchi blushed slightly. "Well, if you call piloting a swoggled ship off-planet sensible and serious, I suppose I must be."

RairaiMela felt like applauding, but she restrained herself. How deftly raiChinchi handled herself in her diffident, self-effacing way. Whether the reply was (as her manner suggested) merely ruminative, or whether it was a deliberate riposte, no one could possibly tell. Applause would have travestied its subtlety.

RaiEvelynn, the fourth brunette aboard, had been detailed to watch the ship's monitors. She ran into the room.

"There are five ships after us," she said, attempting, with some success, to appear unruffled.

"How far off?" asked raiAntala.

"Quite a way, but they're gaining."

"What type are they?"

"I don't know. Long sleek things. They look fast."

"Far-Darters, probably," said raiAntala. "This is more or less what we were expecting. RaiChinchi, get to your post. I'll follow." RaiChinchi turned and walked smartly to the control room.

"Have they got us, Captain?" asked raiClaralin.

"They think they've got us, but they're in for a surprise. They are expecting a pilot who is just feeling her way around an unfamiliar vessel. Actually, raiChinchers probably knows this ship and its systems better than the official test crew. We'll give her a test they weren't expecting. We're doing them a favor really."

RaiAntala turned to go, and raiClaralin made to follow her.

"You stay here," said the Captain. "We don't need a crowd in the control room. Entertain the blondes."

"There are times when raiAnters could almost annoy me," said raiClaralin to raiEvelynn.

"She's simply dreamy," said raiCharmian.

"Let's hope she doesn't dream one dream too many," said raiClaralin darkly.

"How are we going?" asked raiAntala, entering the control room.

"All serene," replied raiChinchi. "They aren't gaining now, and we shall start opening the gap shortly. I don't think they knew the old bucket could do this."

"Haya!" shouted raiAntala exuberantly. "You're a genius, raiChinchers."

"I didn't build the machine," she replied diffidently.

"No, but I don't suppose there's a soul alive can fly her like you."

"Oh, give them a few months, they'll all be able to do it."

"What's that on the fore-monitor?"

"I don't know. Can't be anything significant."

"Are you sure? Take a look."

"Sell my hat!" exclaimed raiChinchi with uncharacteristic vehemence. "That isn't possible."

"Is it what it looks like?"

"It's a Valkyrie-class battle cruiser bearing down on us at full speed."

"Can we turn?"

"Only if we want the Darters up our tailpipe."

"But you said there was nothing within four hours' flight, even at Starship speed."

"There wasn't. There's something wrong about this."

"The Darters are closing again."

"I know. What do you want me to do? Smack into the cruiser's range? We're tagged."

"No, we're not. Head into the aethyr-crease."

"But Captain, no one's ever come out of one."

"Not this side. They must have come out somewhere."

"Not necessarily. The stress might destroy the ship."

"What are you, chicken?"

"No. But there's something wrong about that cruiser, raiAnters. I don't quite believe it."

"We'll take your course in epistemology later, raiChinch. Right now, head into the aethyr-crease. That's an order."

21

Chapter 3

Destroy the Outlander!

THERE WAS no audible crash, but the ship lurched as if she had run into a rock. The monitor screens displaying the great starry vista of the aethyr turned red. The interior lighting turned red. Cocktails were spilled. Blondes gasped. Had it not been for the Raihiralan ethos of imperturbability, there might well have been panic.

"What's happening?" asked raiEstrelle, the youngest blonde present, in a voice just slightly too hasty for the insouciant calm expected of a Raihiralan blonde.

"Looks as if raiChinchi has gone through a red light," said raiClaralin. Everyone laughed.

There were more bumps, felt but never heard. The stars swirled out of focus in the red aethyr depicted by the screens. RaiAntala sauntered into the chamber.

"Strap the blondes in again, if you would be so good. Touch of turbulence."

"What sort of turbulence?" demanded raiClaralin. "This isn't an aero."

"We were nearly tagged by a battle cruiser. We've nipped into an aethyr-crease. We should be out again in a while."

"What do you mean, an aethyr-crease?" asked raiClaralin.

"We can chew the fat later, old acorn. Just now please strap the blondes in."

RaiClaralin stood staring for a moment.

"At the double," said raiAntala, without raising her voice but in the patrician tone of command used by senior military officers.

Almost automatically, raiClaralin touched her right hand to her left shoulder in salute and led the blondes into the safety chamber.

No one betrayed fear or nervousness. One simply didn't. Not only was it beneath one's Estate, but hoverbike bands like this one had an ethos that, while outwardly rebellious, was in some respects super-Raihiralan—taking the old aristocratic warrior-virtues as the basis of their play. But then do not the old books tell us that all worldly action is but play?

The ship shuddered and jolted. The redness turned to orange and glaring yellow. The monitor screens showed curious symmetrical patterns in red and then golden monochrome, and finally, as suddenly as it began, it ended. The colors of things became what we are accustomed to term natural again. The wild yet stately arabesques on the monitor screens became once again the blackness of the cold aethyr and the white pinpoints of the stars. But these were not stars that any eye aboard had seen before, nor the eyes of any of their ancestors.

"What's going on?" asked raiClaralin as the blondes came back into the concourse. "What is this aethyr-crease anyway?"

"If it's what I think it is," said the Princess slowly, "we could be thousands of light-years from home. Is that right, raiAnters?"

"That's about it," said the Captain. "Of course we might not be. We might be in the solar system next door."

"What are the chances of that?" asked raiCharmian nervously.

"Not sure," said the Captain. "RaiChinchi is the expert, but I would guess that since we could as easily be anywhere as anywhere else, the chances of our being anywhere near home are remote."

"Then how do we get home?" asked raiClaralin.

RaiAntala shrugged. "Don't know if we do."

"What about re-entering the aethyr-crease?"

"Might work. Trouble is, a few people have tried this trick before, and none of them got back. I imagine they might have thought of re-entering the aethyr-crease, and if they did, it evidently didn't work."

"You knew this?" asked raiClaralin.

"Of course I knew it."

"Then why did you take us into the g'doinking thing?"

"We had five Far-Darters on our tail and a battle cruiser in front of us. It was the only way out."

"You could have surrendered. They'd only have taken us back home."

"Surrendered?" said raiAntala. There was a cosmos of contempt in the word.

"Yes, surrendered," said raiClaralin. "Wouldn't that have been better than losing us at the rump end of the universe?"

"When I play tag," said raiAntala deliberately, "I don't get tagged. If you want to chicken, you shouldn't ride with me. I told you all when you came that this might be your last ride. I told you to come if you wanted adventure and laughed in the face of death. Otherwise stay at home. Is that what I said or isn't it?"

There was an uneasy murmur of assent from the company.

"Well, if you've changed your minds now, I'm afraid you've changed them too late."

RaiChinchi entered the room. "What's the news?" asked rairaiMela.

"Utterly fascinating," said raiChinchi. "Completely different stars. These aren't the stars we know from another angle. These are stars no one has ever seen before. No one from our world, anyway."

"You two are insane," said raiClaralin. "No wonder the Academy threw you out." The silence that followed this remark was almost tangible. RaiClaralin had broken a taboo, rupturing the fundamental unspoken code of courtesy of the sisterhood.

Finally raiChinchi said simply and coldly, "It didn't."

"Well, threw raiAntala out, then."

"It didn't," repeated raiChinchi.

RaiClaralin turned to raiAntala. "But you said——"

"I said I'd left under unfortunate circumstances."

"So what did happen?"

"It's a bit embarrassing really. They rescinded my commission. Said I had to stay on for two years as an ordinary fleetsoldier. Work off my debt as it were. I asked 'Nettie to buy me out, but she wouldn't. Said the discipline would be good for me. Elders, eh?"

"So what happened?"

"What do you think happened? I left."

"Deserted."

"'Fraid so. What would you have done?"

"So that's why you took us on a one-way trip to nowhere. You're a deserter, and you were afraid of being caught."

"Afraid?" said raiAntala menacingly.

"That's enough," said rairaiMela. "I've never known raiAntala act out of fear. You will not question her honor."

"Won't I, by the Eagle? Who are you to say what I shall do?"

"Your Sovereign," said rairaiMela simply.

"She's right," breathed raiEstrelle. "We are far from the Empire now. We may never return. RairaiMela is the nearest royal blood among us. She automatically becomes our Sovereign."

Silence fell on the company. Slowly the truth grew within them to its full maturity. They were no longer attached to the golden chain of thamë. The chain was temporarily, perhaps permanently, snapped.

Their one mistress under Dea was now Melenhe Celestina Viktorya li'Caerepurh Liante, 54th in succession to the throne of Novarya, several-hundredth in succession to the Imperial throne, but the nearest link now between the company of the *Silver Vixen* and Royal-and-Imperial authority: the sole thread attaching them to civilization and the Universal Harmony.

Here, amid the stars themselves, little rairaiMela was the one link still joining them to the Golden Chain; to the *Axis Mundi* about which turned all the stars "like to dancers in the pattern of the dance"; to the sacred thread upon which all the worlds were threaded "like pearls upon a string".

"I am conscious of the responsibility I bear," said the Princess with a dignity they had never before heard in her. "And by the blood of Sai Rayanna that flows within me, I shall not fail you, as no other of her daughters has ever failed her children."

A hush had fallen over the ship. Everyone made reverence to the Princess.

"Captain Antala, you will in future refer to me before making any momentous decisions such as taking us through aethyr-creases. Is that understood?"

"Yes, Your Highness," replied the Captain.

"With Your Highness's permission," said raiClaralin, "may I point out that raiAntala is a deserter from the Royal Novaryan Aethyr Command."

"I fail to see," said the Princess, "why you feel it necessary to point that out when we were discussing the matter only minutes ago."

"I was bringing up the matter, Your Highness, in relation to her legal and ritual fitness to be Captain of this ship. I know, Your Highness, that you will not allow your personal feelings to interfere with your probity."

"I shall not do so. But I shall certainly do everything necessary to ensure the safety and well-being of my subjects aboard this ship."

"That is the point, Your Highness. RaiAntala has consistently showed her disdain for matters of safety."

"Have you any alternative suggestion?"

"I believe I am capable of captaining the ship, Your Highness."

"Indeed? Well, I shall take your suggestion under advisement. But do not forget that the Captain is now under my instruction, and, now that we are, as it were, an outpost of the Empire, I believe our position on questions of safety and danger—including that of our present Captain—will have to change. Are you satisfied?"

"Yes, Your Highness, since you will consider my suggestion."

"I shall. Have you any other suggestions you wish me to consider?"

"One, Your Highness. As you have said, all great decisions must fall to you: but would it not be wise also to discuss them as a company and reach decisions together. Many heads are wiser than one."

"I shall hold discussions where that seems helpful, Carshalton-chei. But let me make one thing clear. This is now an outpost of Empire, and we shall have proper government: not some sort of debating society or general vote. As a personal matter, I do not greatly relish the authority that is thrust upon me: but be assured that I intend to do my duty and not dilute it. And I shall expect every one of you to do the same. The audience is now at an end."

The company seemed at a loss what to do. Were they expected to disperse? If so, where to? RaiEstrelle broke the silence.

"Are we still to call you 'Your Highness', rairaiMela?"

Everyone laughed. It was a laugh of dissolving tension.

"No," said rairaiMela. "We are back to our normal selves now. We shall have to learn—as all in authority learn—the difference between our high functions and our small selves. For now I am Mela again. But don't forget that your Princess watches over you."

Was that a reassurance or a warning? Either way it seemed curious and out of character. And yet, no one took it lightly. The Princess was another *persona*: another thing-spoken-through, that is, another mask. But high masks are of jade or gold or ivory, carved with eternal forms, while our small selves are but fleeting bundles of impulse and emotion, blown by the winds of the world.

"Oh, thank Heaven for that, rairaiMela-sweetie," said raiCharmian. "Let's have a drink."

"Yes," said rairaiMela, "I think we all deserve one."

RaiClaralin walked a little nervously over to raiAntala.

"I hope you don't take it personally. You know—the things I said. I mean, I was just trying to do what I thought was right for the ship —for the outpost of Empire, you understand. As rairaiMela says, that doesn't affect our everyday selves, does it?"

RaiAntala shrugged. "If the Princess makes you Captain, you're the Captain. Till then I am."

"But that doesn't stop us being friends?"

"Why should it? But rairaiMela can leave off being the Princess when she wants to. I can't leave off being the Captain. Not now."

"Yes. I can see that."

Suddenly raiClaralin threw her hands over her ears. Everyone did. A horrible sound like a harsh siren blared through the ship's speaker system, followed by a voice almost equally harsh. It sounded not like a human voice, but like the barking of a huge dog, somehow translated into speech.

"*This is Captain Kang Shahtha of the* Black Boar. *Shut down your engines and prepare for my crew to board your ship. If you offer any resistance you will be blown to atoms.*"

"It's a pirate ship." The Captain saluted. "Very close. Permission to destroy it, Your Highness."

"Destroy it?" repeated rairaiMela, "But——"

"I know what these creatures are, Your Highness. They are schizomorphs. Probably slavers. Believe me, Your Highness, we do not want to be taken alive by schizomorphs. I must act immediately."

"One moment, Captain," said the Princess calmly. "RaiClaralin."

"Yes, Your Highness."

"If you wish to take command of the ship, you may do so now. Otherwise we shall never consider the matter again."

The speakers boomed once more. "This is your final warning. Surrender your ship."

"Let raiAntala do it," said raiClaralin in a small voice.

"Very well," said the Princess. "Captain. Destroy the outlander."

Chapter 4

Quiet Enjoyment

THE CAPTAIN touched raiChinchi on the shoulder—a long-established sign for her to follow—and they both ran to the control room.

"Prepare a fission-limpet," said the Captain.

"A fission-limpet?" said raiChinchi. "Isn't that using a sledgehammer to crack a nut?"

"Yes," said raiAntala, "and I want to be sure it's cracked before we are."

"Suppose we're caught in the blast?"

"That's where we rely on our acceleration. You said the *Vixen* was pretty zippy. You'd better have been right."

"Limpet ready to fire, Captain. What timing?"

"Thirty seconds."

"Whew!" RaiChinchi was somewhat appalled at how fine raiAntala was cutting it, but she knew better than to argue.

"We're drifting toward them. Fire it, then hit the dear old pedal hard. We fly under them: right between their legs. The *Vixen* can make top speed in ten, and we have twenty to get clear."

The fission-limpet was an experimental weapon designed for use against enemy fleets flying in formation or against the huge cruisers of the Senkharian Empire, which were as large as Herthelan cities would be if their inhabitants, like the Senkhari, were over twelve feet tall. Essentially it was a nuclear device that could be programmed to attract itself to the gravitational pull of a large object with a force many times that of the object's actual gravity: hence the term 'limpet'. If the object—usually a ship—was protected by a force shield, the limpet did not penetrate it, but simply adhered to the limit of the field, pulled by the gravity within it. When it detonated, it would destroy everything within its radius, which was that of a small planet. The fission-limpet had never been used in anger, for the Novaryans were not a warlike people. They just wanted to be sure that if they were attacked they would be able to destroy those who would destroy them. Like most feminine

28

peoples, they had no desire to attack others, but were utterly ruthless in defense of the Motherland.

Using the device at such close quarters had never been envisaged and would certainly be against all guidelines and regulations. Or, indeed, it might not be, since no ship's officer would be imagined capable of attempting anything so *vaht'he.*

The fission limpet hissed along its chute, and simultaneously the hyperthrusts whined at a steadily rising pitch. As the limpet attached itself, unnoticed, to the *Black Boar's* force shield, the *Silver Vixen* accelerated beneath her great hull at unbelievable speed.

"What's happening?" asked raiCharmian.

"We're accelerating," replied raiClaralin. "We're running straight at them."

"Is she playing chicken with pirates?" asked raiCharmian.

"No, we're running under them. We're off into the aethyr," said rairaiMela.

"That's insane," said raiClaralin. "If they can't catch us, they'll bombard us with missiles. We can't survive that."

"Jolly-ho," said raiChinchi. "We're past them and away. The *Vixen's* speed is everything they said, which is just as well, since we really should get clear of that blast. Why only thirty, if I may ask?"

"Our main danger will arise if they try to follow us. Then we *should* get caught in it. We've got to blow them while they're still turning."

"Whoops! Incoming!" cried raiChinchi. "That was quick!"

The speaker system roared again. "We have despatched six fire-and-forget missiles. Turn back and I can call them off. Otherwise you will be——"

The broadcast ended abruptly as the aethyr was lit up by something like the sudden appearance of a sun.

"Haya!" shouted raiAntala. "They fire and they're forgotten! Pity there's no noise in the aethyr: that should have made a rather satisfying pop."

"What about the incomers?" asked raiClaralin, who was now at the door of the control room.

"Four of them went in the blast," said the Captain. "Two seem to be on our tail. Look after the blondes, there's a good girl."

RaiClaralin was nearly back at the concourse, when she and all the blondes were thrown violently to the floor by a terrible concussion. "Sorry, Skips," said raiChinchi. "I'm afraid we copped that one."

"What's the damage?"

"Physical, probby not much. Force shield badly depleted; fuel running down replacing it. We can't take another hit—and the other missile is coming for us."

"Pestilentials. Keep out of its way then."

"Can't do that forever, Skips. Train a beam on it—and as soon as I make enough distance, blow it."

The Captain took control of the main beam cannon. RaiChinchi weaved through the aethyr like a hare through a cornfield, cutting sharp angles and sudden turns, but the homer kept on the *Vixen's* tail. The gap was not closing, but it wasn't opening either.

"I can't blow it," said the Captain. "It's too close—it'll damage the *Vixen*. Run it head on, then chicken over it. It's our only chance."

RaiChinchi swung the *Vixen* in a tight hairpin and headed for the missile's nose.

"Greenies!" cried raiCharmian watching the monitors in the concourse. "She's playing chicken with the missile!"

The *Vixen* and the missile ran for tense microseconds on a head-on collision course, and only when everyone in the concourse had given herself up for dead did she swerve fractionally aside. The two bodies were now carried rapidly apart by their momentum. But not for more than two seconds. The agile missile turned like a fish and, in mid-turn, became a flare of red light and then nothing.

"Popped it!" said the Captain. "Let's plip off and get a drink."

The maids were already mixing cocktails in the gleaming Art-Neo chrome cocktail-shakers. The triangular glasses with their black stems had all been safely strapped into cushioned lockers according to rairaiMela's instructions, so even the unexpected and violent concussions through which the ship had passed had not disturbed their polished, cut-crystal perfection. It seemed to confirm the stewardship of the Princess over all worldly harmony —for, of course, the deepest aethyr still existed on the worldly plane.

"Neat work, Captain," said the Princess as they arrived in the concourse. "And wonderful flying, Chinchi-chei. We all owe you our lives."

"Quite a firework display," said raiClaralin. "I loved the big one."

"Eerie how it is all so silent," said raiEvelynn.

"Ah, the aethyr," said raiAntala. "Where else can one have such quiet enjoyment?"

"Quiet perhaps," said the Princess, "but not exactly smooth. We were nearly shaken to death when the missile hit. I thought force shields were supposed to absorb shock."

"It did absorb about ninety-five percent, Your Highness," said raiChinchi. "If the missile had hit us unshielded—and if our hull had been made of such impossibly hard metal it that was not breached—and if the missile had failed to detonate: then we should have been literally shaken to death."

"Well, thank Dea for force shields."

"Indeed, Your Highness, though I must report that we are running with a very minimal one at present."

"What do you mean by minimal, Madam Pilot?"

"I mean, Your Highness, that we are shielded against light aethyr debris and little more."

"Why is that?"

"Force shields, Your Highness, are made of energy. That is why they are called force shields. They draw energy from the same crystals that power the ship. Well, actually that isn't quite true. They have their own crystal bank, but when that is depleted they draw on the main power bank. The shields' own power banks are completely exhausted and the shields have begun drawing from the main banks —those that supply not only our propulsion but our light, warmth, artificial gravity, and air circulation. Without them we die. I have therefore reduced the shields to operating minimum. In an emergency we can restore them to about half-power, protecting us from heavy debris, and from some blasts and beam weapons. We could not maintain that for long, and we could not sustain another missile strike like the last one."

"There ought to be spare crystals, Madam Pilot."

"There ought, Your Highness, but there are none. This is an

experimental craft. I am maintaining a notebook that I shall present to the research guild when we return."

"*If* we return," put in raiClaralin.

"Quite so. One of my recommendations will be for at least one reserve crystal bank. At present, however——"

"At present, ladies," said the Captain, "if our late lamented friends aboard the *Black Boar* have any shipmates kicking about nearby, we are in the borscht right up to our diamond earrings."

"Can't the crystals make more power?" asked the Princess.

"The crystals don't make power, Your Highness," said raiChinchi. "They only store it. We have a solar generator that can recharge them, but that takes time—and, of course, we need to be near a sun to do it."

"Mildly pestilential," said the Princess. "What do you recommend, Captain?"

"I think our next move should be to get within charging radius of a sun; and also to look for a habitable planet within its system. We can't last for long on the food and water supplies aboard."

"How long will it take to reach a sun?"

"At the speed we are traveling," said raiChinchi, "we may have passed one already. We shall have to go to the control room and start navigating."

"Madam Pilot, may I ask why we are making such tremendous speed through the aethyr when you aren't even—um—steering or whatever you call it?"

"Energy again, Your Highness. We attained top speed in escaping the blast that destroyed the *Black Boar*. Since there is virtually no friction in the aethyr, and since a body in motion tends to remain in motion, it costs us no power to maintain that speed, whereas it would cost power to slow down. Once we know where we are heading, we can try to navigate and slow her with minimum energy consumption."

"Not to mention," said the Captain, "that, at this speed, any of the *Black Boar's* cutthroat chums would have to be pretty zippy to catch us. Which, of course, they may be; but it's always worth a try."

"Very well. To the nearest suitable-looking sun then."

"Chalwë, Your Highness," replied the Captain, and departed with her Pilot.

"You've a good Captain there, Your Highness," said raiEstrelle.

"And a good Pilot. And I can't say I'm sorry. Indifferent officers would be rather a drawback on a trip like this."

If the remark was in any way intended for raiClaralin she gave no sign of noticing it. "All rather fun though, isn't it?" she said. "Of all the people who set off to bask in the sun, how many of them get a choice of suns to bask in?"

There was a little more banter, but after a short time the company fell surprisingly silent, watching the stars on the monitor screens.

The close brush with death had bothered them more than they would care to admit, but not too much. All of them had ridden near the edge of destruction on hoverbikes. It was the enormity of the aethyr that gripped their minds now. The unimaginable distance between themselves and all that they had ever known, and their separation from the next links in the Golden Chain and from the great *Familia* of Nation and Empire.

They looked to their Princess now as the only living representative of *lhi Matrilan Raihir*, Mother Empire; and their Princess was but a child who stood with her eyes upon the fore-monitor, gazing into the vastness of the aethyr in silent prayer.

Chapter 5

A Hot Time in Ranyam Astarche

RAIANTALA strolled back into the concourse, but as she drew near to rairaiMela she stiffened and saluted.

"One fat juicy sun, Your Highness," she reported. "We are orbiting it now as close as is consistent with safety. Generators running, crystals charging, all serene. RaiChinchi is scanning the system's planets for anywhere we might land to take on provisions—water at least. We have large reservoirs on board, but they aren't filled."

"What are the chances, Captain?"

"Well, only a small minority of planets are capable of supporting life of our sort, but water is a little easier. We might find an ice planet, for example."

The speakers boomed into life again. The voice was again deafening, but this time sounded human.

"Please identify yourself, spacecraft. You are in the aethyr-territory of Ranyam Astarche."

"Greenies!" said raiAntala. "Go and tell raiChinchi to turn that thing down, will you, raiClaralin? It's set so the technis could hear it over their machinery."

With only a small grimace, raiClaralin ran off on her errand. RaiAntala took her transceiver from her pocket and tuned it to the *Vixen's* coordinator.

"This is the *Silver Vixen*, a ship of the Royal Novaryan fleet. Captain Antala FiaMartia speaking. We are off course and are recharging our power crystals from your sun. Permission requested to continue."

"Rayati, honored Captain FiaMartia. It might have been politer to request permission before beginning." The voice was quieter this time and easier to assess. It was feminine and civilized-sounding. The translation indicator was showing very low output. The speaker was clearly using a language very little removed from our own.

"Rayati, noble defender. Apologies. We were unaware that we were close to any inhabited planet."

"Apology accepted, honored Captain, and permission granted. We

34

are not aware of Ranyam Novarya, and you appear unaware of Ranyam Astarche. You must be very much off course."

"It seems we have entered an aethyr-crease."

"Understood. Why does your ship bear the Imperial insignia, honored Captain?"

"Novarya is part of the Nevcaeren Empire."

"Is that in any way connected to the Caeren Empire?"

"It is its direct descendant."

"On what planet?"

"On the same planet. Sai Herthe."

"The same planet as the original Caeren Empire? It still survives?"

"Certainly."

"Have you need of provisions?"

"Great need."

"I am sure our Ranyam will provide them for you. Please continue recharging. I shall report to my superiors."

"What do you make of that?" asked rairaiMela.

"Well, they know about the Caeren Empire, that's for sure, but they must have been out of touch with Sai Herthe for a long time. Probably millennia."

"But there was no aethyr travel millennia ago."

"Not among our people—at least not in the form it exists today."

"What do you mean?"

"Remember that the magic of former times was at least as powerful as the technics of today. Magic is still strong today in the East, but at the time of——" RaiAntala trailed off.

"Go on, Captain," commanded the Princess.

"Well, say at the time of the Caeren Empire, Your Highness. The original one. Magic was a very great power. They could have put people on other planets if they had wanted to."

"But they didn't think that way."

"Not as far as we know, Your Highness. But perhaps in some great crisis."

"Are you suggesting that these people might be related to us?"

"It might explain why we were able to understand them."

"Surely that was because of the translator-things built into the ship's communication system—isn't that right, Madam Pilot?"

"I have been wondering about that, Your Highness," replied raiChinchi. "We certainly have a powerful cognitor wired into the reception system. It translates all known languages instantly and can analyze unknown ones. But we seem to be in a wholly unknown sector of the universe. One would expect languages here to be completely unrelated to any we know, in which case such an instant relay-translation should not have been possible."

RaiChinchi's swift right thumb was moving deftly over the screen of her hand-transceiver. "In fact the cognition unit was only working at about five percent. The language appears to be relatively close to our own—some differences of vocabulary, more of pronunciation, and a slightly different grammatical structure, but it is actually more like a dialect of Herthelan Westrenne than most languages known in our own aethyr-sector."

"But at the time of the Caeren Empire no one spoke a language like ours."

"Suppose theirs had evolved from High Caeren in a similar way to ours," suggested raiAntala.

"That is an extraordinary idea, Captain."

"It is, Your Highness, but it does answer the facts. Never mind. We shall probably learn more in due course."

"And what of the schizomorphs?" asked the Princess. "Were they speaking a language like ours too?"

RaiChinchi continued to examine her transceiver. "They were using a polyvox—that is, a polyvocative transmitter rather like ours, Your Highness. It converts spoken transmissions into a beam containing streams in all languages known to the unit. Even the simplest cognition engine on the receiving end can locate and separate the known stream. One of the streams was the language we have just been discussing: that of this Ranyam Astarche—but that is to be expected since they were operating in this aethyr-sector. Our cognitor selected this as the most prehensible stream and made an instant analysis and translation. The source-vocation, however, was in a very different language."

"But isn't it rather a great coincidence?" put in raiClaralin. "I mean, that we should be pitched clean across the universe and land on the doorstep of people who speak a language related to ours and recognize our Imperial insignia—and even know about the Caeren Empire."

"Very great," murmured raiChinchi. "Almost too great. Why did we enter the aethyr-crease at all?"

"Because we were being chased by five Far-Darters and our path was blocked by a Valkyrie-class battle cruiser," said raiAntala somewhat irritably.

"Exactly," said raiChinchi, "and I am perfectly sure that a battle cruiser—of any class—could not have been in that place at that time."

"But I saw it," said raiAntala. "You saw it. Everyone saw it."

"I know. And the instruments registered it too."

"Then what are you trying to say, Madam Pilot?" asked the Princess.

"I don't know, Your Highness," replied raiChinchi. "I really don't know. But I do recommend caution. There may be more going on here than meets the eye—or the instruments."

"What do you mean by 'going on *here*'?" demanded raiClaralin. "The cruiser was near to Sai Herthe, and this Ranyam Astarche is probably so far from there that even a ship traveling at the *Vixen's* speed couldn't get there in a lifetime. How can the two sets of events be connected?"

"I agree that the cruiser was that far away from here, if there *was* a cruiser," said raiChinchi.

"Then you mean——" began raiEvelynn and stopped. "What *do* you mean?"

"I don't mean anything," said raiChinchi. "I just don't know."

Another voice rang out from the speaker system, older-sounding and more authoritative than the last.

"Rayati, honored Captain FiaMartia. You have full clearance to land your craft in Ranyam Astarche. All assistance will be accorded to you, and your ship will be fully provisioned. Captain FiaMartia and her senior officers will be treated as the personal guests of Queen Ashhevala the Third. What kind of landing area do you require?"

"This ship can land just about anywhere," said Captain FiaMartia.

"Very well. We shall bring you down in the Palace Airfield. A pilot ship has been dispatched to escort you. It was launched when we first spoke and will be with you in a matter of minutes. Please follow it into our planet's atmosphere. Her Captain will guide you to a landing place within the palace grounds."

"Thank you," said Captain FiaMartia. "You are more than kind."

"Efficient, aren't they?" remarked raiClaralin.

"Highly," agreed raiAntala. "RaiChinchi and I had better start slowing the ship's orbit about this sun, and if I could trouble you, raiClaralin——"

"I know. Look after the blondes."

"If you would."

As the Captain and her Pilot left the concourse, raiClaralin made reverence to the Princess. How much she resembled raiAntala and raiChinchi, though their hair was as raven black as hers was platinum white, against that same copper skin and dark, reserved almond eyes.

Suddenly an unworthy thought entered her mind. *They don't trust a Westrenne,* she thought. *That is the truth of the matter. When we were at home on Sai Herthe, Quirridips were good enough friends to ride with and make devilment. But now that things are serious and rairaiMela is our Sovereign, they cannot trust a shallow Westrenne to uphold the Golden Order. Of course the Princess would never even consider a Westrenne for the captaincy of a Novari ship, and raiAntala would never trust her with anything more than looking after the blondes. Everything has now taken on a ritual significance, and a Westrenne could not be trusted with that.*

"Rayati, honored Captain FiaMartia," a voice came over the speaker system. "This is Captain Susarin of the *Sun Hawk*. You should have visual contact. Please follow us toward Astarche."

"Rayati, honored Captain Susarin," replied raiAntala's voice. "Visual contact confirmed. Please proceed. We shall follow you."

RaiClaralin watched as one of the planets visible from the monitor became larger than the others. She made reverence to the Princess and requested her and the rest of the ship's company to come to the safety chamber.

The process of harnessing the ship's company took a few minutes and seemed not to be complete before time. The pilot Captain spoke again: "Rayati, honored Captain FiaMartia. Please reduce your speed for entry into the planet's atmosphere. You are traveling too fast."

"Rayati, honored Captain Susarin. Apologies. We seem to have taken damage in an encounter with a hostile ship. Retro-boosters are not firing. We can't decelerate quickly enough."

"Then enter orbit, honored Captain. You must not enter the atmosphere at that speed."

"We are trying, honored Captain. Momentum and gravity are carrying us toward the planet. The *Silver Vixen's* hyperthrusts are not responding."

"You are overtaking us, honored Captain. Please try to avoid entering atmosphere. You are very close now."

"We are aware, honored Captain. Are trying everything in our power to avoid entry."

"What will happen if we enter the planet's atmosphere?" asked the Princess. "Why do they sound so urgent? Might we crash or something?"

"Crash?" said raiClaralin. "At this speed, friction with the planet's atmosphere will heat the ship very rapidly. We shall burn to a crisp long before we reach the planet's surface."

'Lannie, the younger maidservant, began softly to cry.

"Be brave, child," said the Princess calmly—though 'Lannie was probably two years her senior. "You have been a very brave girl so far. Please go on being brave. If Dea is calling us to Her arms now, then we must go to Her with smiling faces."

"Yes, Your Highness," said 'Lannie a little weakly. She set her mouth into a smile, and did not cry again. She was still afraid, but she wanted to be a credit to her Princess.

"We have entered the atmosphere, honored Captain Susarin," said raiAntala. "Temperature gauges are rising rapidly. We are still trying to pull out of free fall. If we manage it, we shall make whatever landing we can."

"Understood, honored——"

There was silence as the communications system shut down.

Chapter 6

Blood Sisters

FOR THE longest minutes of their lives, the ship continued to free-fall in eerie silence. Then they heard a dreadful sound: a deep, juddering roar, so low in tone that it seemed to make their bones vibrate. The sound rose in pitch until it became the high, full-bodied whine with which they were all familiar. The hyperthrusts had engaged.

There was the horrible lurch of rapid deceleration that seemed to pull them inside out, and then the ship's course leveled. The *Silver Vixen* was still moving very fast by planetside standards, but the danger was over. They sailed in toward Astarche. What had been a ball was now a horizon, and soon they found themselves over ocean, which was visible through breaks in the cloud cover.

"Stay fastened for now," said raiClaralin, unfastening her own harness. "I am going to the control room to find out what's happening, since we seem to have lost the comm system. RaiEvelynn, look after the blondes."

She entered the control room and was greeted with a broad grin from Captain Antala.

"All serene?" she asked.

"All serene," replied raiAntala.

"RaiEvelynn is looking after the blondes."

"Glad to hear it. You should have seen the temperature gauge on *this* blondie!"

"I bet you could have fried eggs on the hull."

"Fried eggs? You could have incinerated the entire waste-disposal of a large city."

"Where are we now?"

"Somewhere planetside. Definitely in Astarche, we think, and going by the *Sun Hawk's* course, we can probably land not too far from the palace. That is, within a hundred miles or so, in all likelihood."

"You had time to plot the *Sun Hawk's* course while you were pulling us out of a death-drop?"

40

RaiAntala grinned slyly. "Oh, we're just brimming with resourcefulness."

RaiClaralin gave her a slightly quizzical look.

"We're coming in to land," said raiAntala. "Do you want to stay and watch?"

"Thank you, honored Captain."

She watched fascinated as raiChinchi descended below cloud level into a densely wooded region and piloted the ship into a small clearing in the dark forest. The ship whispered to the gentlest touchdown imaginable.

"Perfect flying, Madam Pilot." said raiClaralin.

"Thank you," said the Pilot.

"Why here?" asked raiClaralin.

"It's a nice safe place to put down," said raiAntala, "since we don't know exactly where we are. Pop and release the blondes, would you, then we'll all meet up in the concourse."

RaiAntala seemed more cordial than before, and yet raiClaralin's sense of exclusion was growing. Who knew exactly what raiAntala and raiChinchi were up to? They seemed to have their own little secrets, even within this shared adventure, that no Westrenne would ever be privy to.

"The Captain says all serene," she announced to the safety chamber. "We have landed like a feather and are all free to meet in the concourse. Cocktails are in order, I think."

"But not strong ones," stipulated the Princess. "We are on a strange planet and we need to be clear-headed."

It was enough for raiClaralin to say anything to ensure she should be immediately contradicted and countermanded by one of the Estrennes.

Captain Antala made deep reverence as the Princess entered the concourse.

"We are safely landed, Your Highness, and await your further instructions."

The Princess perched herself elegantly on the edge of a chair and looked intently at her bubbling, freshly shaken cocktail.

"Thank you, Captain. Thank you, Madam Pilot. Since we have an invitation from the Queen of this land, I imagine our first task will be to find the palace."

"We have our hoverbikes docked in the ship," said the Captain. "I suggest that I locate the palace and make initial contact."

"Not dressed like that, Captain," said the Princess. RaiAntala was wearing a circular skirt with a white polo-necked sweater and a black leather zip-fronted jacket open half-way. Typical attire of the less respectable café-teens of Quirinelle.

"No, I suppose it might not make entirely the right impresh."

"You are representing the Empire and you are representing me. Fortunately there are some Royal Novaryan Aethyr Command uniforms aboard, including one with Captain's insignia. Please try it on."

RaiAntala disappeared and reappeared shortly afterward in the blue-and-gold uniform with front-pleated skirt and high boots.

"A touch on the large side, I fear," she said.

"Yes, it is," agreed the Princess. "Have we a morphing-box aboard?"

"Nothing configured for couture-work," said raiChinchi.

"If it please Your Highness——" ventured Sharan, who was refilling cocktail glasses with the rather mild concoction ordered by her royal mistress.

"Yes, Sharan?"

"If it please Your Highness, I have my sewing things with me. I could make a few alterations for the Captain if that would be in order, ma'am."

"Sewing," said the Princess. "With scissors and needles and things?"

"Yes, ma'am. We still do it in Quirinelle."

"Doesn't it take an awfully long time?"

"I could probably get that uniform altered in an hour, Your Highness. Perhaps even less. It isn't a big job."

"Very well. Take any measurements or whatever you need. The Captain is yours."

Sharan giggled. "Thank you, Your Highness."

In a few minutes the Captain reappeared in her café clothes. "All serene, Your Highness. Uniform alterations under way. With your permission I should like to leave the ship for a short while. I wish to check the atmosphere and terrain."

"Permission granted, Captain."

"RaiClaralin, please accompany me. I wish to speak with you."

"I have been wishing to speak to you too, Captain," replied raiClaralin.

"Very well."

The woods surrounding the ship were every bit as dense as they had looked from the air. They smelled richly of some aromatic alien foliage in the midday heat. The heat itself was such that they were not sorry for the shelter of the trees.

"We wished to speak to each other," said the Captain. "You take the first shot."

RaiClaralin felt a little uneasy. It was hard to raise the subject. She had known it would be: that is why she had committed herself in advance.

"I know what's going on——" she began.

The Captain smiled. "Do you, indeed?" she said.

"I mean, I know what you think of me."

"How clever you are. What do I think of you?"

"You think I'm a Quirridip."

RaiAntala laughed. "You *are* a Quirridip, aren't you?"

"Yes, but you think that's all I am. You think I am a shallow Westrenne, not to be taken seriously. Oh, we Quirridips are fun to play with, but when it comes to the real things of life, we are little better than outlanders——"

"Hold hard, old thing," said raiAntala. "Don't get yourself carried away. I never called a Westrenne an outlander in my life. I never met a Novari who did. Perhaps that is the way some of you Westrennes talk about us——"

"Don't talk rot. Of course it isn't. We may have our differences, but an outlander is quite another matter."

"But you think I don't know that?"

"No—look, I'm not putting this very well, but you know what I am trying to say. Now that we have to manifest the Golden Order ourselves—well, you don't think a Westrenne is up to the task. We don't think in traditional ways like you. Even when you've been running with the maddest of Westrennes, you still think like the ancients at root. I know that. But we are sound in the West too. For all our modern ways and everything. I mean, we aren't ritually impure or something. You think we are. Her Highness thinks we are. But——"

"Ritually impure?" said raiAntala suddenly. There was a sardonic, almost a bitter, smile on her face.

"Well, I probably used the wrong expression, but out of thamë or something."

"What about me?" asked raiAntala.

"What do you mean?"

"Don't you know what I mean? You stated it yourself, very forcibly, not long ago. I am a deserter. Out of obedience. Out of thamë. How can I be the second link in a Golden Chain?"

"Only through the grace of Dea," said raiClaralin, "and the grace of Her Highness."

"You Westrennes are sound enough—when you stop thinking about your own silly grievances and let the truth come through you. Of course you are completely right. Through that grace, and through obedience. Well, I haven't been obedient to Her Highness today. Not even after I accepted her commission."

"Really? How could you——"

"Never mind how. I'll talk to you about that later. Just accept that I have put myself out of obedience again. Immediately after what I promised myself would be a fresh start. That's one reason I asked you out here. You see those trees? I want you to cut a switch from one of them and whip me with it."

RaiClaralin stood dumbfounded.

"You know how to do that, I suppose," said raiAntala.

"Yes, I know, but I can't. I mean, I just——"

"All right, you can't," said raiAntala in sudden anger. "Then I'll have to deal with myself." With unbelievable suddenness, speed, and accuracy, raiAntala whipped out her knife, pulled back her sleeve, and slashed her left arm from wrist to elbow. Blood began to drip rapidly upon the alien soil.

RaiClaralin felt giddy and shocked. Why did raiAntala have to be so hasty, so angry, so sudden? The thing she had asked her to do was an incredible thing, a bonding thing. RaiClaralin cursed herself for a fool. The moment was gone now. The opportunity for something of great importance was wafted on the breeze of raiClaralin's hesitancy and burned up in raiAntala's anger.

RaiAntala looked at raiClaralin's horrified countenance and said in a hard voice, "It's all right. I've avoided the artery."

An impulse seized raiClaralin, and she knew this time she must not hesitate. She had not the raw courage of raiAntala, but she must not hesitate. She took out her own knife, pushed back her sleeve, and slashed her own arm, just as raiAntala had done. The pain sickened her; the blood horrified her as if she had been a blonde; but at the same time she felt exultant.

"You fool," said raiAntala. "What did you do that for?"

"Because I let you down, honored Captain. Because, like you, I had to put something right."

"Come here."

RaiClaralin stepped close to raiAntala, who seized her bleeding arm and pressed it close to her own. "Grip my elbow. Hold it tight. This is the bond of blood, raiClaralin. No Estrennes or Westrennes now. Sisters. You understand?"

"Sisters," repeated raiClaralin.

"Now, I want you to be my second-in-command. I am going away from here, and I need you to be in charge. It may be more important than you think."

"Me? Not raiChinchi?"

"You, raiClaralin. RaiChinchi is Haiela. You are Raihira." The words struck raiClaralin forcibly. Of course she knew the old distinction between the Haiela, the priestly and intellectual Estate, and the Raihira, the aristocratic and military Estate, but in the West the two were now largely merged in an indistinct 'upper class'. How closely and naturally the Estrenne mind adhered to these ritual distinctions.

"Of course," said raiClaralin. "You can count on me."

"I knew I could, sister. Now, you asked how I could have disobeyed Her Highness. I will tell you. She ordered me to consult her on all major decisions. Well, I did not consult her on the decision I made as we approached this planet. The decision to cut the engines and let the ship go into free fall, losing our escort and breaking wireless contact."

"I had a feeling that little incident wasn't all it seemed."

"I know you had. That is one reason I want you with me."

"Why did you do it?"

"The most obvious reason is that we are in charge of a Royal and Imperial ship. A new and experimental one. It is our duty not to let it fall into the hands of outlanders. Not even apparently friendly ones."

"These people seem to be intemorphs like ourselves, and even to have some lineage back to our own Empire."

"Well, we shall see. If they are truly representatives of a forking branch, as it were, of the Empire, our whole position may change: we may have to give our allegiance to them. But at present we know nothing for certain.

"We don't know the level of their technics—although we do know that their pilot ship wasn't equipped with a tractor beam, otherwise they could have pulled us out of our fall. If they get to know—or know already—how we destroyed the *Black Boar,* they may regard the *Silver Vixen* as a threat—or as an opportunity."

"By the Eagle, you are absolutely right, sister. I owe you another apology. I could never have been Captain in your place. You think so clearly and so quickly."

RaiAntala tightened her grip on raiClaralin's elbow, and raiClaralin did the same. They both experienced a sharp stab of pain, but both smiled.

"Thank you, sister. But you see my problem? I had to act quickly. It wasn't easy to discuss the matter, and I was afraid Her Highness would think me unduly distrustful of our kind hosts and overrule what was certainly a bit of a wild plan—to bring the ship down in a feigned emergency landing.

"But I came on this trip in a state of athamë. I was out of obedience to the Golden Chain. That was my personal affair then, but now it isn't. The only way I can function as a legitimate part of the Chain now is in obedience, through Her Highness's grace. I have to be her right hand. I can't keep acting without her will."

"Sister," said raiClaralin, "when a blow is aimed at the face, the right hand may often move to protect it without being commanded. That is part of the function of a right hand."

"Sister, you are right. Still, I must learn not to act outside Her Highness's will so easily. That is why I had to make penance. To show myself physically that there is a price to pay: for I am one who lives too much in the realm of the physical, with too little regard for the spirit."

"You are hard on yourself, sister."

"Listen to me, sister. I have told you before to look after the blondes; I tell you so again. It is the highest commission I could give you. It is more important than what I am about to do. Look after the ship and look after its company. If anything goes wrong, get it off the planet immediately. I'll give you more specific orders later. But these are your standing orders. Look after the ship and look after its company. At all costs. I am trusting you, sister."

"I understand, sister. Various people might see the *Silver Vixen* as both a threat and an opportunity."

"That is right, sister. And we have that aboard which could be seen as an even greater threat—and an even greater opportunity."

"What do you mean, sister?"

"Hello, darlings," said a blonde voice, "what are you blathering about all this time? And you call us blondes chatterboxes! Anyway, Sharan wants the Captain for her final fitting. She thinks the uniform is ready."

"We're coming," said raiAntala.

RaiCharmian screamed. "Is that blood? What have you been doing?"

"Making a Bond of Sisterhood," said raiAntala, speaking lightly and smiling reassuringly. "Nothing to panic about."

"Sheltering Heaven! What a time to do it! And why do you brunettes have to be so excessive? Look at the mess you've made. You'll be scarred for days!"

"Brunettes can be excessive, I fear," said the Captain apologetically. "'Were there no blondes, there were no temperance', as the poet says. Lead me to my uniform."

Chapter 7

The Captain's Sword

A SHORT time later, raiAntala entered the concourse resplendent in dark blue and gold. She looked somehow taller than she had before. Was it just the heels of the long military boots and the fact that she was carrying herself more erect?

For the first time, rairaiMela saw the Captain. No, she had caught glimpses of the Captain before, but always with raiAnters's bright, mischievous eye winking through her. Now she was every inch an Imperial Officer, as different from dear old raiAnters as rairaiMela was from the Princess.

"You are looking splendid, Captain," she said.

"Your Highness is too kind. But if I am to represent her, no splendor could be great enough," replied the Captain.

"But they were cutting themselves, Your Highness," said raiCharmian, who had not quite grasped the nature of the occasion. "Blood everywhere. Making a Bond of Sisterhood. Can you think of a worse time for such a business?"

"I cannot think of a better time," said the Princess. "But we must deal with the more immediate matters in hand. Captain, what are your plans?"

"I propose to take my hoverbike and find the palace, Your Highness. I shall keep in regular touch by means of my hand-transceiver. In fact, may I have it back, Madam Pilot?"

RaiChinchi took a moment to respond. It was the first time raiAntala had addressed her like that. "Yes, here it is, Captain," she said. "You will need to wear these wireless earbuds and this tiny throat-microphone. The microphone will pick up the speech of others and transmit it to the transceiver. I have installed translation software for the language used by Ranyam Astarche, so you will get an immediate translation through the earbuds. They block out all sounds from normal sources, but you will get non-vocal sound transmitted through the earbuds too. You can fade the non-vocals if you want. Very handy for hearing what people are saying in a noisy environment. Quite useful for eavesdropping too. The way this works is the same as with the mainframe translator. You will hear the sampled voice of the speaker translated into Westrenne. You will be able to hear all her vocal intonations, so you will know, for example, if she is speaking in an angry tone or a tearful one. However, it can't *translate* intonation, so where tonal conventions differ, you will have to learn by experience what a particular tone of voice implies with this people."

"Easier than learning the language," said the Captain.

"And a great deal quicker," added raiChinchi. "The microphone-set incorporates a speaker and an absorption crystal. It will absorb around ninety percent of your voice's sonority. In other words, you will be nearly silenced. Your words will be conveyed to the transceiver, translated, and broadcast through the speaker. The system is sufficiently sophisticated that most casual listeners will not realize they are not hearing your voice direct."

"Excellent," said the Captain.

"As you requested, I have programmed in a keyword. Whenever you speak that word, a beep will be transmitted to my transceiver."

"That will be my signal that all is serene, Your Highness," explained the Captain, "or at least relatively serene. I shall transmit this signal about once an hour if I am not in voice contact during that hour. If I go more than three hours without giving a signal, you are to take the ship off-planet."

"Without you, Captain?" asked the Princess in some alarm.

"Without me. I shall only fail to transmit if I am in serious trouble and unable to, which is likely to mean I have fallen into enemy hands. This ship and its company must be kept out of enemy hands at all costs. With Your Highness's permission, I am appointing raiClaralin as Commander in my absence. Under her direction, I want the ship's company to stock the *Vixen* with water and, if possible, some food, and to stand ready to leave the planet should I order it or be out of contact for over three hours. Are those orders acceptable to Your Highness?"

The Princess hesitated. "Yes, Captain—but—but these people seem friendly. Why such precautions?"

"They are merely precautions," said the Captain. "I am not anticipating your sudden departure from the planet. However, this is an unknown world, and just in case things should not be as they seem, I want us to be ready."

"Very well, Captain. I respect your judgment and approve your appointment of Commander Carshalton. The rest of you, please withdraw. I desire a private word with my Captain."

Mildly surprised, the others left the concourse.

"I have something to ask you, Captain, and I do not want an evasive answer."

"Evasive answer, Your Highness?" queried the Captain innocently.

"That is right. This little blood-letting ceremony with Commander Carshalton: was it in any sense a dare or chicken-game?"

"I can tell you, Your Highness, quite unevasively, that it was not."

"I am glad to hear it. I wish to make this clear. So long as we are on this side of the aethyr-crease, and until and unless I say otherwise, there are to be absolutely no dares or chicken-games or anything of that sort. You are not the toughest cat in town any more. You are my Captain. Do I make myself understood?"

"Understood and obeyed, Your Highness."

"Good." RairaiMela allowed herself a smile. "I don't say I shan't miss the toughest cat in town."

"You are not required to say that, ma'am," said raiAntala, returning her smile. "I shall miss the zippiest chick in town myself."

"Whatever you have done up to the point of putting on that uniform, I now expunge. For what you do from this point on, I hold you accountable." Whether it was luck or royal instinct, or whether blonde intuition (or acuity) ran a little further than the Captain had suspected, the Princess had hit on exactly the right formula. RaiAntala, weighed down by the sense that she had already confirmed her reprobate status, now felt that she had both made penance and received absolution. She felt renewed, cleansed, and ready to begin afresh in the service of her Royal Mistress.

"Thank you, Your Highness," she said simply.

"And now, in token of your status as my servant and the servant of the Empire, I have something very important for you." With considerable reverence, the Princess lay on the table a long shape wrapped in red silk edged with spun-gold thread. "Unveil it," she said, "for you shall bear it in my name."

RaiAntala approached with something like trepidation. It was the first time rairaiMela had seen the smallest hesitation in her. Carefully and with an uncharacteristic delicacy, the Captain drew off the silken veil to reveal a long, slender blade of a steel that shone brighter than the finest silver. A steel that had been forged and re-forged in a sacred flame to the high inchanting of an hereditary sword-creator whose craft was somewhere between sorcery and priesthood, and of her virgin apprentices who were like temple acolytes of the holy flame. A steel folded and re-folded until it was compounded of literally a million infinitesimal laminations, hard and sharp enough to cut a floating leaf in twain and yet supple enough to bend into a crescent and spring back always to the same absolute straightness. This sword was no mere object, but a living thing: an embodied spirit of justice and rectitude; an ensouled bringer of protection and of death.

RaiAntala fell to her knees before the sacred blade. "I cannot bear this sword, Your Highness," she said. "I cannot even look upon it. I beg that you will cover it again."

"I have said you shall bear it in my name," said the Princess. Already she was in awe of the ritual weight of her own words, and knew that what she said must be.

"And I shall, Your Highness, when I am worthy; but I am not worthy yet. If you command me to bear it now, I shall do that. But weigh me in your heart, I pray you, and see if I am worthy."

In taking this sword of an Imperial Captain's rank from the ship's vault, the Princess had acted not lightly, but still with too much of rairaiMela about her. She had spoken the words of the Princess that the Captain should bear this sword, and she had spoken true. But for the first time the weight of her great office was borne in upon her in its fullness. She looked upon raiAntala and knew that she was not yet worthy; and she knew also that, in bringing the Captain face to face with this sacred vikhelic majesty, she was forcing her to face the things she had avoided in her headlong career of disobedience and death-defiance, and that it was right that she had done so.

"You are not yet worthy, my Captain," she said, "but you will become worthy. We shall become worthy together."

51

Carefully she laid the red silken veil with its spun-gold edging over the beautiful and terrible blade, and raiAntala breathed again.

"I think you should wear some sword nonetheless," said rairaiMela. "You are visiting a Queen after all."

"Yes, I shall take a practice sword."

"A practice sword——"

"I noted an exceptionally fine one in silver with a chased blade. I imagine it has been used for ceremonials before. It will look nice enough, and I imagine I shall have to remove it before seeing the Queen in any case."

"That is true, and after all we were not expecting to visit royalty. There is no reason why a True Sword should have been aboard."

"Why was it aboard, I wonder?" said raiAntala.

"Do you mean how did it come to be aboard?" asked the Princess. "Or *why* is it aboard?"

A slight shiver passed over raiAntala as she considered the distinction between these two questions.

RairaiMela changed the tone completely. "You are being very cautious, Captain, with your talk of the ship's leaving the planet at a moment's notice. What do you expect to find here?"

"Our Pilot has warned us that things may not be what they seem, Your Highness. Of course, they also may. My conjectures run to two extremes. I fancy that either our hostesses are something very different from what they are affecting to be, or they may well be legitimate representatives of the Line of Rayanna."

"Of our own Empire?"

"Or some sort of descendant thereof. Yes, it is possible."

"And if they are, that would put us in an interesting position. Should we not have to accept their authority? Would not this strange position of being our own thamë be at an end?"

"It would seem likely, Your Highness: though of course we should all await your word on the matter."

"And then we should be orphans in a strange land."

"Well, don't worry too much about that," said raiAntala. "I'm still the toughest cat in town."

The Princess laughed. "Not till I say so."

Chapter 8

Three Friends and a Foe

It felt good to be astride a hoverbike again. This part of the planet was green and fertile. Its afternoon was progressing, and it was not quite so hot as it had been during the Captain's time with raiClaralin. Besides, the air rushing past her cooled her considerably.

As they flashed by, she took in the tall, strange trees and the cultivated fields, some with curious-looking crops, some that looked almost like those at home. In the far distance was a range of mountains rising majestically against the azure sky. She was heading toward them, in the direction indicated by raiChinchi's calculations.

She passed several villages before she came upon wider roads and, after a time, the first sizable town. Here she stopped, both to ask directions and to get a feeling of the nature of this world.

A number of motor vehicles were parked. Internal combustion, wheeled vehicles. They recalled the less technically advanced nations of her own home planet; indeed they were somewhat redolent of Quirinelle. She parked the bike and began walking down a wide street. There were shops with bright fascias selling all manner of goods. The signs were incomprehensible to her, though written in an alphabet not too far removed from the Westrenne one at home. She wondered vaguely if they would ever come up with a visual translator.

People were dressed in light summer frocks that were very different from those at home, but recognizably of a style that one would identify as generally "modern" and "Western". They were of much the same size as our own people—a shade shorter on average—and distinctly a people of the same type: all feminine and clearly of two sexes, one fair-haired, frailer, and smaller, one dark-haired, taller, and more robust-looking. People were shopping, chattering, loitering, or going about their business. There was a generally peaceful and contented air.

She saw three young brunettes of school age. They were dressed in neat uniforms with calf-length skirts and two rows of brass buttons on their high-collared, double-breasted tunics. They were marching in strict step, with delightful precision, as raiAntala herself had been taught to do in her schooldays whenever there was more than one brunette in uniform. How different, and yet how very familiar, everything seemed.

"Chalwë," said raiAntala sharply as they drew close. The three halted and saluted, arms across chests, in perfect unison, looking quizzically at the tall, almond-eyed stranger in strange uniform.

RaiAntala saluted. "Rayati Raihiranya," she said.

The three brunettes glanced among themselves, suppressing giggles. "Rayati lhi Rayin," said the tallest of the three. "Rayati lhi Rayin," echoed the others.

"I wonder if you would be so gracious as to direct me to the royal palace," said raiAntala.

This time they did giggle.

"It is not in this town, honored officer," said the tallest of the three.

"I know it is not. I just need to know the direction in which I must ride. I have an appointment to see your Queen."

More glances passed among the three, combining incredulity and excitement. Was this stranger insane? Or was she someone terribly interesting?

"You must ride the Great Road toward the mountains, honored officer," said the tallest of the three. "It is a long way from here."

"You are very kind," said raiAntala. "I should buy you coffee, but I have none of your money. Only this." She showed them a few Novaryan coins at which they gazed in fascination.

"May I enquire where you are from?" asked the tallest of the three.

"I am from another world. I am Antala FiaMartia, Captain of an aethyr-ship from many light-years away. Would you care to see my bike?"

The giggles became more open. A maid claiming to come from the stars and arriving on a bike. This was becoming silly.

"By all means, honored officer, show us your bike," said the tallest of the three, grinning broadly.

They accompanied raiAntala a hundred yards down the road to where her bike was parked. The chrome-glittering machine never failed to make an impression—not even here, where the name Chandra-Alarente meant nothing. There were appreciative sounds from the brunettes even from some way off.

"But it has no wheels," said the tallest of the three as they came closer.

"No," explained raiAntala. "It is a hoverbike. It rides about six inches off the ground. It is as happy over water as over land. It can handle most rough country without difficulty, and it turns on a penny."

"You're joking, aren't you?" said the tallest of the three.

"I'll tell you what. If you'll buy me a coffee, I'll take you for a spin."

"All right," said the tallest of the three. "Spin first."

"But of course." RaiAntala mounted the bike. "Jump up behind and hold 'round my waist. Tight."

The brunette mounted with ease and grace. Her arms about raiAntala's waist were surprisingly strong for her slightly spindly frame. RaiAntala kicked down the starter and the machine lurched forward. She rode out into the suburbs, noting the strange and yet somehow pedestrian architecture. She found a long, empty stretch of road and took the Chandra up to 150 mph, then made her celebrated spin turn that, as the thrusters reversed, gave the appearance, and sensation, of the bike's having shot out on a piece of elastic and snapped back in the other direction.

"Rayati, honored Captain. Having fun?" asked raiChinchi.

It was a bit surprising to have raiChinchi address her as if she had been on the bike too. Her voice came through the earbuds from which raiAntala was receiving other voices and all ambient sounds, which gave the eerie effect of raiChinchi being as much present as her other surroundings.

"I take it you aren't at the palace yet," raiChinchi continued.

RaiAntala revved the engine so that she could talk without being overheard and lowered the non-vocals on her sound unit.

"Rayati, raiChinch. No, I'm not. How did you know?"

"Well, the sound of your bike is a slight clue. Besides, you aren't even on your way. You stopped at a small town and are cruising about. I've been tracking you on the scanner. By the looks of things you've got a passenger. What are you up to, honored Captain?"

"Making friends with some local brunette schoolgirls."

"Whatever for? You shouldn't keep a Queen waiting, you know."

"Since they've lost track of us completely, they'll be impressed with how quickly I get there. But I'd like to know a little about this place other than what they choose to tell me, and brunettes from a good school are always terribly knowledgeable. They have just learned all the things adults have forgotten. And these girls are from a good school. I tell you that because I know you would worry dreadfully if you thought I were in bad company."

"Bosh. Anyway, how can you tell if alien girls are from a good school?"

"Immaculate uniforms, marching in perfect step. Some things never change. Anyway, they aren't that alien."

"Have fun, honored Captain. But don't be too sure about not being tracked. There's a mascûl on your tail."

"Are you serious?"

"This isn't a social call, honored Captain. Someone has been following you for the last fifty miles. Heavy biped, according to the scanner. Not an intemorph and not a saurian. From the readings I would suspect a mascûl."

"Where is it now?"

"Lurking about outside the town under cover of some trees, I think. Probably waiting for you."

"Well, well. Isn't it nice to be popular? Rayati."

"Rayati."

In a length of time that seemed like forever, and also absurdly short, raiAntala's passenger was back with her companions.

"Coffee?" said raiAntala, dismounting.

The passenger dismounted in an affectedly easy style, trying not to totter as she dizzily made her reunion with *terra firma*.

"My name is Lihashte Chavran," she said. "May I present my comrades Schionte Tennara and Tivrate Ariet?"

Each of them made in turn a deep reverence. They were ashamed now of having giggled so rudely.

"Miss Chavran, Miss Tennara, Miss Ariet; I am greatly honored," said raiAntala, bringing her heels together and dropping her head.

"Where would you like to have coffee, ma'am?"

"Oh, wherever you normally go."

"The Copper Kettle," suggested Miss Tennara. "We can't take her to the Java Jive."

"Oh, but I should love to see the Java Jive," said raiAntala.

Miss Chavran grinned. The opportunity to show off this stranger at the Java Jive was a triumph almost greater than the bike ride itself.

RaiAntala fell instinctively into step with the three youngsters as they marched to the café. It was down a cobbled side street: a curious place with tinted windows and a pink and pale blue neon sign. The design of everything was strange, and yet it reminded raiAntala of a dozen coffee bars she had haunted in Quirinelle. The strong rhythmic beat of the music that could be heard several doors away was very unlike Quirrie rock and roll, and yet had a certain decided kinship to it.

They entered a darkish room filled with a curious scented smoke. Tables and chairs in gleaming chrome were occupied by groups of brunettes, often dressed in black and with hair swept off their faces and rolled up into a coif with a spray of hair stiffened to stand up like a plume. Among blondes the fashion seemed to be for various shades of pink lip enamel lined with red. Among both sexes, heavy "temple-style" eyeliner seemed to be in fashion, often with cute curlicues emerging from the corners. Several customers were in school uniforms and were more conservatively coiffed and painted.

Miss Tennara and Miss Ariet commandeered an empty table and motioned raiAntala to join them. RaiAntala turned down the non-vocals on her transceiver, cutting the pounding beat of the music by about half.

"Double espressos?" asked Miss Chavran. Everyone assented. "Double espressos, fair serving girl," she called to a blonde waitress.

They took their seats amid considerable curiosity from the regulars. RaiAntala was not only a stranger, but she looked very foreign and was wearing an unrecognizable uniform.

RaiAntala acted as though she were oblivious of the attention. She was used to creating a stir in cafés.

"Do you know anything about schizomorphs?" she asked.

"Certainly," said Miss Chavran. "They are a humanoid race—or rather several humanoid races, because as far as we know all humanoid races are either intemorph or schizomorph. They look almost indistinguishable from ourselves; or at least, half of them do. They have two sexes called femīn and mascûl. The femīns look fully human. Their hair can be either dark or fair, but it is not a secondary sexual characteristic. And the mascûls are larger and more angular and look like a cross between people and wild beasts. Some of them even have fur on their faces."

The waitress arrived with steaming cups of a curious design. "Four double espressos, noble child," she said.

Miss Chavran flushed slightly. RaiAntala guessed that the address "fair serving girl" had been a shade presumptuous on the part of a schoolgirl and that the waitress was taking revenge. Miss Chavran paid nonchalantly. "Keep the change, miss," she said.

"Thank you, miss," said the serving girl. Order was restored.

"Anyway," said Miss Chavran hastily, "in the early millennia of a schizomorph historical cycle the femīns are predominant, but toward the end of the cycle the mascûls come to the fore, and schizomorphs become very ferocious and even kill their own kind. At this stage some of them even believe themselves to be descended from gorillas."

RaiAntala smiled at this naivety. "I doubt that they believe it literally. I imagine the gorilla is a sort of totem animal and the notion of descent expresses a symbolic filiation."

"It is said that the more civilized ones cut off their face-fur terribly close to the skin with very sharp blades in order to make themselves look more human," put in Miss Ariet.

"That is obviously a fable," said Miss Chavran. "Clearly they would consider their fur completely human—I mean human in their terms. Why should they cut it off in order to conform to *our* standards of humanity? The fur-cutting stories are obviously invented by humans like ourselves because we find the idea of facial fur repulsive."

"I'm not so sure," said Miss Ariet. "I have read that all schizomorphs are conceived as femīns but that half of them take on mascûl characteristics as a result of exposure during gestation to a particular hormone. In the early part of their historical cycles the femīns are always predominant, and even in the later part the race may still have an unconscious urge to conform to the universal human norm."

"Where did you read that?" asked Miss Chavran somewhat tartly. She was not accustomed to being challenged in argument by her followers and suspected Tivvie of showing off for the newcomer.

"In the *Weekly Pictorial*."

"The *Weekly Pictorial*," said Miss Chavran disdainfully.

"Probably the fur itself is just a yarn," suggested Miss Tennara. "People have seen them without face-fur and said they must have cut it off. I don't suppose they ever had it in the first place."

"Miss Chavran's reasoning is perfectly brilliant," said raiAntala, "and Miss Tennara's supposition makes perfect sense. But in point of fact, mascûls *do* have facial fur, and many of them do cut it off—so it seems the *Weekly Pictorial* must be good for something after all."

She hoped she had pacified all parties, not only from her natural good manners, but because she wanted facts from these young pups, not theories and arguments. She took a sip from her cup. It was peculiar stuff. Certainly not coffee. Slightly bitter; decidedly aromatic and rather viscous. Not exactly unpleasant—but odd and very surprising. These idiomatic translators could be too clever by half. Clearly this scented goo held something like the role of coffee in the society of this land, and so whatever its name actually was it had been rendered as "coffee" by the cognitor.

"In any case," she said, trying not to look too dubiously at her cup, "what are the chances of encountering a schizomorph—specifically a mascûl—here in Ranyam Astarche?"

"Absolutely nil," said Miss Chavran. "There are none here." She thought for a moment. "Well, actually there are a few at the Fearalyan Embassy in the capital. The Fearalyani are a schizomorph race that has diplomatic relations with Ranyam Astarche. Most of the servants and such are femīns, but the actual diplomats of some Fearalyan nations are all mascûls, so they have to be allowed in. They aren't on Astarchean soil, though, because the Embassy counts as Fearalyan soil. They aren't allowed to wander around out of the Embassy though, so you would never see one. I never have."

"So why is this Embassy here at all? My people tend to keep contact with the outlander to a minimum."

"So did we until recently, but lately there has been a good deal of trouble. Aethyr-pirates have attacked our ships and some of our outposts. They seem to be highly organized and are led by a devil called Kang Shahtha. They have been attacking the Fearalyani too. Some people believe they are supported by a powerful force much greater than themselves. So you see, some cooperation between ourselves and the Fearalyani has been necessary in order to fight these pirates."

"I see. Is this authorized by the Empress?"

"Which Empress?"

"That is what I have been wondering. When we first met, I gave you rayati Raihiranya and you gave me rayati Ihi Rayin. Have you no Empress—only a Queen? Who is your Queen's mistress?"

"You *are* a stranger, aren't you?" said Miss Tennara. "Do you come from Sai Esterline?"

"Of course not," said Miss Chavran. "If she came from Sai Esterline, she would *know* about us Astarcheans, whatever she *thought* of us."

"Yes, I am a stranger," said raiAntala. "I have not heard of this Sai Esterline. You must teach me as you would a child."

"And yet you have an audience with the Queen?" said Miss Chavran.

"Indeed I have, and I should prefer not to go to her in complete ignorance. You see, I chanced on this land accidentally, and your Sovereign has shown me the greatest civility."

"Well, gosh," said Miss Chavran, immediately wanting to kick herself for her *gaucherie*. "I mean, where can I start?"

"From the beginning," said raiAntala. "Start with the Caeren Empire."

"The Caeren Empire? Which one?"

"The original and best."

"You mean the one on the Mother World? The one that was destroyed three thousand years ago?"

"Who told you it was destroyed?" asked raiAntala.

"Well, everyone knows that, surely."

"I don't. But then I am a stranger, and I have the disadvantage of coming from the Mother World, and from the Caeren Empire."

"You're joking!"

"If I were, it wouldn't be all that funny, would it? But leave that aside. Just humor me. Give me a history lesson."

"All right. The Caeren Empire was pretty much the start of everything. Before that it was a different Age, I suppose. Great demons came to attack the Mother World, and Sai Rayanna, the Daughter of the Sun, came to drive them away. She was the first Empress of the present Age."

"We're all in agreement so far. Then what?"

"Well, hundreds of years later the demons came back. They laid siege to the city of Caere itself. The Empress then was Ashhevala—dawn-rider. She was great, but she was not Sai Rayanna. The mighty demons of darkness destroyed the city, laid waste the country, and murdered all the daughters of light. After that only demons lived on the Mother World and a few strange maidens that coupled with demons to make half-demon kindred.

"But before the Great Destruction, the Great Conjuress Shelatinhe drew up a thousand blondes and a thousand brunettes in a great cloud and took them to another world. That world was Sai Esterline, the land of the New Dawn.

"Of course all this happened in times very unlike our own. There were no ships of aethyr. It was all a kind of magic."

"Does it strike you that if your ancestors left Sai Herthe before the Great Destruction, they cannot have seen it happen? And that therefore it is pure conjecture?"

"You are not the first to suggest that. The Cathrians hold the same view."

"Who are the Cathrians?"

"Well, that brings us to the history of this planet, Neverthe. The Cathrians are one of a number of sects who believe that Sai Shelatinhe betrayed the True Empire by leaving Sai Herthe. Therefore they reject the sovereignty of the High Empress of Esterline. When aethyr-travel became possible, some of these sects left Sai Esterline for other worlds. The Cathriani came here and colonized a great continent to our east which is very rich in mineral resources. They built great cities and named their land Cathria.

They traded with other Old-Loyalist sects and became extremely rich.

"After a time, the Empress Chantrine IV sent an expedition to Neverthe to look for mineral deposits. The Cathrians refused them permission to enter their land, so they came to this continent and founded a new colony which they called Astarche. Eventually Astarche became great enough to have its own Queen. One of the Imperial Princesses was sent here to become our Sovereign, and her line has ruled ever since."

"Then surely your Queen is the servant of the Empress, in accordance with the law of thamë?"

"That was true until about fifty years ago when aethyr-piracy became such a problem that communication with Sai Esterline and the Imperial Command became difficult. Then our nearest allies were the Cathriani, and we began to have much greater co-operation with them. In this new atmosphere of friendship, the Cathrians put forward their views on the illegitimacy of the Esterline Empire to our Queen."

"And your Queen accepted these views?"

"No, but eventually she adopted a position of formal neutrality between the Empire and the Old Loyalists, which allowed Astarche to cooperate with all parties."

"And the Empire accepted this?"

"As you'd expect, the Empire was not entirely happy, but our Queen is still the only Sovereign of any consequence in this region who does not actually reject the claims of the Empire."

"I see," said Captain Antala. "Thank you very much. You have been wonderfully informative. I feel much less ignorant now about your beautiful country."

Miss Chavran made a sitting bow.

Seeing that their conversation was paused, a slightly older brunette approached the table carrying a slender, smoldering stick, rather like an incense stick, from the tip of which rose a strangely scented smoke.

"Ophrasti?" she asked. The word was untranslated as there was no very close equivalent in Herthelan Westrenne. RaiAntala had noticed a number of the young people here holding these sticks and breathing deeply of the smoke.

"Thank you, no," said Miss Chavran, nodding her head in the curtest of reverences. "I am in training. So are my friends."

"As you please," said the brunette with a deep bow and an unctuous smile.

"She *is* in training too," said Miss Tennara to raiAntala. "Miss Chavran is our school's champion in the art of two-sword fencing."

"How interesting," said raiAntala. "That used to be my vikheli when I was at school. Some day I must teach you the Twin Swallows style—if you are interested."

"I should be deeply honored to learn a style from the Mother World," said Miss Chavran excitedly.

"For now, though, I fear I must keep my royal appointment. I am sure we shall meet again."

"I do hope so," said Miss Chavran.

All of them stood, made reverence, and gave each other rayati. RaiAntala stepped out into the fresh air and bright sunlight. She beeped raiChinchi.

"I am getting a better picture of this place," she said. "My schoolgirls were very helpful. I'll tell you more on the road to the palace."

She mounted her Chandra and took the open road. There was very little traffic. Either private cars were a relative rarity or people did not travel much, she thought. However, after a short way she found her path barred by a sleek tail-finned sports car, presumably stolen, deliberately parked across the road. Beside it stood a very large mascûl dressed in some form of heavy leather clothing that may well have been reinforced as protective armor. It wore a long sword at its side.

"I think I've run into our mascûl-chum," said raiAntala to raiChinchi. "It is trying to bar my path."

"What are you going to do?" asked raiChinchi. "Can you get by?"

"I could, but I think I might as well find out what it wants."

"Be careful then."

"Oh, you know me, raiChinchers. Cautious to the point of timidity."

She dismounted and the mascûl stepped forward aggressively.

"Beautiful afternoon," said raiAntala, smiling pleasantly.

"It might not be for you," said the mascûl.

"Oh, but it is, I assure you," said raiAntala. "And I hope I find you enjoying it equally."

The mascûl walked forward and seized the handlebar of raiAntala's Chandra with a fist that was easily the size of both her hands combined.

"Kindly remove your hand from my bike," said raiAntala with undisturbed politeness.

"And why should I do that?" asked the mascûl.

"Because your greasy palms may smear the chrome," said raiAntala. "And I shouldn't like that."

"You've got a lot of lip for a pretty girl. What do you think you are with that toy sword? A warrior?"

Unfortunately, the silver-plated practice sword with which raiAntala had insisted upon arming herself was little more than a toy. She hoped that the mascûl could not be too certain of that, though it really was not a terribly convincing weapon.

"I am a warrior in the service of my Princess," she replied.

"A warrior." The mascûl laughed in a way that had more unpleasantness in it than any laugh raiAntala had ever heard. She wondered if mascûls were always like this. "How many people have you killed?"

"Killed? Why, none."

"And you call yourself a warrior?"

"I have never been off my homeworld until now."

"What of that?"

"My people do not kill their own kind."

"A warrior that never killed anyone. You women make me laugh."

"I am not a woman."

"I know what you are. One of these dark-haired melini. But you look like women, smell like women, and fight like women. You're only good for doing what women do."

"What an unpleasant creature you are. Please unhand my bike and I shall be on my way."

The mascûl stood insolently, firmly gripping the handlebar.

"You know," said raiAntala, "now that I think of it, I have killed a few creatures. They were Captain Kang Shahtha and all its crew—I don't know if they count as people."

"You're a liar."

"No, I assure you it is perfectly true. They became rather impertinent, and I found it necessary to kill them."

"I call you a liar."

"Have it your own way. It doesn't matter to me."

"I call you a liar, and you are afraid to fight me."

"Afraid? Why would I be afraid?"

"Because where I come from we fight to the death."

"But that is quite all right. I have no objection to killing outlanders."

With a single movement, the mascûl drew its long, cruelly sharp blade and raiAntala drew her silver-plated practice sword.

Chapter 9

An Audience with the Queen

RAIANTALA saluted with her blade and made a courteous bow as all civilized people do before commencing swordplay. The mascûl took advantage of these courtesies to aim a powerful stroke at raiAntala's lowered head. RaiAntala knew that if she tried to deflect the blow with her own blade the silver practice sword would be sheared in two, so she managed to spring backward out of range.

The mascûl grinned and swung its sword back for a lateral cut while charging forward. It was not a subtle style, and with a real sword raiAntala could have responded very effectively and without great difficulty. As it was, she knew that any sweep of that razor-keen blade could be the last thing she saw in this life.

She gained a little distance and then practised some flourishes, spinning the blade in her hand like a parade-fencer. She moved in, and, as she had hoped, the mascûl stepped back from the whirling silver. It did not look a formidable blade, but this melini wielded it with speed, skill, and confidence. Who knew what secrets might inhere in this alien steel or in the vixen who plied it?

With the balance of battle restored, raiAntala had gained space to consider her strategy. Each regarded the other with caution now, looking for an opening. RaiAntala was hampered by the knowledge that not only would her sword not withstand contact with the tempered warblade in her foeman's hand, but also that it had been designed specifically not to cause injury in practice combat.

With a look of determination that had in it a little of desperation, she attempted a slightly awkward thrust at the enemy's face. The warblade swept in and sheared the silver blade clean in two at a sharp angle. RaiAntala stared at her ruined weapon with a look of horror and disbelief. The mascûl grinned and drew back its sword for the *coup de grâce*.

As the deathblow descended, raiAntala swiftly stepped in and thrust the now-sharpened point of her sword-stump into the underside of the mascûl's upper arm, through the leather clothing. She hoped the pressure points on these humanoids were the same as those on real people. They were, and the warblade dropped from the mascûl's temporarily paralyzed hand.

With a single neat movement, raiAntala dropped her own sword and caught the foeman's as it fell. She stepped back, felt its balance, and took a few practice passes.

"A fine blade," she observed, making once more the salute and bow of which her foe had taken such disgraceful advantage. "And an excellent combat, if a little brief. I thank you, honored warrior."

The mascûl stared at her as she sheathed its sword.

"To the victrix the spoils and all that," explained raiAntala, patting it lovingly. "Hope you don't mind. You can have mine if you like. Dab of glue and it'll be as right as a trivet—or at least as right as it ever was."

As she walked toward her Chandra, raiAntala's enhanced hearing picked up a movement behind her. She turned to see the mascûl withdrawing some form of blaster from its leather coat. "I said to the death!" it barked.

Fortunately, its hand was still numb and slightly shaky, giving raiAntala the fraction of a second she needed to close the gap between them with a leap, drawing her new blade.

"To the death," she said. "So sorry, it quite slipped my mind for the moment." The mascûl's dark-bearded mouth grinned back at her from the place on the ground where the head had fallen.

"Stupid, stupid, stupid!" cursed raiAntala. "I forgot one cannot treat schizzies as if they were civilized. Never turn your back on a live one. How many times did I hear that at the Academy?"

"Never mind," said raiChinchi. "You got away with it that time. Just don't forget the lesson. Now, in the name of Sai Thamë, get on to the palace, and don't stop for any more distractions."

"Chalwë, Madam Pilot," replied raiAntala.

SHE was as good as her word. At full speed, the capital city was another hour's ride toward the mountain range, but long before she reached the mountains great golden-capped white towers rose before them. From the perspective of the approaching road, the lofty spires of nature were dwarfed by the heaven-piercing monuments of human splendor.

The city was laid out radially, with the palace at the center. All roads in the city led to the palace, even as all roads in the Ranyam led to the sacred city. This was the traditional pattern on Sai Herthe too, expressing the symbolism of the city as the sun and heart of the realm; the palace as the heart and hearth of the city; and the sacred monarch as the sun at the center of all. All this was right. All this was thamë. All this was in accordance with the Golden Order laid down from the beginning. Why, then, did it seem to raiAntala to have too much in it of human pride and too little of pure reflection of the sacred order of the cosmos? Was there a nuance of excess in the proud thrust of those spires—which were, after all, *supposed* to be resplendent, in imitation of the true Sun Herself? Or was it merely raiAntala's own prejudice: her unfamiliarity with an alien land, coupled with the account of this planet's history she had received from Miss Chavran?

RaiAntala shrugged. She was not one to make hasty judgments. She trusted her feelings up to a point, but did not idolize them. Young and rash as she was, she came from a family of diplomats, courtiers, and military theorists. Both from her background and from her mother wit, she knew that things were often far more complex than they at first appeared.

The city was large compared with the town she had just come from, but small by the standards of the great cities of Sai Herthe. It was no Trintitiana or Chelverton or Nevrayapurh, and yet it was impressive. There were many great town houses, all built from the same white stone as the palace. Unlike most Herthelan capitals, this city, it seemed, had little lay-life of its own. It was there almost solely to serve the palace: to house the great ladies who lived within it and those who lived outside it: the Cabinet and the courtiers; the socialites and the supplicants; the embassies and the trade delegations; and then all the many who fed and clothed and served and entertained them. So much seemed evident to the Captain on her first brief tour of the city. But brief it was, for she knew that she should delay no longer. She approached one of the great gates of the palace complex. They were high wrought-metal gates set in white stone archways, gilded with pure yellow gold. Each one terminated one of the wide radial roads of the city.

The gate she rode up to was, like all the others, closed and guarded by two uniformed brunettes. The gates were opened quite regularly as people passed in and out on the extensive business of the palace, but each incoming traveler unknown to the guards must identify herself and give account of her business. If this world was like Sai Herthe, such a procedure would be more to keep out the idly curious than from any more serious reasons of security.

RaiAntala dismounted and saluted the guard. "Ehr Chalwë," she said. "I am Captain Antala FiaMartia of the *Silver Vixen*. I have been graciously invited by your most honored Sovereign to enter her light-bestowing presence."

Both guards saluted, and the senior of them spoke: "Ehr Chalwë, honored Captain. You are expected. Please pass."

The gates swung open automatically.

"Should I park my bike inside the gate, noble defender?" asked Captain Antala.

The senior guard smiled. "It will be a long walk if you do, honored Captain. Ride toward the palace and you will come to another gate. The guard there will instruct you."

"Thank you, noble defender. Rayati."

"Rayati lhi Rayin."

The palace complex was indeed vast. It could have passed for a small city in itself. RaiAntala passed the various stages of gates and portals, was divested first of her bike and then of her sword. The outer guardians had been briefed to expect her. As she came to the interior of the palace itself, she was greeted by blondes, exquisitely robed and painted, who reverenced her deeply and treated her as if she were a person of considerable importance, though this might perhaps have been merely the etiquette of the court toward any visitor.

As they passed down magnificent corridors, often lined with white marble columns and decorated with statues and reliefs of peacocks and other emblems of royalty, she began to grow curious as to what the inner sanctum would be. A vast hall with raised throne and guards in splendid array, perhaps? A more modern reception hall, oak-paneled and businesslike? Quite suddenly, as it seemed, they came upon a small iron-bound, almost rustic, wooden door. Two guards saluted and stood aside, and the courtier who was escorting her—a charming and exquisitely mannered blonde—laid her hand on the door handle and said: "Her Majesty awaits within."

The Captain reverenced deeply to her conductress. The handle was turned and the door opened. It was clear that the Captain was expected to proceed alone.

She stepped through the door and was surprised by sunlight; for, after the long corridors of the palace, she was now in a walled garden, open to the heavens. Birds sang and a fountain played, and seated at a small table with a chessboard set out upon it was a young blonde, who could only be the Queen.

The Captain knelt and touched her forehead to the ground.

"Rayati. Please rise," said the Queen. Her voice was sweet and gentle and perfectly modulated, like a musical instrument in the hands of a mistress-player.

The Captain rose to her feet, made deep reverence, and gave rayati.

"Stand straight, pray, and let me look at you," said the Queen.

"As Your Majesty commands," said the Captain, standing to attention. The Queen looked upon a maid tall above the common height of this world, copper-skinned and almond-eyed, radiant in the uniform of a full Novaryan Captain, and with the air of a fine and fearless warrior, and found herself impressed.

"Welcome to our humble court, honored Captain," she said.

"Far from humble, Your Majesty, it is resplendent as a thousand suns. The eyes of a poor provincial such as myself are dazzled by its magnificence."

"Hardly provincial, honored Captain. I am told that you come from the True Empire itself. The Empire which many hold to be passed these long millennia from the realm of things palpable and yet from which all our thamë derives: the source and fount of the Golden Order by which we all have our being."

The Captain reverenced low. "I have that honor, Your Majesty, yet I am but a simple Captain in the navy of a Queen who serves the High Empress. And even in the court of that Queen have I never been privileged to place my unworthy foot. How deeply honored am I then to receive Your Majesty's most gracious invitation to enter this image of Paradise upon the realm below and to look upon its very sun incarnate."

"But they have spoken true? You are from holy Caere?"

"Not from Caere itself, Your Majesty," replied the Captain. "Caere is far from where I lived and is no longer the center of the Raihir. The present Empress dwells far to the West, in the holy city of Ladyton. Ladyton lies at the meeting-point of three great nations, and in one of those, named Novarya, I was born."

"Yet Caere is in that same world?"

"It is, Your Majesty, but far to the East, and it is difficult of access, for as one travels eastward in my world, the machines and devices of the West cease to function, for the East belongs yet to another time and another order of things."

"It is someway similar in this world," said the Queen. "To the land of Cathria Maya no airplane may fly, no train or autocar may run, but there, they say, the enchantments of old still keep a force far greater than here in the West. Is it not strange that ships of the Aethyr may fly to other worlds, but not to the other half of this one?"

"There are many kinds of distance, Your Majesty, of which simple miles and light-years are but one. The East of my world, and no doubt of yours, is near in space, but in other ways much further than the sun, which I was circling this morning."

"You are wise, honored Captain. And I hear that your ship met with a mishap on its way from the sun to here."

"It did, Your Majesty."

"We have heard nothing from you from that time to this. Are you all safe? Were any hurt?"

"None were hurt, Your Majesty."

"But your ship is grounded? You came on alone?"

"I did, Your Majesty."

"Where is your ship? We shall send out a party to help your crew and to bring them here as guests."

"Your world is unfamiliar, Your Majesty. My crew is small and is about necessary tasks. I shall fetch them here soon, with your permission."

"As you wish, honored Captain. Do you play chess?"

"I think so, Your Majesty."

The Queen laughed a charming golden laugh. "You do or you do not, honored Captain. How can you be unsure?"

"I was unsure, Your Majesty, whether the game we call chess at home is the same game that you call chess."

"Pray see for yourself," said the Queen, extending a slender hand toward the chessboard before her. "White is to move. What move would you make?"

The Captain studied the board for a full minute.

"And is the game the same, noble traveller?"

"It is the same, Your Majesty, and white is in a perilous position."

"And how should she move, think you? You need not fear it discourtesy to defeat me, for I myself am white, and black is my Vizier, Telarmine. She defeats me quite regularly, and it would delight me for you to turn the tables on her."

"It is late in the game for that, I fear, Your Majesty," said the Captain.

"Then answer me something else. It is a question about the nature of the game that has long troubled my mind, and I feel you may be the one to answer it. The Queen is the most important piece on the board, is that not so? If she is taken, the game is lost."

"That is so, Your Majesty," said the Captain.

"Why is it then that the Queen can move but one square in any direction, while her Princess or Vizier can move the whole length of the board in any way she pleases?"

The Captain suppressed a look of surprise. "Because, Your Majesty, the Queen is the yerthing of the Spirit Herself. Every possibility is latent in her; but hers is the Unacting Action. Is it not written: 'Earth moves but Heaven is still; the rim revolves but the Center remains without motion'? The Queen is that unmoving Center containing all potentialities; while those potentialities are enacted outwardly by her servants, each in the manner of her own capacity."

The Queen moved her hands as if to clap them but restrained the childlike gesture. "That makes it perfectly clear, honored Captain. I wonder why no one has explained this to me before."

"I wonder too," said the Captain. It did indeed seem very strange. At home it would be questioned whether a people who lacked a basic grounding in the Metaphysics of Polity could be fit to govern a village, far less a Ranyam. Princess Melenhe, like every royal person, even those far from the throne, had been brought up from her earliest years on the Science of State. RaiAntala had no such background, but like every educated person, she understood the symbolic principles on which all life is founded.

She had heard of peoples who had lost these principles, who even had no true Royal Line. She knew also of peoples who termed the aethyr "space"—as if all that great distance she had travelled to this world were not pervaded by the fifth and immaterial element, but were a void of simple nothingness—a "space". RaiAntala felt a sudden vertiginous lurch in the pit of her stomach as she stood for a second, in imagination, upon the precipitous void of this empty universe. She knew that the two voids were one: that which was enacted in the State and that which was imagined in the Aethyr. Could it be that the people of Astarche were so far strayed that they were less of a State than the tiny polity of the *Silver Vixen*?

It did not seem so. The palace was constructed according to true Principle. There was another possibility, a little less frightening but equally serious. Could it be that the Royal Science was known, but was for some reason being withheld from the Queen herself?

A maidservant entered, bringing a golden tray with glasses of cordial, and the Queen bade the Captain drink with her.

"Tell me more about the Royal Pieces in chess, wise warrior," she commanded.

"In the high days of Caere, Your Majesty, in the days of the Outlander Wars, after the first Warrior-Queens, there was a division between the two functions that were both fulfilled by Sai Rayanna. There was a High Queen or Raihiranya and a War-Queen or Princess. The High Queen directed all things from the still Center, and the Princess rode forth, commanding the armies in all the eight directions of space. It is from this, they say, that the two Royal Pieces are derived: though the Principle behind them is universal."

"And is the Princess also a Vizier?"

"The ancient name of the piece, Your Majesty, is *li Frist,* which can be translated as Principessa, or Princess, the First of subjects, or as the Queen's First Minister. Whoever carries the will of the Queen from the serene Oneness into the world of the ten thousand things may be called li Frist."

"How do you come to know all this, honored Captain?"

"In my country, Your Majesty, all Raihira are taught these things. My family have all been servants of our Queen—how, indeed, could a Captain serve her Queen if she knew not the principles whereby she served?"

"You shall teach me more, Captain. You shall bring your crewmaidens to be my guests. You shall meet with me tomorrow. But I forget. You are not my Captain to command."

"Not your Captain, Your Majesty, but yours to command, most certainly," said raiAntala, making deep reverence.

"You are too kind. Then I shall see you tomorrow in the morning?"

"If Your Majesty wishes it."

"She wishes it."

The Captain looked at the young Queen, a little older than herself in years but younger in many other ways. She looked again at the chessboard, picked up a white knight and moved it to another position.

"If your rules are the same as ours, Your Majesty, white may find that move helpful."

The Queen studied the board. "How clever!" she exclaimed. "Wait until Telarmine sees that! Until tomorrow, noble warrior."

The Queen rang a bell, and the blonde who had escorted the Captain thither appeared.

"Show the Captain to her rooms. I wish her sword to be restored to her. She shall wear it on the morrow."

"By all means, Your Majesty, only——"

"She shall wear it on the morrow in my presence."

"As Your Majesty commands."

"Rayati, warrior."

RaiAntala knelt once more and touched her forehead to the ground. "Rayati, Your Majesty."

She left the lovely garden backward and was once again led through high corridors until she came to a suite of rooms hung with rich tapestries. It had a marble sunken bath, a canopied bed, and a terrace looking out over some of the palace gardens.

"You may wish to rest and bathe, honored Captain," said her conductress. "When you ring this bell, your dinner will be served." She made deep reverence and left.

Captain Antala surveyed her quarters. She toyed with the thought of making a report to raiChinchi, but decided to do so later in a place where she could be sure of being unheard. For now she simply sent a beep to let her know all was in order.

She drew aside the long curtain that partly veiled the terrace, and there behind it stood a mascûl in military uniform. It was less ugly than the last one, but that was no great feat. RaiAntala sprang backward, adopting a modified form of the First Defensive Position in the White Dragon Style.

Chapter 10

An Audience without the Queen

THE MASCÛL covered its right fist with its left hand and made deep reverence. She covered her own fist and returned a lesser reverence.

"Forgive me," said the mascûl. "This is ungainly entrance, but discretion was necessary. My mistress wishes to speak with you."

"I am a guest of Her Majesty," said the Captain. "Why would I go in secrecy about her house upon the business of outlanders?"

"I assure you, most honored Captain, it is not from Her Majesty that we wish to conceal anything. You are a stranger here and know little of what passes. Will it harm Her Majesty if you hear what my mistress has to say? And may it not be part of your duty to your own Royal Mistress?"

"You speak fair, outlander, and you may have the right. Pray honor me by telling who is your mistress."

"She is the Lady Entresne Selvar, Ambassadress of the Chenri Confederation."

"You must forgive my ignorance, but what is the Chenri Confederation?"

"I think my mistress will explain matters better than I. Will you not come?"

"I see no harm in it," said the Captain.

RaiAntala allowed herself to be led along a maze of passages, for which in itself she was not sorry. She was beginning to form a picture of the layout of the palace, which might always prove helpful in the future.

Eventually she was ushered into a pleasant suite decorated with fine statues and paintings. A few of the paintings included mascûli in a style and in attitudes that could be seen to be idealized—they looked graceful, smooth, almost human until one looked more closely. Whatever effect was intended, raiAntala found it rather creepy.

A mature person who had a strange look, like a blonde with something of the manner of a brunette, and with dark hair, arose from the leather chaise longue on which she had been seated and made a curious sort of curtseying reverence.

"Rayati, honored Captain," she said. The word rayati was unchanged from Herthelan Westrenne to Astarchean, being an ancient and sacred greeting from long before the Esterlini had left Sai Herthe. On the lips of the Lady Selvar, however, it had the distinct ring of an alien greeting used for courtesy.

The Captain responded with a crisp military reverence. "Rayati, my lady," she replied.

"Thirin, you may leave us," said Lady Selvar to the mascûl who had conducted raiAntala to her.

Thirin spoke words in the dialect of its homeland, supposing that the Captain would not understand them: "This is a dangerous warrior, my lady. I think I should remain." The translator handled them perfectly.

Lady Selvar replied in Astarchean: "I have scarcely more strength than one of their blonde chelani. The honored Captain is a gentilmaid. She would not harm me. Please leave."

Thirin made a strange salute with its hand toward its head and left the room.

"Pray be seated, honored Captain," said Lady Selvar, gesturing toward a chair. "Will you honor me by taking cordial with me?"

"The honor will be mine, my lady," said the Captain, taking the seat indicated.

"You look at me strangely, I fear, honored Captain."

"I most humbly beg your forgiveness. I am just getting my bearings. I have not—that is, I have never——"

"This is the first time you have seen a woman, perhaps, honored Captain."

"It is, I fear, my lady."

Lady Selvar smiled comfortingly. "It is an unnerving experience, is it not? We all find it so at first. We are so very like each other—and yet so very different."

"So very different," agreed the Captain.

"And yet the same Dea made us all, in Her wisdom."

RaiAntala touched the fingers of her right hand to her forehead and her chest, honoring the mention of the Divine Name.

Lady Selvar clapped her hands twice, and a serving maid appeared bearing a tray with beautiful small glasses and a cut-crystal decanter of golden fluid. The girl looked very like a blonde serving maid except that she was dark haired.

"Forgive me, my lady," said the Captain, "but are all your people dark haired or is hair color quite random? Or has it some other significance than sex?"

"There are genetic factors, honored Captain, but for practical purposes it is random, having no significance beyond the aesthetic. People who look like you, though—Estrennes, I mean—always have dark hair. Your white-haired Estrenne blondes look quite startling to us at first."

"It is true that I am from the east of my world, my lady—or at any rate my people come from there. My particular branch has its own nation in the West—but why do you call me Estrenne, as if I were from the east of this world or of yours?"

"People who resemble you tend to gravitate to what is termed the east of a planet. It has to do with the nature of the directions. You are rising-sun people everywhere, while we are setting-sun people on any planet. You see, despite our differences, we all have much in common."

"As you say, my lady."

"But I see you are a businesslike Captain. You wish to know why I invited you here."

"Only a little, my lady. The honor of your company is more than reason enough for being here."

"I come from the world called Fearalya. You have heard of that perhaps?"

"I heard a little this afternoon."

"What have you heard?"

"That you are a schizomorphic people ruled by your mascûli, as all schizomorphi come to be in the late times of a world-cycle."

"That is but partly true, honored Captain. The great nations of Fearalya are mascûl-ruled, it is true; but others are ruled by their femîni; in others again the rule has not been settled and vacillates between one system and the other; in still others compromises have been found, and both mascûli and femîni share in rulership, each having their areas that they govern best."

"Thank you, my lady. I understand your world a little better now."

"The great divide among the Fearalyani is on religious grounds. Some follow the mascûl God and some remain loyal to Great Dea. From this most fundamental alignment, all other outlooks upon life follow."

"Thank you again, my lady."

"I see that you came not here for a lesson in alien polity, honored Captain. Please humor me a little further, for if you are truly a stranger to this planet and to all the worlds nearby, there are things that you were well to learn."

"I am in great eagerness to learn them, my lady, and I thank you for being my teacher."

"There is another god, honored Captain, if I dare sully the word god with that name. Indeed the name itself I do not mention, but everywhere it is known as the Dark Lord.

"Now Fearalya is a great world of many nations—great nations spanning the larger parts of continents and smaller nations both within the continents and on many islands; and in the islands to the South, the Cult of the Dark Lord has taken hold and is rapidly spreading northward. They have many ways of wooing people, but if a people is not won quickly they simply begin killing until an island is ready to accept their rule.

"Even in some of the great nations they are gaining adherents. Most particularly in the United Republics, where a strong political party is controlled by sympathizers of the Dark Cult——"

"Forgive me, my lady, you said a political—what?"

"A political party. It is a faction or interest group that competes for the rulership of the State. The United Republics are entirely ruled by these parties and have no monarch at all. Other States have monarchs but are still largely controlled by the parties. These operate on the late-masculik principle of perpetual opposition and adversarial government.

"But let me not trouble you with the endless complexities of the polity of the masculik part of my world, which, frankly, are as strange to me as they are to you. I represent the Chenri Confederation, which gathers together the femīnil nations of my world, all of which have Queens and some also mascûl-Queens, which are known to us as Kings; and all of which operate on the

79

femĭnil principles of concord and harmony rather than opposition and factionalism: principles akin to your own Golden Order, or thamë. So you see, my peoples are in some ways closer to yours than they are to the masculiki of our own world."

"In some ways, perhaps, my lady."

"This is a long preamble, but it has been needful. Let me now come to the matters that may directly affect you. These followers of the Dark Lord are not confined to my world. Far from it. They control a mighty empire that has its center in the far world of Nokht. The pirates that plague these worlds also are followers of the Dark Lord, and whether they are indeed merely pirates who hold the Dark faith, or whether they are mercenaries and forward troops of the Dark Empire, even I cannot yet be sure—and believe me, it is my business to know these things.

"The Dark Ones have taken many worlds by many means. They appeal to the weaknesses in all schizomorph peoples. They appeal to the worst natures of masculi. They preach a creed of violence and the rule of the strong over the weak; and where they cannot tempt, they threaten; and when their threats fail, they begin to destroy; and when destruction does not bring submission, they destroy all."

"I can see, my lady, that they are a terrible danger to your people and a considerable nuisance to this world."

"They are a terrible danger to all peoples, honored Captain; schizomorph and intemorph alike. You know nothing of these worlds, but if you are from where you claim to be from, I think you will know the name of the Dark Lord if I speak it."

"Then speak it, my lady."

"It is Mordhûl."

RaiAntala's eyes grew wide. "That one."

"I see you know the name, honored Captain, for you do not speak it."

"It is accursed, my lady. It is the name of the arch-demon that tried to overrun my world three thousand years since. Is that one not dead?"

"The Dark Lord cannot die. Its followers call it a god; but your people and mine know it for what it is. And believe me when I say that it intends to overrun all the worlds, including this one and, eventually, your own homeworld. Recently the pirates abducted a whole ship full of Astarcheans, and the Government here paid a massive ransom to get them back safely and prevent them from being sold into slavery on Darkheld worlds. Such attacks only become more frequent and more audacious; and all this is only the beginning. I know. I have seen; and your people also have seen."

"Madness to pay these creatures!" exploded raiAntala. "It only makes them stronger. Who was advising the Queen?"

"What can one do, honored Captain? Allow one's own people to be sold into the horrors of the Darkness?"

"What can one do, my lady? Blow them out of the sky. That is what one can and must do."

"Spoken like a Caeren, noble warrior. And I hear tell you have begun this policy yourself."

"What mean you by that, my lady?"

"Rumor holds that you blew the great flagship of Kang Shahtha out of the sky."

"Does it indeed, my lady?"

"It does, and if that were true you have placed yourself in great peril. The Kang are a terrible warrior tribe, and they will not rest till they have destroyed the perpetrator of such an outrage upon them."

RaiAntala shrugged. "Why should I care whether they rest or not?"

Lady Selvar laughed almost gleefully. "Oh, I like you, honored Captain. But I also fear for you. I hear tell that a mascûl was found dead on the road not far from here and that you came in bearing a Kang sword. Why do you not bear your own sword, Captain?"

"I have my reasons, my lady."

"Then have a care also. Next time they might not send a single assassin."

RaiAntala snapped her fingers in scorn for her enemies. Then she blushed, stood up, and made deep reverence, for this was the sort of gesture she made naturally among her friends, but it was wholly out of place in a royal court.

Lady Selvar took advantage of raiAntala's discomfiture to press a more personal question. She laughed kindly and reassuringly and then said in the friendliest of tones, "Forgive me, noble warrior, but how comes one so young to be full Captain of an Imperial ship?"

"Perhaps I am less young than I look," said raiAntala.

"Who has sent you here, honored Captain? What is your mission?"

"No mission, my lady. I am far from home by accident, having entered an aethyr-crease. I have no business here. I wish only to return my crew and passengers."

"Your passengers, honored Captain——"

"Indeed, my lady," said the Captain, determined to cut off this line of questioning. "And if I may respond with a like question, how comes a girl so young to be Queen of Astarche?"

"Her honored mother, the late Queen, and several royal personages took a State-ship to Cathria Mena to negotiate alliance. The ship was destroyed by pirates." She bowed her head. RaiAntala touched her forehead and her chest.

"I am distressed to hear that, my lady. And if I may ask one further thing: who was charged with the education of the Princess, before she became Queen?"

"The Lady Telarmine, Vizier to the old Queen and to the young, who fortunately was unable to be present on the fated ship."

"I have not yet had the honor of meeting her."

"She is away at her lodge in the mountains entertaining delegates from the United Republics. She does much of her work there. But, honored Captain, our time grows short and there is more that I would have you understand."

"I am learning much, my lady."

"Have you considered the question of why you were invited to the palace and granted immediate audience with the Queen herself?"

"I have meditated upon that question, my lady."

"And what answer have you found?"

"Only that the Astarcheans are an extraordinarily hospitable people."

"You are playing games, honored Captain. Are you unaware of the stir you have caused by your claim to be from the True Raihir?"

"In truth, I assumed that to have something to do with the invitation."

"Do you not see how it could change everything? If the True Raihir still exists, if you represent it, if indeed there were a Princess of the Blood Imperial in your party——"

"Who has suggested that?" asked the Captain.

"Mere vulgar rumor. I take no cognizance of it, of course. But if it were true, or were believed to be true, it would place a claim upon the loyalty not merely of Astarche, but of the Cathrias and their allies, and even upon that of Esterline itself. It might upset many ambitions in Astarche, but give rise to new and greater ones. And then there is the story that you have killed Kang Shahtha. Do you not realize that to some of the younger officers of the Royal Fleet you will appear like a Daughter-Knight of old Caere smiting the enemy as they have long wished to do?"

"I had no intention of causing such a stir. I merely flew off course into an aethyr-crease."

"And there is one more thing. Part of the power of the Cult of the Dark Lord lies in its reputation for invincibility. Once a nation or a world is breached by them, it is only a matter of time until it falls. Once it falls it can never be reclaimed."

"My lady, the True Raihir was breached millennia ago, but the Hordes of Darkness were utterly destroyed there."

"That is well known, honored Captain. But they were destroyed not by mortal maids but by the Sun Herself come down upon the world of things palpable."

"By Sai Rayanna: that is true. But centuries later they came again."

"And everyone here—except a few—believes that the Raihir was then destroyed."

"It is not so. The descendants of Sai Rayanna came close to defeat, it is true; but they rallied and destroyed the Hordes. The Dark Lord itself, if not killed as it now seems, was certainly laid low."

"And if that is known, the hypnotic belief in the inevitability of the Darkness once it takes hold will be destroyed."

"If so, my lady, I shall regard that as my good deed for the week."

"You are playing in a game with stakes far higher than you knew, young Captain."

"They always say high stakes make the game interesting, my lady."

"Whoever has sent you here, be sure to obey her and be not tempted upon some wild enterprise of your own."

"No one has sent me, my lady. I am simply off my course. It may be that Providence has sent me, but no person has."

"I could wish you had been more frank with me, honored Captain, but I understand that frankness toward me may not be your first duty. If you ever need my help, please return here."

"Thank you, my lady. I may indeed avail myself of your kindness. Rayati, madam."

"Rayati, honored Captain."

RAIANTALA was conducted back to her rooms by Thirin—a procedure that was hardly necessary, since her fine directional sense had already assimilated the pattern of the tortuous corridors. Still, her instinct told her not to be too free in showing her strengths.

Back in her tastefully opulent apartment she lay on a long couch and found herself suddenly very tired. She rang the bell and a little blonde serving maid appeared. She ordered a light repast, for it was long since she had eaten.

The blonde returned shortly with a tray most artistically arranged. How pleasant it was to be in the company of a simple, genuine blonde after this strange femīn who was neither blonde nor brunette.

She spoke to the serving maid, who instantly knelt and touched her forehead to the floor. She had expected to have a little conversation with her as she set out the food from the tray on a small carved table, but the blonde finished her work with great deftness and then knelt demurely before the Captain to answer her questions. RaiAntala asked about her work, her friends, and her family. It all seemed very sweet and normal. Suddenly Ranyam Astarche felt rather a lot like home.

She finally dismissed the maid, who cleared the things and left. RaiAntala turned toward the great canopied bed where a silken nightdress lay neatly folded on the pillow. It was a curious thought that the last time she had slept had been in a little hotel in Ushasti County, Novarya, on dear, distant Sai Herthe.

Chapter 11

The Invasion of the *Silver Vixen*

SHORTLY after the Captain's duel with the mascûl assassin, Commander Carshalton had returned to the *Silver Vixen* from a brief hoverbike reconnaissance of the area.

"There's a village nearby," she said. "They are very kind and helpful, but I haven't been very informative about the *Vixen*. The Captain prefers discretion at this stage. They really are the most delightful people, though—very happy to give us food for the night and tomorrow's breakfast. There's also a small lake nearby from which we can draw water. So I want Madam Pilot to move the *Vixen* over to the lake while raiEvelynn takes raiEstrelle and the Paxit-maids into the village. A blonde will be best at dealing with these people; the Paxits will know what they want for feeding us. RaiEstrelle can ride a hoverbike, so you'll take one of the Paxits each."

She looked expectantly at raiEvelynn, who was a little taken aback by raiClaralin's sudden air of command.

"Chalwë, Commander," said raiEvelynn a little belatedly.

"Where is the lake, Commander?" asked the Pilot.

"About ten miles east of here, taking the nearest pole as north."

"Do you mind if I see the area first, Commander?"

"I was about to suggest that, Madam Pilot. We'll do a quick recce on our bikes, and you can work out the best and most discreet way of positioning the ship to take on water."

"Should I be doing anything, Commander?" asked raiCharmian.

"I want the Princess to stay aboard, and you will look after her."

"Chalwë, Commander."

The members of the company moved about their business. The Princess retired to the small room set aside for her, to attend to her hair and makeup. She felt it part of her duty to look impeccable. RaiCharmian accompanied her.

"Commander Carshalton seems rather efficient, doesn't she, rairaiMela—I mean Your Highness?"

"Mela will do while we are alone," said the Princess. "Yes, she does. I am so glad raiAntala appointed her Commander. It is good for both of them and for the relationship between them."

They chattered idly for a while. It felt rather artificial somehow, talking as if they were on the homeworld and everything was normal. Finally raiCharmian broached the matter that was preying on both their minds.

"What do you make of the attack on raiAntala?"

"Was it a planned attack, do you think? Perhaps it was just some aggressive mascûl."

"I know that's what raiChinchers said, but, rairaiMela, there *aren't* aggressive mascûli on this planet. That is pretty clear from the Captain's report. Those school-brunettes have lived here all their lives and never even *seen* a mascûl. That one must have tailed raiAntala. Where from? Does it mean they know where we are? What else do they know? What do the brunettes think about it? They will never discuss these things with blondes for fear of worrying us. Don't they imagine we can think of these things for ourselves?"

"I know how you feel, darling, but at a time like this they need more than ever to maintain the order of things."

"I understand that, rairaiMela, but it makes me so nervous. That bang I heard a minute ago. I felt for a moment that it was something dreadful."

"It scared me too, but——" The Princess stopped and listened. "Are those footsteps?"

"Yes, they are. Someone's in the ship."

"Surely not."

"Listen. They're opening and closing doors as if they were searching the place."

"They must have some kind of electronic override device to work the portals. I'm going to go out and see."

"No, Your Highness! I am here to look after you. Those are my orders. Stand against the wall beside the door where you can't be seen, and I shall open it a little and peep out."

The Princess obeyed her appointed guardian, truly impressed at how the ship's company was already functioning as a true polity.

RaiCharmian reached for the door-control, but before she could touch it, the door slid back. Framed in the silver portalway was a huge mascûl with no hair on its head but abundant black fur on its face. It was dressed in heavy leather clothing and had a sword at one side and a blaster at the other. It moved into the room and took raiCharmian by the shoulders. Its manner was unfathomable, for it seemed both amorous and aggressive at the same time. It barked words that neither of the blondes could understand and pushed raiCharmian further into the room, while closing the door behind them with a flick of the small controller unit on its wrist.

The Princess, now standing behind the mascûl and as yet unseen, looked in horror as the creature rammed raiCharmian up against the far wall of the small chamber and began to paw her body. Silently, rairaiMela stole up behind the mascûl, which was both too obsessed with what it was doing and far too noisy to notice her. She managed to remove the creature's blaster from its holster and felt for the triggering-point. The mascûl suddenly became aware of her and turned. RairaiMela ran backward, and there was a flash of light. For a fraction of a second the mascûl's body was irradiated, almost like a neon tube, and then it fell to the ground, lifeless.

RaiCharmian was dead white, wide-eyed, and trembling. "How did you know how to work that thing?" she asked in a strange, distant voice.

"I didn't," said rairaiMela. "I was trying to work it out, and it just went off in my hand." She put her arms about her friend. RaiCharmian was cold and clammy.

"What now, Your Highness?"

"We aren't far from the ship's outer portal. We try to get out as quickly and quietly as possible. Stay close behind me, raiCharmie. Stay quiet, and don't worry. If anything spots us, it's dead."

"But what if there are lots of them?"

"Just be quiet and follow me. Those are your orders."

"Chalwë, Your Highness."

The Princess opened the door. Fortunately, the ship's doors were silent. The corridor outside was empty. The mascûl they had just killed was probably detailed to this one, and it would not have been missed yet. She moved quickly to the end of the corridor. She felt raiCharmian behind her. She felt the girl's cold terror. She stopped at the corner at the end of the corridor and patted raiCharmian's arm. "It's all right," she whispered. "We're very close. Just do your duty."

She peeped into the next corridor. It was the last one before the outer portal. One mascûl. She blasted it as it reached for its weapon. Thank Dea for silent blasters. The great ramp leading to the outer world was down. There was one mascûl holding a large long-range beam weapon and facing away from them. RairaiMela blasted it from behind.

"We don't go down the ramp," said rairaiMela. "Just do what I do."

"Chalwë," said raiCharmian in a voice that seemed to come from miles away.

Very quickly, rairaiMela got onto the ramp and, lying on her stomach, let herself down over the side of it until she was hanging on by her hands. She then dropped onto the grass a few feet below. Like an automaton, raiCharmian followed her.

"We move around the ship close to the hull, toward those trees, and then break and get into their cover. That way they will have very little chance to spot us visually. Pray they haven't got the ship's scanners working."

"Might they have?" asked raiCharmian tremulously.

"Very unlikely. The ship's systems are very tightly encoded, and if I know raiChinchi, she's made them even harder to crack."

The two blondes attained tree cover quickly. They half-ran, out of sight of the road, in the direction rairaiMela thought was the way to the lake. Within minutes they heard the approaching roar of two hoverbikes.

"A Range-Runner and a Chandra," said rairaiMela, who knew her bikes. "RaiChinchi and the Commander."

They ran out onto the road and flagged down the two brunette riders.

"What are you doing out of the *Vixen*?" demanded Commander Carshalton.

"The ship's full of mascûli," gasped rairaiMela. "No idea how many are in there. I've killed three of them. Don't know if they're on alert yet."

"They're probably trying to crack the ship's systems," said raiChinchi.

"All right, Madam Pilot, let's get in there," said the Commander.

"You may want this," said the Princess, handing raiClaralin the blaster.

"Thank you. Don't worry, raiChinch, I'll bag you one when I kill the first mascûl."

"I am Haiela," said raiChinchi. "I don't use weapons."

"Greenies!" exclaimed the Commander. "You wouldn't care to tie our hands behind our backs while you're at it, would you?"

"I am sorry, Commander," said the Pilot.

RaiClaralin made reverence even as she ran. "I am sorry too, white Haiela. That remark was enormate. Please forgive me."

"Forgiven and understood," said raiChinchi.

They were running toward the ship as they spoke. The guard rairaiMela had shot still lay sprawled on the entry ramp.

"It looks clear," said the Commander. "We go straight up the ramp and hope it isn't an ambush."

"Chalwë, Commander."

The two brunettes ran up the ramp and into the ship.

"We need to get to the control room as fast as possible, Commander," said the Pilot. "May I precede?"

"Yes, but stay close to me and fall back at the first hint of an encounter. You are unarmed, and we need you alive."

They made their way swiftly along the corridors. Suddenly a siren sounded and a mascûl voice barked orders.

"That's the alert," said raiChinchi, who was wearing a translator earbud. "They've found one of the bodies, but they don't know where we are. Let's keep moving and try to shoot before anyone can report our position."

They had only progressed a dozen yards when the amplified voice barked again.

"What is it this time?" asked the Commander.

"They are throwing a null field over the ship. Nothing crystal-powered will work."

Commander Carshalton tried the blaster. "That's right. It's dead. What's the idea?"

"They think we are like their femīni and that they will have the advantage of strength. Also that once we get mired in a fight they will be able to mob us. What they don't know is that we have no swords."

Around the next bend was a huge mascûl with its great Kang sword already drawn.

"Stand back," said the Commander to raiChinchi. "I'll deal with this."

RaiClaralin fixed her eyes on the aggressor, ready to react to the first movement. The mascûl came in with a swift downthrust that could have cloven her head in two. RaiClaralin twirled aside at the last split second and thrust her second knuckles spear-like under the creature's ribcage in a perfect inverse Cobra Strike. Even with so large a creature, the blow might well have rendered it unconscious had it been unprotected. As it was, the leather clothing absorbed most of the impact. Even so, the creature staggered backward, slightly winded, and eyed the Commander more warily.

They watched each other closely. RaiClaralin knew that only split-second timing stood between her and a bloody death. Suddenly two things happened at once. The mascûl came in with a forward thrust. RaiClaralin sidestepped with perfect timing and aimed a paralyzing stamp kick just above the knee. Simultaneously, raiChinchi dashed past the mascûl, turned, and with dizzying rapidity and accuracy hit a series of pressure points on the creature's neck and body. It slumped to the ground.

"Zippy business," said raiClaralin, "but I thought——"

"I didn't say I can't fight; only that I can't carry weapons."

RaiClaralin retrieved the mascûl's sword and tried its weight. "Very fine piece of steel," she said. "Heavy, too."

"Too heavy for you?" asked the Pilot.

"For my style, yes. If I fought like them, it would be ideal. It's a hack-and-slash weapon." She made a few practice passes. "Still, it'll do the job."

"The control room is just on the next corridor, Commander," said the Pilot urgently.

The door of the control room was open. There were five mascûli inside: four with swords, one studying the control panels. On the

90

floor near this one was a fat tubular device emitting a faint blue light, which raiChinchi surmised to be the null-field generator.

"Can you engage the warriors while I shut off the null field?" asked the Pilot.

"I think so," said the Commander.

"Good. As soon as it's off, I shall shout 'haya'; then you can blast them before they know where they are."

The Commander leapt into the room flourishing the Kang weapon. The swordsmascûli advanced upon her. She executed some fancy parade-fencing flourishes. One of the mascûli moved in with an abdominal thrust. It was a hasty, ill-considered move. The Commander parried it easily and spun in one smooth movement into a death-cut to the neck. The other three realized that overconfidence was misplaced, but also knew that with three against one they should be able to kill their prey. They began to maneuver into a surrounding formation that would ensure that she could not defend against them all at once. One covered the door, since the closed space would work to their advantage.

In the meantime, raiChinchi slipped into the room and walked in a brisk but calmly businesslike manner toward the null-field generator. The unarmed mascûl watched her with incredulity. RaiChinchi saluted jauntily, made slight reverence, and turned her attention to the generator.

The mascûl advanced and put its arms about her body, tightening its grip into a ferocious bear hug that would have killed the femîn it believed raiChinchi to be in seconds. RaiChinchi's strong, deft fingers drove swiftly into a series of pressure points on the head and neck, and the mascûl fell.

She turned to the null-field generator and within twenty seconds shouted "Haya!"

The Commander, who was now hard-pressed, drew the blaster and killed two of her assailants with astonishing rapidity, and threw herself to the floor. The third realized the situation and loosed off a blast just as raiClaralin dropped out of the line of fire. She fired from the ground and the fight was over.

RaiChinchi already had the *Vixen's* systems fired up and was pressing buttons intently.

"Phew. You worked out how to use that alien machine pretty g'doinking quickly!"

"No, I didn't. A null-field generator requires power like any other machinery. It beams its field outside its own radius so it doesn't self-nullify. I just opened the crystal-hatch and removed the power crystal. I may not carry a weapon, but I do carry a multifunction screwdriver."

"You clever old Pilot!"

"Thankies, Commander. I've closed the outer portal and all interior doors. I'm running the scanner now. Let's see what we've got."

The mascûl raiChinchi had downed regained consciousness and, stealthily drawing its blaster, took careful aim at raiChinchi's back. The Commander spotted the movement out of the corner of her eye, drew, span, and killed the creature just in time.

"RaiChinchi, you g'doinker! Why can't you kill these things?"

"That's your job, Raihira."

"You mean the one you downed in the corridor is still alive?"

"'Fraid so. But that's the least of our worries. I'm just checking the scanner. As I thought, there are several of them about the ship, but there are also over a dozen in the main crew concourse. What are they doing there, do you think?"

"Never mind that—how long will it take them to rush this room?"

"About as long as it takes to blast the doors and get here."

"Listen, raiChinch, I'm pretty good, but I don't think I can sustain a firefight with over a dozen mascûls. Aren't there any internally directed weapons systems? Ducts of poison gas or something?"

RaiChinchi pressed a series of keys on the main control console. "Complete invasion of the ship wasn't one of the contingencies the Guild provided for. I'll have to make a note of that in my book."

"Never mind your book—we're going to lose the ship, not to mention our lives."

"Oh, don't be pessimistic, Commander. They won't make it to the room, thanks to you."

"Thanks to me?"

"Yes—I just took your idea and did the opposite. I hope you don't mind."

"My idea?"

"The one about the gas. There are no provisions to pump gas into parts of the ship: but one of the contingencies that *is* provided for is oxygen shortage If necessary, one can withdraw oxygen from selected parts of the ship to conserve it for others. I have just withdrawn the oxygen from every area except the control room."

"You really are shining today, Madam Pilot."

"Thank you again, honored Commander. What now?"

"They obviously know where we are. We'd better pick up the others and move the ship. Can you cloak her so they can't track us?"

"I can try. I'm just scanning for the others."

The Commander dropped into a chair. "I must be out of condition. Fencing with those critters has exhausted me. That sword is heavy, and they are so strong. Their technique is poor, but I think they must be so much stronger than ordinary mascûli that they rely on brute strength."

"Are they stronger than ordinary mascûli?"

"They must be. I was always taught that a schizzie femîn is stronger than a blonde and a mascûl weaker than a brunette. These critters aren't noticeably weaker than us, I'd say."

"You're right there, honored Commander," said raiChinchi, feeling her bruised ribs. "Rather the reverse, in fact."

"Exactly. I think an ordinary mascûl would have trouble wielding one of these swords. I knew a girl who fought like them back at Selastine. One of those big West Arkadyani peasant girls by background. She was a bit out of place at Selastine. Anyway, when she was fourteen she used to smash her way through the fencing tournaments. You could parry her great thrusts easily, but she smashed straight through the parry. I think that is what these critters rely on. They haven't encountered brunettes in combat before, so I suppose they think that even if we aren't femîni, we can't be stronger than mascûli. I suppose they'll know by now, though."

"Not quite yet, honored Commander. Not one we've tangled with has so far lived to report back."

"How's the scanning going?"

"I've got raiEvelynn's party, but I'm having a bit of trouble with Her Highness and raiCharmian."

"Good. As soon as we've got everyone back on board, we move out. We'll take on water elsewhere. I want the ship cloaked as soon as we are all in order."

"Commander, we've got a problem. Her Highness and raiCharmian are gone."

"What do you mean, gone?"

"I mean they aren't where we left them and they aren't in this area of the forest at all. They are nowhere they can possibly have gotten to on foot. Commander, they've disappeared."

Chapter 12

Commander Zhendel

As the brunettes ran toward the *Silver Vixen*, raiCharmian turned to the Princess.

"What now?" she asked in a quiet voice.

"Not much to do now except wait for the brunettes to clear out the *Vixen*," replied the Princess. "Let's sit down." In truth she felt raiCharmian had best sit down before she fell down. She took her hands—still ice-cold—and settled her against the trunk of a great tree of some alien species.

"Can they do it?" asked raiCharmian tremulously.

"Our brunettes? Clear out a few schizzies? Of course they can."

"Only one armed brunette," said raiCharmian.

"Don't you worry about raiChinchi," said rairaiMela. "There is no one better to have by one in a tight spot."

"You are right——"

"Sshh!" hissed rairaiMela. RaiCharmian opened her mouth, but rairaiMela squeezed her arm tightly and put a finger to her lips, warning her to stay silent.

Two creatures were making their way through the undergrowth. As they came nearer, it was clear that they were human in shape but very bulky. They could well be more mascûli. As they were not headed directly toward the blondes, rairaiMela felt the best course was to keep silent and hope they were not seen.

RaiCharmian stared ahead. She seemed unaware of what was taking place, almost as if she were in a trance. As she became more aware of the mascûli—for they now decidedly were mascûli—she began to moan very quietly and rhythmically as if in abject terror. RairaiMela held her arm firmly both to reassure and attempt to restrain her. The girl seemed to have no awareness of her own actions, and rairaiMela feared she might do something to signal their presence.

The mascûli trod heavily through the undergrowth. They were a good fifty yards off and facing in another direction. Provided they didn't turn and look in the blondes' direction, they should be safe.

RaiCharmian was breathing heavily. Her frightened moans were too quiet to be heard at any distance. She seemed to be in some state of mental shock.

The mascûli were approaching the point where their path placed them directly in line with the blondes—though not facing them. After that they would be walking away from them and would soon be gone.

RairaiMela tightened her grip on raiCharmian's arm, scarcely daring to breathe. Suddenly, a strange bird screeched, and one of the mascûli turned toward them. It was looking high into the branches of the trees, searching for the source of the sound. It did not see the blondes, but its harsh, furred face was clearly visible at this distance.

Then the unthinkable happened. RaiCharmian screamed—a long, wailing scream full of fear and despair. The two mascûli turned toward the blondes and then started running at them.

"Get up!" commanded the Princess. "Come on—we've got to run."

She leapt to her feet and dragged raiCharmian after her. The mascûli were bearing down upon them with a speed that belied their bulk. RairaiMela ran, dragging raiCharmian behind her, but raiCharmian ran like a girl in a trance. RairaiMela felt as if she were pulling a dead weight behind her.

Suddenly raiCharmian screamed again. One of the mascûli had caught up to her and seized her arm, crushing delicate blonde flesh and sinew in its huge paw. RairaiMela had already flipped the cap off a slender gold pen-like tube. Now she released the lever. An ear-splitting scream rent the air as something streaked skyward, leaving a thin trail of black smoke. Then the heavens were illuminated by a dazzling white light, and a deafening explosion caused the very ground to tremble.

The two mascûli threw themselves down in the long grass, thinking they were under aerial attack.

"Come on," shouted rairaiMela, pulling raiCharmian's hand. The shock of the assault together with the terrible explosion seemed to have cleared raiCharmian's head. The two blondes ran fast across the rough ground.

Despite its ferocious noise, the skyflash had no offensive potential. It was simply a distress signal with which rairaiMela had been equipped by raiChinchi. It could be seen and heard for miles and should bring help running—but with raiAntala away, raiClaralin and raiChinchi fighting inside the *Vixen,* and the others in a village some miles away, it seemed doubtful that help would come.

As they reached the road, the masculi were already up and after them. One of them drew a blaster and shouted a command at them. They could not understand a word of it, but "Stop or I'll shoot" seemed a rather probable guess.

The two blondes stopped running as they reached the roadside. The masculi slowed their pace and walked toward them, each holding a blaster leveled at their helpless prey.

The one closest to them leered unpleasantly through its facial fur, and then its expression changed. They all became aware of a clangorous ringing sound, like that of several electric bells, distant at first, but coming rapidly closer. The nearest mascûl looked at its companion, which was already turning back into the forest. It turned to follow, and they disappeared into the trees as two large black cars pulled up, their bells drowning all other sound.

"I never thought I'd be so glad to see the rozzers," said rairaiMela.

The bells were shut off, but the ringing continued in raiCharmian's head. She heard car doors banging, saw uniformed brunettes. One of them saluted. Words swam in and out of her mind.

"Rayati, ma'am…"

Then words that were completely meaningless. She heard rairaiMela answering in Herthelan Westrenne. One uniformed brunette pointed at the sky, spread her fingers, and made a loud noise.

And then everything was black.

COMMANDER Zhendel put down the receiver and drew deeply on her long black cigarette holder.

"Get a car, Machirta. We are going to Linton immediately."

Lt. Machirta saluted. "Chalwë, Commander."

"Well, get moving, Lieutenant."

"When you say Linton, Commander, do you mean that little village between here and Mena Chavran?"

"That is the only Linton I am aware of, Lieutenant."

"If it isn't an enormate question, Commander, why are we going there?"

"It is an enormate question, Lieutenant, but since you are a Rose, I will answer it. As you know, I was sent out here to be out of harm's way. I was considered to be what they call a radical. They didn't want people like us near the center of things, interfering with their double-dealings and appeasements."

"I understand that, Commander, but what has that to do with Linton?"

"They sent me here because it is a backwater, out of the stream of vital events. Well, my dear Machirta, by Dea's good grace, they may just have sent me to exactly the right place—or, from their point of view, exactly the wrong place."

"That sounds rather exciting, Commander."

"It could be, Lieutenant. It could just be very exciting indeed. It could even be the turning point we have been seeking."

LINTON was a charming village. A cluster of traditionally built houses gathered about a few shops, two inns, and a little temple. A stranger in Linton was a remarkable event that happened perhaps twice in a year. Today they had been overwhelmed with strangers— and strangers, too, who would have seemed remarkable even in Mena Chavran: first the very young, very dashing, and very foreign Commander, and now a whole group of foreigners—all of them on motorbikes that rode above the ground with no wheels. This was talking material for the coming decade.

The *Silver Vixen* party, for their part, were wonderfully impressed with the kindness of the villagers, who insisted upon supplying them not only with a little food as they had asked, but with stocks of tinned goods, cakes, sweetmeats, cookies, and presents of various sorts.

"You really are too kind," said raiEstrelle. "Really, we just need food for tonight and tomorrow morning."

"And where will your next food come from, honored stranger?" asked Lady Deranyin, the highest-ranking blonde of the village. "A ship must be well stocked, or who knows what privations you may encounter? You must have been long and long upon your voyage that your ship has run out of all provisioning."

RaiEstrelle made deep reverence. "But, my lady, it does not fall to your good people to provision our ship."

"It falls to them by the hand of Providence, honored stranger, and by the unsearchable will of blessed Dea. It falls to them by the words of Scripture that bid us care for the stranger at our gates. It falls to them as a welcome opportunity to make a good werdë for their undying souls, and it falls to them to uphold the honor of this humble but most ancient village. But more than all, fair and honored stranger, it falls to them by the love that is in their hearts, for see how they smile and how happy they are to serve your dear people."

RaiEstrelle thought carefully for a moment. For years she had talked the slang and colloquial speech of North Quirinelle—an *argot* that caused consternation even to her parents, who themselves used a more respectable form of that Northern vernacular which sounded so casual even to most Westrennes. Yet she knew, at least in theory, how a more traditional person should speak. She only hoped the translator would not pick up any awkwardness in her expression. "Yet, my lady," she said, "our honor also is involved, and our werdë. It were ill for us to cause hardship either to strangers or to our kind friends, and your village people are both to us."

"You cause no hardship, honored stranger, for as you see, each of our people brings a little contribution from her larder, and between them a sufficient provision is made. The laws of hospitality bid you do us the honor of accepting our humble offerings."

"How are we going to carry all this back to the ship, ma'am?" said Sharan to raiEvelynn.

RaiEvelynn looked at the stacks of provision that continued to be brought by the kindly villagers. The prospect of transporting them with hoverbikes certainly presented a problem.

As she pondered it, a large sleek black car pulled up. A brunette in uniform got out, walked around to the front passenger door, and opened it. She stood to attention and saluted as another brunette in a more elaborate uniform emerged, a long black cigarette holder projecting elegantly from between her small white teeth. Combined with the confident smile on her dark-rouged lips, it gave her an air of swashbuckling poise and dashing determination.

She walked toward raiEvelynn and saluted. "Chalwë, honored stranger," she said.

RaiEvelynn saluted and made reverence. "Chalwë, most honored officer."

"I am Commander Zhendel."

"I am Lieutenant Appelbeam," said raiEvelynn uneasily. She had been supplied with a Lieutenant's uniform from the ship's store. It seemed to regularize matters, and after all, she would have been a Sub-Lieutenant if she had continued with her cadetship at Chelverton College. But actually claiming the rank to a senior officer—she was unprepared for that and felt quite dreadful about it. Still, what could one do?

"Rayati, Lieutenant," said Commander Zhendel, saluting again.

"Rayati, honored Commander," said Lieutenant Appelbeam, saluting and making military reverence.

"I am delighted to see the villagers are looking after you very well, Lieutenant. They are a credit to our nation."

"They are indeed, Commander."

"These provisions are for your ship, I suppose."

"Yes, Commander."

"Oh, don't look surprised, Lieutenant. The local Constabel reported the matter to me as soon as your Commander came to the village. It is a naval matter, after all, isn't it?"

"Yes, Commander, I suppose it is."

"And I am sure you will allow me to arrange transport for these provisions."

"That is very good of you, Commander. Would you mind if I wireless my ship?"

"By all means, Lieutenant."

RaiEvelynn moved her fingers over the screen of her transceiver, looking increasingly frustrated.

"I am afraid I can't get a response, Commander."

"No matter, Lieutenant. We can speak to your commanding officer when we get to the ship."

"Yes, of course——" said raiEvelynn hesitantly.

"Get those provisions into the back of the car, Machirta."

"One moment, Commander," said Lt. Appelbeam.

"What is it?" asked the Commander patiently.

"It is just—well——"

"You are not sure that your Captain would want you to reveal the whereabouts of your ship?"

"No, not that exactly, ma'am," said raiEvelynn slowly.

"Then what, Lieutenant?"

Lt. Appelbeam stared dumbly at the Commander, for it was exactly that, and she was at a loss to think of another excuse.

"I do understand, Lieutenant. I suspect your Captain was at considerable pains to conceal her landing place. And wisely so. However, you are going to have to confide in somebody, and I think you will find that you are lucky that somebody turned out to be me. Let me explain a little——"

The Commander's words were cut short by a flash of blinding light and the sound of a terrible explosion that left their ears ringing. Looking in the direction of the explosion, they saw a slender column of black smoke still streaking upward into the clear summer sky.

"What was that?" asked the Commander, hardly expecting an answer.

"A distress flare from Her—— from a member of our crew," said raiEvelynn.

"It sounded like an aerial assault," said the Commander.

"Those flares are pretty hefty devices. They are only to be used in serious emergencies. I am afraid we shall have to go."

"Get on your bike. We'll follow you," said the Commander.

"But——"

"What are you planning to do, Lieutenant? Answer that distress call with your party of blondes? Or rush in single-handed? Your 'crew member' may be in serious trouble. Do you want to save her or not?"

"I am sorry, ma'am. I was being foolish. Please come with me."

RaiEvelynn's Chandra and the black staff car raced down the

open highway in the direction of the explosion. It had been a fair way off, near to where the *Silver Vixen* lay, which is why she had been hesitant about letting the Commander accompany her. Naturally the Commander would have worked that out. RaiEvelynn cursed herself. She was handling this situation abominably, committing every *gaucherie* imaginable. The other brunettes—the Captain, Commander Carshalton, raiChinchi— were so terribly capable. RaiEvelynn felt like the ship's fool.

It had taken about twenty minutes to get to Linton from the ship. They made it back to the nearest part of the highway in less than ten, but there was no sign of rairaiMela or anyone else. Remnants of the black smoke still hung in the windless sky, giving a rough indication of the spot from which the flare had been fired. They searched the nearby forest, but with no success.

"Could she be back at your ship?" asked the Commander.

RaiEvelynn hesitated. If she was back at the ship, she was probably safe. What would Commander Carshalton say if she led a stranger to the *Silver Vixen* for no pressing reason?

The Commander looked fixedly at raiEvelynn. She was clearly determined to get to the *Vixen*.

"Let me try to wireless again," said raiEvelynn, getting out her transceiver.

Again, there was no response, but as she pressed the keys, desperately playing for time, she heard a sound that she had heard twice before: the strange, chirruping throb of the *Vixen's* hyperthrust engines. The silver ship rose slowly above the woodland canopy and high into the sky, and then she disappeared. She did not disappear into the distance. She was still clearly visible when she winked out of sight, like a candle flame being extinguished.

"Where did it go?" asked Lieutenant Machirta.

"A cloaking device," replied the Commander. "The most sophisticated I've ever seen. Quite a ship you've got there, Lt. Appelbeam. Do you think your Captain was that anxious not to see me? I really do begin to feel like the Uninvited Guest."

Lieutenant Appelbeam blushed deeply. "No, Commander, I am sure——"

Two heat-seeking missiles came in at incredible speed from the far distance, homed in on the spot where the *Vixen* had disappeared, and then continued eastward. They were out of sight by the time two more explosions rent the air.

"I hope they didn't get your ship," said the Commander.

"I doubt it," said raiEvelynn. "They obviously knew in advance that the missiles were coming, and with raiChinchi aboard, I think we'll be all right."

"RaiChinchi?" asked the Commander.

"Our Pilot. She's about the best there is," said raiEvelynn and then stopped. She was talking too much.

Commander Zhendel smiled. The young Lieutenant was starting to open out. "What are you going to do now?" she asked.

"Well, I suppose——" RaiEvelynn looked nonplussed.

"You have a fine collection of supplies, but no ship to deliver them to. You are in an alien land with no base to return to. But you will find my people very friendly."

"Oh, yes, ma'am. They have been more than friendly."

"I suggest we go back to Linton. You can put up there and wait for your next orders like a good vikheli. And we can have a long talk."

"I should be delighted to enjoy the company of so noble an officer," said raiEvelynn.

"Very well. That is settled. Back to Linton."

Chapter 13

The Sisterhood of the White Rose

THE RED DRAGON was the finest inn in Linton—that is to say, the other one was not quite so well-appointed. The maids were dressed in fetching blonde uniforms of red and gold, and the cuisine was up to the standards of the Royal City itself.

Commander Zhendel treated raiEvelynn and raiEstrelle, as well as Lt. Machirta, to a splendid meal on the wooden terrace that overlooked the quietly flowing River Seftan. The terrace was netted in to keep out the insects that could be particularly bothersome by the riverside as the summer evening approached.

"I do hope the ship is all right," said raiEstrelle.

"If your Pilot is all that Lt. Appelbeam says, and your ship is all that I believe her to be, then I have no doubt she is perfectly safe," the Commander assured her.

"Do you think rairaiMela got aboard before it took off?"

"There was no sign of her in the surrounding woods, so that would seem to be the most likely thing," said the Commander comfortingly.

RaiEvelynn noted that raiEstrelle was turning to this foreign officer and not to herself for reassurance. Somehow Commander Zhendel had the air of being in charge of the situation. She was the sort of person to whom a blonde would turn for answers. RaiEvelynn had asked no questions, but she found herself inwardly turning to her too.

"But who would fire missiles at our ship? And why?" asked raiEstrelle a little plaintively.

"Do you not know, madam?" asked Commander Zhendel.

"No—I don't think so."

"You are a very sweet blonde. I am sure honored Lt. Appelbeam could tell you, or at least make as good a guess as I, but perhaps she would prefer not to do so in my presence, so let me do it. I think we may be almost certain that the attempt to destroy your ship was made by the Kang, a group of schizomorph pirates who have infested the aethyr in this part of the galaxy for several years."

"Is this sort of attack common, honored Commander?" asked raiEvelynn.

"In the aethyr there have been a number of disgraceful incidents, Lieutenant. In Astarchean airspace such things are virtually unknown. There has been only one such incident before today. However, your ship was responsible for the destruction of the Kang flagship, the *Black Boar*, and the death of Kang Shahtha, the late unlamented head of the Kang clan, for which I pause to tender my deepest thanks and greatest admiration. An unfortunate disadvantage associated with this noble and meritorious act is that the Kang will undoubtedly be seized with the desire to destroy your ship, its Captain, and preferably its entire crew, and they will pursue this objective relentlessly until the day it is achieved or the Kang are wiped out."

"Is that a large task?" asked Lt. Appelbeam. "I mean, how long would it take to wipe out these Kang?"

"Haya!" shouted Commander Zhendel suddenly. "I knew I was going to like you people."

"Not that it's really any of my business, of course," added Lt. Appelbeam hastily.

The Commander laughed. "Honored Lieutenant, deception and discretion are not your long suits, if I may be allowed a gaming analogy. And I salute you for it. You are a fine and frank warrior; yet your duty bids you guard your tongue in a way that is unnatural to you, and like a good vikheli you seek to obey your Captain. I understand. But fortunately you have found the right company. You give yourself away because you are no deceiver, but Dea has led you to the place where your natural frankness is most needed.

"But you need attempt discretion no more, not only because you are among friends, but because I know all that you have to tell in any case."

"How would you know what I may or may not have to tell?" said the Lieutenant, struggling hard to maintain discretion.

"Let me continue with the gaming analogy and lay all my cards on the table. I shall give the briefest of accounts at present. Later you shall hear more detail, for I fancy we shall be working closely together. As you will see, I will tell you that which could put myself and my friends in peril, for I know that I may trust you; and, though it would be unfair of me to ask you to return this trust, you will see that it is unnecessary.

"Let us then begin with your friends the Kang. Who are they, you wish to know? They are a foul and vicious gang of schizomorph pirates that has come in these latter years to infest this part of the aethyr. They have been more trouble to other schizomorphi than to us for the most part, but in recent years things have grown much worse. One of our ships was taken about ten years ago, in the days of the old Queen, and the crewmaidens sold as slaves to a planet influenced by the Dark Ruler. Our Queen ordered an expedition against the pirate fleet and stationed three dreadnoughts in orbit around the planet where the crewmaidens had been sold. The Grand Council of the offending nation explained that they had been bought in error and returned them with apologies.

"After that, there were occasional attacks on our ships when they were far from home. There was a notorious case when a Kang boarding party actually got aboard the HMAS *Brightwind* and the Captain scuttled the ship with a nega-blast, destroying ship, crew, and boarders and badly damaging the Kang ship that lay nearby. After that, the Queen began a program of strengthening the Navy, seeking out and destroying Kang vessels, and negotiating with various non-Astarcheans—principally the Mena Cathriani on our own planet, but also various off-world powers—about cooperation against interstellar piracy.

"It seems the Kang became deeply worried about Queen Ephranaria of Sai Astarche, and one day, when she and several of her Ministers were undertaking a State Visit to Cathria Mena, the Royal Skyship, the *Sai Rayanna,* was destroyed within our atmosphere by a sudden missile attack. The aggressor ships were annihilated, but how they penetrated so far into our defenses remains a mystery to this day. Our Queen and much of her Government were lost in a single stroke."

Lt. Appelbeam and raiEstrelle touched their fingers first to their foreheads and then to their chests.

"It was a terrible blow to our nation. The Crown Princess and Princess Cantarmine, the Admiral of the Fleet, were also aboard, and so the succession passed to Princess Ashhevala, who was little more than a child. The Queen's High Vizier, Raya Telarmine, also survived. A sudden illness had prevented her from taking the fatal journey. She became the Vizier and chief advisor to Queen Ashhevala the Third.

"The new administration favored peace and began to reduce spending on the armed forces. The Kang grew bolder. One day they attacked an Astarchean ship very close to the homeworld. They took several crewmaidens as slaves, and the Queen paid a huge ransom to have them returned to Astarche."

"Do you think she was so terrified by the slaughter of her mother and sisters that she dared not resist the Kang?"

"I think, madam, that she was badly advised. I think she has been kept in partial ignorance of the noble traditions of our own people. However that may be, it is undoubted fact that the great work of strengthening the Fleet begun by Queen Ephranaria has been halted. It is rumored that other ransoms have been paid in secret, and you may be sure that there are many in the Government and in the Forces who wish to see all this change. They wish to build the Navy, pursue the Kang, cooperate with all the enemies of the Kang, and punish any who deal with the Kang—certainly in intemorph slaves."

"And they are right," said Lt. Appelbeam forcefully.

"Certainly they are right. But who is to say our Queen is wrong?"

"But if she is ill-advised——"

"It is a problem, as you see. And into this tangled web comes a new factor. Suddenly the Kang flagship is destroyed and the head of the Kang, the terrible Shahtha, is killed. The very action is taken that every red-blooded officer of the Fleet has been talking about over the mess-table these two years.

"But there is more. This action is taken by a ship bearing the insignia of the Old Empire. The Empire believed to have been destroyed three thousand years ago in a galaxy far away. It is a small ship with new weapons, powerful enough to atomize the feared *Black Boar,* and—most remarkable of all—it is rumored to be carrying on board a Princess of the Blood Imperial. A direct descendant of Sai Rayanna, the Supernal Sun incarnate."

Commander Zhendel stood and bowed very deeply to raiEstrelle. "Indeed, madam, I perhaps have the honor of addressing her at this moment."

"No, not I!" cried raiEstrelle in astonishment.

Commander Zhendel clapped her hands. "I thought so! But right about all the rest!"

"You thought so," said raiEstrelle petulantly. "Do I not look like a Princess?"

"Madam," said Commander Zhendel, bowing again, "you look like the noblest and most beautiful of Raihira blondes, but a Princess is something different: for the solar light shines in her as it shines in no ordinary being. That is true even of our Princesses here in Astarche, but it must be even truer of a Princess in the direct line of the ancient Blood Imperial. You have looked upon it, madam. You must know. I fancy that the 'modern' spirit of the latter Age of Iron has come upon your people as on ours, and perhaps your Princess is an old school friend whom you treat familiarly. And yet, does not the radiance of the Sun-Blood shine in her every movement?"

RaiEstrelle nodded. She had hardly considered it before, amid the rough talk and banter of the Road Angels. But of course it was true. It was true even when she was rairaiMela, riding behind raiAnters; and when it fell to her to take up her royal responsibilities, it was that which had thrown the entire crew into a state of something like awe before her.

"How do you know all this?" asked Lt. Appelbeam.

"The Royal Ministry of Vigilance is still the best intelligence agency in this galactic quadrant. All ship-to-ship transmissions are routinely monitored by ships and stations across a huge network. Kang Shahtha's threats to you were picked up. After that, they managed to get a lock on your internal communications. Now there is another mystery. Why did this ship allow internal aethyr-waves to carry sensitive information? Such waves are subject to eavesdropping. At times the crew members were not even communicating to different parts of the ship—they had simply left their transceivers active. Any ship well enough armed to destroy the *Black Boar* must know enough about conflict to have a policy on communications. Why was this policy disregarded even when such an important person was aboard?"

"I really don't see——" began Lt. Appelbeam.

"Please," said the Commander. "Do not trouble yourself. You

have told me enough already. I have my own views on this slightly embarrassing matter. Perhaps we shall discuss them at some time if it interests you. But for the present we have far more important things on hand.

"As I have indicated, the coming of your ship has introduced new factors into the situation. Important and incalculable new factors; perhaps far greater than even you are aware of.

"In the first place there is the destruction of the *Black Boar*. Not only was that ship the Kang's most powerful, but it carried Kang Shahtha, the hated head of the Kang. The news of Shahtha's death will send reverberations around this whole quadrant.

"The Kang will be anxious to exact vengeance. They will also be unsure what has happened. Various naval fleets have been seeking the *Black Boar* without success. Was your small and apparently relatively harmless ship set as a deliberate bait to catch the Kang? I am sure it was not, but the Kang will not be sure.

"Then there is the ship itself. How did it destroy the *Black Boar* and escape destruction itself? The Kang will want either to destroy or to take that ship, and preferably to take it. Other parties will be highly interested in it too.

"But more important than any of this is the Princess of the Blood Imperial. I take it you know a little of the history of our world. There has long been a rift between the Esterline Empire and the Old Loyalists. That rift is ultimately based on the question of whether the Old Empire was destroyed and whether those who followed Shelatinhe, the Great Conjuress, from Sai Herthe were saviors or traitors. If the origin you claim for yourselves and your ship is correct, then the matter is settled in favor of the Old Loyalists. What happens next?

"In theory, a Princess of the Blood Imperial would claim the allegiance of all parties. The Old Loyalists would have to acknowledge her as the authentic representative of the Authority to which they have always proclaimed their loyalty, while the Esterlini would have to admit that they were returned to the true Imperial jurisdiction. If the truth of your claims were generally admitted, you see what all this might mean?"

"I think so——" began Lt. Appelbeam.

"Well, this is an unfamiliar situation to you, so let me suggest a few things. The Old Loyalists would see this as a validation of their claims and might want your Princess to head a loyalist federation, perhaps based in Cathria Mena or Cathria Maya or one of the Old Loyalist planets. The Esterlini might want to return Esterline to True Imperial rule and thus legitimize the Esterline Empire and consolidate its claim to rule all the children of the Herthelan Exile. If your Princess became the Esterline Empress, the Old Loyalists would have to return to Esterline rule. Alternatively, the Imperial House of Esterline might be very loath to recognize a Monarch who must displace it.

"The Kang, on the other hand, would fear the uniting of all the intemorph peoples of this quadrant into one great Empire. If they understood the situation—which eventually they must—their wisest policy would be to assassinate the Princess before her claims become established.

"The Kang are relatively unimportant. For all their nuisance value, they are only a bunch of pirates. But there has long been a suspicion that they are in some sense an arm of the Dark One."

"The Dark One——" breathed raiEstrelle.

"Yes. The Dark One. I mean precisely what you fear. That Dark One you must have read about in your history books. The Demon-Ruler who nearly destroyed your world—whom we thought *had* destroyed your world—three millennia ago."

"That one still lives?" asked Lt. Appelbeam.

"That one cannot die. And its devilish influence is now spreading over many of the schizomorph worlds in this quadrant."

"Are there many schizomorph worlds?"

"Too many. They have never been a trouble to us. Schizomorphi are natural warriors and tend to plunder and conquer their own kind and all other kinds. But the aethyr is vast, and our peoples have maintained strength sufficient to make attacks on us ruinous to them. There are better and safer places for them to go a-plundering.

"But you know that the Dark One is not merely a schizomorph. It is perhaps not a schizomorph at all, though it seems like one to us. It is the Great Darkness. It cannot leave the light to shine anywhere in creation. In the end it must destroy us. Its one true will is to destroy everything and to extinguish every light."

"Those worlds that are Darkheld must eventually attack us, no doubt when the Dark One's hold on the schizomorphi has been made near to complete. And then the divisions among our intemorph nations will be their greatest strength. And yet in this quadrant we have one advantage. All our intemorph nations derive from the same world—Sai Herthe. All trace their thamë to the same Empire. All acknowledge themselves to be daughters of Raihiranya Sai Rayanna."

All touched their fingers to their foreheads and then to their chests.

"Whew!" said raiEstrelle.

"Indeed," said Commander Zhendel. "You begin to see what a position of affairs you have sailed into—and what forces you yourselves bring to bear upon it whether that is your intention or not."

"I thank you for telling us all this, honored Commander," said Lt. Appelbeam, "but I imagine no action is required on our part for the present. Our Captain has gone to the palace of your Queen. No doubt they will be discussing these matters at this very moment."

"I wonder," said the Commander. "Queen Ashhevala makes no decisions without the advice of her Vizier, and the Vizier is not currently at the palace. She is at her mountain retreat, and as far as I know she has not hastened back to the capital. I am wondering why not. She must be aware of the importance of this situation and will want to shape matters to her own ends."

"That is strong talk, honored Commander," said Lt. Appelbeam.

"It is," replied the Commander. "I have outlined the situation for you, and now the moment for strong talk has arrived. I promised to lay my cards on the table, and I shall, even at risk to myself. I have thought about this. I have prayed on our motorcar journey for guidance. I believe Dea has guided you to me and me to you precisely so that I may tell you what I am about to tell you.

"I have told you already that our Queen is ill-advised. I have told you that our Government is weakening our defenses and strengthening our enemies by paying large ransoms to them. I have told you that many of Her Majesty's most loyal servants wish to reverse this policy. Now I will tell you that a number of those servants have formed a secret organization called the Sisterhood of the White Rose.

"A year ago, I was outspoken in my criticism of the present policy. I was then an intelligence officer at the heart of the military and governmental network in our capital, Astarcheana. As a result of my frankness, I was sent to a small command post not far from this village. Many others who expressed similar views were despatched much further from the center of events. Perhaps I was considered relatively unimportant.

"However, there are others who hold the same views but were more discreet about them, and many have joined the Sisterhood of the White Rose. That is how I know all that the Ministry of Vigilance knows about your ship. The Ministry is full of White Roses. The movement becomes stronger each day, and that is because more and more of those close to the Government begin to suspect that there is something more afoot than a weak and foolish policy. They suspect actual treason."

"Is such a thing possible among people so much like our own?" asked raiEstrelle.

"You must understand, madam, that the Dark One is ultimately behind all this. Very far behind, it is true. There are agents and agents of agents, and agents of agents of agents. There are whisperers and compromisers. I do not know, for example, if the Kang themselves are much enamored of the Dark One, but they do its work because their advantage lies that way.

"The Dark One is adept at playing upon the weaknesses of human souls. Whoever is not impeccably honorable is vulnerable to corruption, even as a mere scratch on the skin may let in a vile disease. The re-awakening of the Dark One is like a great stone thrown into the center of a pond, and every ripple that reaches the shore—even those that seem unconnected with the great disturbance that bore them—is touched with corruption."

"You make things sound terribly dark," said raiEstrelle.

"Where the light does not shine strong and true, things *are* terribly dark, fair lady. In distant worlds a darkness has fallen whereof I cannot even speak in the presence of your sex. Here all seems in order and relatively serene. And yet those same ripples of corruption, faint as they may seem, and far removed from the crushing impact at the center, are rolling over our lives and profaning the sanctity of the royal palace itself.

"Wherever the influence of the Dark One exists, there is deception and confusion; and even quite good people may be beguiled by the fairest-seeming arguments. When the shadow fell across Sai Herthe, it was so———"

"No, never in Sai Herthe," protested Lt. Appelbeam.

"Come, come. You are living proof of it."

"What do you mean, madam?"

"The Old Loyalists have always claimed that Shelatinhe, the Great Conjuress, was beguiled by the Darkness, and that all who followed her deserted their true Empress in the hour of need to come to a place of safety. They claim that her prophecies of the inevitable destruction of the Mother World were false: snares laid by the Darkness to tempt maidens from the path of obedience and thamë. The Esterlini and their allies have contended that those prophecies were true. But if you are who you claim to be, then it is clear that the Old Loyalists were right, and that the Darkness had suborned our people with false prophecies from the way of loyalty and truth. And our people were your people then, and still are now."

Lt. Appelbeam bit her lip. To one raised in the belief in the divine thamë, the order and goodness of the Universe and the Empire as a perfect reflection thereof, and in the fundamental goodness of maidens, this evidence of corruption came as a disturbing blow.

"You chill my heart, honored Commander," she said quietly. "How can one trust in anything?" She placed her forehead in her hands.

The Commander laid a hand on her shoulder. "Listen," she said. "Why do you think your Princess is so very important in all this?"

"Because a Princess of the Blood Imperial could unite the descendants of Sai Herthe," said Lt. Appelbeam wearily.

"Yes: and because there is no other representative of the Rayannic bloodline among all our different peoples. There are various minor royalties such as those from which the Esterline Empress and our own Queen are descended. But no one even remotely related to the

Sun-Daughter—no distant cousin, no eighth-blood great-grandchild followed Shelatinhe here; and remember that was three hundred years after Sai Rayanna's great victory. What does that tell you?"

Lt. Appelbeam looked up and began to smile. "It tells us that the holy line of the Sun-Daughter is incorruptible," she said.

"That is right, Lieutenant. It tells us that more than three millennia after Sai Rayanna's coming to destroy the outland hordes, she is still the Bane of Darkness. In her sacred bloodline is that which defies corruption, resists confusion, and makes all the wiles of the enemy worthless. It tells us that a Princess of the Blood Imperial is more than a unifying figurehead: she is a very Daughter of the Maiden-Sun, in whose light the black and dizzying shadows of the Evil One must vanish.

"And, Lieutenant, it tells us that in a world where talk of practicality and compromise and convenience, and of doing bad that good may come, and of fleeing the inevitable end, or paying the slaver, or whatever else Darkness may place upon the lips of certain maids—in a world, I say, where all these things seem like to turn the mind and make the soul unsure where lies the right—there is yet a single light that will dispel these shadows, and whenever the Darkness threatens to descend, that light will come."

"You speak as if our coming were Providential. Perhaps even directed by something beyond ourselves."

"I think perhaps it was."

"When you say that, I suddenly remember that what brought us through the aethyr-crease was something rather strange. Something that appeared to be there and yet——"

"Please excuse me, I am terribly sorry." A maidservant had come suddenly onto the terrace and rushed up to the table where Lt. Appelbeam was speaking. It was Sulannie from the *Silver Vixen* party. Her face was flushed and she made deep reverence.

"What is it, 'Lannie?" asked raiEstrelle.

"It's Miss Sharan, ma'am. She's gone. I didn't mean to interrupt you, ma'am, but I don't know what to do."

"Calm down, dear," said raiEstrelle. "What do you mean by 'gone'? Where has she gone?"

"I don't know, ma'am. There is a little temple down at the end of the village, and Miss Sharrie said she wanted to go down there and pray. She was gone about an hour, so I went down to find her, but she wasn't there. There was an honored Priestess there, ma'am, and she said she was there all the time, but Miss Sharrie had never been there. We looked all 'round, some of the village girls and me, but she isn't nowhere, ma'am. She's just gone."

Chapter 14

The Palace in the Mountains

RaiCharmian came to, turning her head from side to side and trying to sit up. A cool hand was laid on her brow and her head was pushed gently back onto a deep slightly scented silken pillow.

"All serene," said rairaiMela's voice softly. "Please relax. Lie back down for a moment. We are safe. Everything is calm."

"Where are we?" asked raiCharmian. RairaiMela came into focus. She was wearing a green silk robe decorated with elaborate figures in gold thread.

"I don't know," said rairaiMela. "The people we thought were rozzers—they certainly looked like rozzers anyway—took us to this place. It assuredly isn't a police station. Not even an alien one. It is more like a small palace in the mountains. I've been given wonderful refreshing drinks and delightful snacks on a gold tray. Would you like a drink?"

"Just a sip of water, if you have one."

Rairaimela poured slightly sparkling spring water from a heavy glass decanter into a cut crystal goblet and held it to raiCharmian's lips. She was still cold to the touch and rather shaky.

The sip became a long, slow drink which left raiCharmian feeling a little more like herself.

"What a lovely room," she said, looking around at the sumptuous hangings, the fine furniture, and the delicate little statues in wall niches.

"Isn't it?" said the Princess. "Perhaps a shade excessive, but one can hardly set oneself up as a critic of alien taste."

"I love it," said raiCharmian.

"They have been terribly kind to us," said the Princess, "though I have absolutely no idea who they are or where this is. I have only to pull that bell cord to bring serving girls into the room, and they will get us anything we want—providing we can make them understand what we do want. The trouble is, I can't understand a word they say, and they can't understand me."

"If only raiChinchi had configured our transceivers with the translation software."

"She wasn't expecting us to leave the ship."

"Can't you turn yours on and contact the ship—or the Captain?"

The Princess lowered her voice to a whisper. "The Captain said she wouldn't use hers except where she couldn't be overheard. I'd rather not do it in this room. We really don't know where we are or what is going on. At least raiChinchi has configured an 'all-serene' blip like the Captain's, so I have discreetly let the *Vixen* know we are unharmed."

Rairaimela arranged raiCharmian's pillows and helped her to sit reclined against them. They ate exotic fruit and chatted. RaiCharmian was amazed at the Princess's easy composure. It was at times like this that the Blood Royal really told.

After a time, there was a respectful knock at the door of the room.

"Rayati," called the Princess. It was the one word she had so far discovered common to her own language and that of her hostesses.

Two uniformed officers entered the room. Each had a rather bulky electronic box on a cord about her neck. They made reverence and gave a similar box to the Princess and gestured to her to put it on, demonstrating the use of a pair of small earphones connected to it by a wire. The technics felt very primitive. One of the officers spoke a few unintelligible words, and a moment later a synthesized voice sounded in the Princess's ears.

"Can you understand me, honored one?"

"Thank you, honored officer," said the Princess. "I understand you perfectly."

There was a moment's pause and the officer spoke again. After a slight delay the synthesized voice translated: "Much good, honored one! I understand you also."

"That is excellent, honored officer," said the Princess. "Your technics are truly remarkable." Admiration seemed to be in order.

The officer made reverence. "Our people have our little triumphs, revered lady. Now you are understanding, please do great honor to accompany us to our mistress."

"The honor would be mine."

"Your companion also?"

"She must rest a little longer," said the Princess. "She will sleep deeply."

RaiCharmian took this as an instruction to feign sleep and not to attempt or accept any communication in the Princess's absence.

The Princess was led along several corridors, all as lavishly appointed as the room she had just left. Finally they arrived at a great double door guarded by two elaborately uniformed brunettes who saluted and opened the doors with some ceremony.

"Please to enter, honored one" said the Princess's escort.

The room was exceptionally long, with a high vaulted ceiling and a deep red carpet running down the center of a white stone floor. At the far end was seated a brunette at a large oak desk with national flags and insignia behind her. One was conscious of every step down the deep red carpet.

This must impress the yokels, thought rairaiMela, slipping mentally into the Quirrie vernacular of the hoverbike gang.

As she approached the desk, the brunette stood up and made reverence. She appeared to have difficulty rising, as if her leg gave her pain. She was the most remarkable brunette rairaiMela had ever seen. The aliens were a little strange—smaller on the whole and different in the cast of their faces, but not that unlike Herthelans. This brunette, on the other hand, was very different. One was not certain she was actually melin at all, despite her hair color. She seemed strangely ambisexual in a way that felt rather unhealthy.

When she spoke, however, even though the words were unintelligible, her voice had a warmth of persuasion that was quite remarkable.

A moment later the translation came through.

"Rayati, most honored lady. Accept my humble greetings. My name is Telarmine. I have the honor to be Vizier of this realm."

The Princess made reverence. "Rayati. I am honored to meet Your Excellency. I am li'Caerepurh Liante."

"And have I the rare privilege to address a Princess of the Blood Imperial of Holy Caere?" asked the Vizier.

The Princess was taken aback. She had no idea that the Astarchi knew so much, and the sudden thrust of the question was clearly intended to catch her off guard, though it was easily justifiable as a necessity, since the Vizier would have to use a very different protocol in addressing a Princess.

RairaiMela surprised herself by showing not a flicker of discomposure. "You flatter me, Excellency. My Royal Mistress is not here," she answered, privately thinking of her own Royal Mistress, Queen Viktorya of Novarya.

"She is perhaps asleep in the room from which you have come, honored li'Caerepurh Liante."

"No, Your Excellency, she is far from here."

"We all have our Royal Mistresses," said the Vizier, indicating that she was not unaware of the possible ambiguity of the Princess's answers. She turned to a large ornately framed picture on the wall beside her of a very young lady in the robes and crown of coronation and made reverence. The Princess made reverence to the picture also.

"I fear that one so lowly as I must be unworthy of an audience with the Queen's Vizier," said the Princess.

"On the contrary, honored lady," replied the Vizier, "it is an honor to speak to any member of the company of the ship that destroyed the feared *Black Boar* of Kang Shahtha."

The Princess cast a quizzical eye at her interlocutor. The Vizier smiled reassuringly.

"Oh, yes, madam. We know these things. Your encounter with the *Black Boar*; the fact that you have a Princess of the Blood aboard. Routine intelligence, I fear. I hope you do not consider it too intrusive, but it is an unhappy necessity in these difficult times. It is likely that your own Government monitors unknown vessels that come within its sphere of security."

"It is possible, Your Excellency. I am a child in these matters."

"As a matter of fact, you have done us a considerable service. Kang Shahtha was becoming a nuisance, preying upon our shipping and making impudent demands. The firebrands among our own people were demanding violent action against the Kang. That would have been inadvisable. We are a peaceful people, madam, and while we stand ready to defend ourselves, it would be unwise to involve ourselves in the wars and conflicts, politics and counter-politics, of the mascûli. The elimination of the Kang leader and flagship by a force that was clearly not our own achieves our ends without leaving us open to reprisals or making us appear to take sides in the conflicts of alien peoples."

"But surely no one approves of piracy, even among the masculi, Your Excellency."

"The politics of the schizomorphi, dear lady, are not like ours. There are endless complexities and oppositions. Some find ways of justifying piracy, or while not justifying it, still opposing actions taken against it. There will be wars very soon, and it is not the place of Sai Astarche to be taking part in them. I am sure you will agree with that, madam."

"It is certainly not the place of intemorphic peoples to be drawn into the endless conflicts of the schizomorphi, Your Excellency."

"Good, good. I had hoped your people would take that view. Indeed I felt sure of it, for you are clearly advanced in so many ways."

"Advanced, Your Excellency?"

"I mean, madam, that your technics are highly developed and so you would doubtless be developed in other ways."

"That is an interesting line of thought, Your Excellency. I have not encountered it before."

"I trust it is pleasing to you, honored lady."

"We are but a simple people, Your Excellency. You flatter us."

"And yet you are the unbroken heirs of the Old Empire. To many here that would mean a lot. A Princess of the Blood Imperial; and the destruction of the Kang flagship. To some you might seem like the very Daughter-Knights of Sai Rayanna returned to set an ailing world to rights."

The Princess smiled. "That would be a very romantic thought, Your Excellency."

"Indeed it would, honored lady. It could also be a very dangerous thought. It could encourage those who would emulate old legends: rush to arms; seek to solve problems with unthinking force, pitching us into unending conflict: conflict that should be none of our affair.

"These are not the Times of Legend, good lady, if indeed such times ever were. These are times when calculation and good sense may keep us safe and free and at peace, but when rash violence may embroil us with our schizomorphic neighbors whose continual warfare never ends."

The Princess nodded. "Yes, Your Excellency, I understand."

"I am greatly relieved to hear it. If your voice carries any weight with your Princess, I beg you to explain these things to her and to persuade her to allow me to explain further. And if your Princess may be closer to you than you have given me to think, please know that I understand the need for discretion and that my door stands open to you—and of course to her—at any hour of the night or day. My aim is to bring peace to my people, and in the pursuit of that aim I never rest."

"A laudable aim," said the Princess. "May Dea guide you in it."

"I thank you, honored lady. But you must be fatigued after your many trials. An aethyr battle; a crash-landing on our world; being pursued by murderous masculi. It has been a strenuous day even for a brunette, how much more for one of your delicate sex. No doubt you will wish to return to your rooms and rest. Be assured that your every request will be quickly fulfilled by my servants."

The Princess made reverence. "Your Excellency is more than kind."

The Vizier returned reverence. "Rayati, madam."

"Rayati, Your Excellency."

The Vizier touched a button, and the great double doors at the far end of the room were opened by two silent guards. The Princess walked the long carpeted way from the presence of her hostess with a grace and unassumed poise with which few had passed this subtle ordeal.

As the doors closed, the Vizier touched another button, and a smaller door behind her slid open, admitting a brunette of middle years, severe of countenance and dressed in the uniform of an admiral of the Royal Astarchean Navy. She was one of the new Government's controversial non-hereditary appointments.

Admiral Tenvil saluted. "Rayati, Excellency. Is she the one?"

"I am not sure. She was very cautious. If I were led by the old superstitions, I should say she was. She has a bearing unlike any I have seen, and though she says little, she looks upon one as if she were weighing one in some celestial balance. The superstitious might well imagine that the light of the Solar Angel burns in her."

"Or that perhaps that she has been brought up with the habitual arrogance of a royal caste, Excellency."

"The superstitious would not say that, honored Admiral; but I take it you are cautioning me against leaning toward that superstition myself. Fear not. I must see with many pairs of eyes if I am to understand what moves the wheels of things; and none of those pairs of eyes is my own."

"And yet you must possess a pair, Excellency."

"Must I? I suppose I must. However that may be, we shall find out soon enough if she is the one: the one they call rairaiMela. Her companion will undoubtedly let it slip. And whether she is or is not the one we seek, I believe I have made her understand our position. It is important for their people to understand that, for the firebrands will doubtless try to win them to their side."

"And if she is a Princess of the Blood, Excellency?"

"Then she could prove very useful, or else very dangerous, to our cause, and in either case we shall have to act accordingly. But do not fall into superstition yourself, good Admiral. A Princess of the Blood is just another girl, no different in essence from a serving maid or a secretary. Her sole value, for good or ill, lies in the web of illusion that is spun about her. In practice, her place could be taken by any other girl and it would make no difference."

"Not quite, Excellency. She would have at least to look like one of them and not like, say, an Astarchean or a Cathrian."

"But of course. I was making a merely hypothetical point at this stage. Though if necessary, it may be possible to make provisions. Let us see how things develop."

"And what of this remarkable ship, Excellency? And what, come to that, of its Captain?"

"The ship we have not yet found, and, fortunately, neither has anyone else. The Captain I cannot imagine to serve any useful purpose, even if she were not by character likely to side with the firebrands. Fortunately again, I doubt she will survive the wrath of the Kang for very much longer."

Chapter 15

Fire from the Skies

DAY DAWNED bright and clear. The second day in Ranyam Astarche.

Captain Antala awoke soon after first light, rested and ready, knowing that her first act must be to make contact with the *Silver Vixen*, but not from within the confines of the palace. She rang for breakfast, partly because she wished to show no sign of haste or to behave in any way unlike a gracious guest and partly because she did not believe in acting on an underfed stomach.

Having broken her fast, she ordered her hoverbike to be made ready for her.

"I wish to take the air before my meeting with Her Majesty this morning."

The Captain rode out of the town and into the open country, enjoying the early morning freshness and brightness. Once well clear of the town, she paged the *Vixen*.

"'Mornin', Madam Pilot. Rayati."

"Rayati and 'morning to you, Captain."

"How fare ship and crew?"

"A good deal has happened since we were last in communication, Captain. The ship has been attacked by a large party of masculi."

"You dealt with them, I take it?"

"Yes, they are all dead. After that, there was a missile attack on the ship. We had to cloak her and relocate her. We maintained radio silence overnight. This morning we are acting as communications center, but that means we'll have to relocate again. The enemy is not slow in tracing us down. Do you approve the Commander's decisions so far?"

−1, "Sounds as if she is doing a splendid job. I knew she would. Pass her over."

RaiChinchi felt a pang of reluctance. There was an almost telepathic rapport between herself and the Captain. They communicated and made decisions together with uncanny ease and rapidity. But raiClaralin was the Commander now. She must be the one to report to the Captain.

"Rayati, Captain. Commander Carshalton reporting."

"Is there more to report?"

"I fear so, Captain. In the first place, we were forced to leave behind the whole of the ship's company besides ourselves. It was the only way of avoiding the missile strike. In any case, Miss Liante and Miss Kerrice had already disappeared. They were outside the ship when we fought the intruders, and by the time we had defeated the enemy, they were gone."

"What of the others?"

"They are in a village called Linton. Lt. Appelbeam has made contact with an Aethyr-Commander who is a member of a clandestine group called the White Roses. Their aim, it seems, is to combat what they believe to be a policy of near-treasonable appeasement pursued by Her Astarchean Majesty's advisors."

"I think I have some understanding of the situation that gave rise to that group. But on whose orders is Lt. Appelbeam making these contacts?"

"It seems that her hand was somewhat forced, Captain."

"And you have no idea of the whereabouts of the—Miss Liante and Miss Kerrice?"

"None as yet, Captain; we have had an all-serene blip from them, but their transceiver is on no-receive. We could override, but we take it they feel it indiscreet to communicate at this stage. We are hoping they will be able to make contact soon."

"Couldn't you trace the blip?"

"Afraid not, Captain. It was saved to memory, and we didn't get it until our cloaking was dropped."

"Is that all?"

"Not quite, Captain. The maidservant Sharan was with the party at Linton. She has also disappeared."

"Under what circumstances?"

"It appears that she was simply walking along a village street toward a temple, not more than a few hundred yards from the other maid and several friendly locals. She never reached the temple, and she hasn't been seen since. No one has any idea what can have happened."

"Are disappearances of this sort a known local phenomenon?"

"Completely unknown, Captain."

"But they make an exception in our case."

"So it seems, Captain. I have further to report that the White Rose organization appears to know all about us—at least our encounter with the *Black Boar* and your visit to the palace, not to mention a rumor that we have an Imperial Princess aboard. It seems they have access to the local State Security. We weren't any too careful with our comms, I'm afraid."

"I know, Commander. We were acting like a gang of bikers. Our affairs seem to be public knowledge. Even off-world ambassadors know all about us. I am surprised there isn't a set of dissected photos of the *Silver Vixen* in the morning papers."

"Actually, they don't know all they'd like to about the ship. That's the impression I get, anyway."

"Poor darlings. Perhaps we should do a special broadcast for them."

"We very possibly are."

"I know that. How are you enjoying the show so far, folks?"

"Don't worry. RaiChinchi has been playing with encryption. We think she has locked them out for the moment. What are your orders, Captain?"

"Do everything you can to trace Miss Liante, Miss Kerrice, and Sharan using scanning equipment, but do not expose the ship. Relocate after communications; scan for hostiles at all times but especially during communications. As far as possible, you should initiate communications at your discretion, but incoming overrides should be allowed in case of extreme emergency. Lt. Appelbeam should use her new connexions to try to locate the missing persons.

"Your first priority is to protect the ship. Orders about retreating off-world are terminated. Off-world will hardly be safer than here, but you have full discretion in an emergency."

"Chalwë, Captain."

"Rayati, Commander. You are all doing fine work. Keep it up."

"Rayati, Captain. And thank you."

SHARAN awoke with an unusual weight of giddy drowsiness upon her, but otherwise with an extraordinary sense of well-being.

Her head lay upon a beautiful silken pillow such as she had never even dreamed of preparing for a mistress. It was slightly scented with a fine tincture of roses, and there was faint but delightful music in the air. The sun streamed in through a tall window, and for the first time she became aware of a uniformed maidservant quietly opening the long velvet curtains. She watched her silently for a moment, feeling too heavy either to speak or move. But it was a very pleasant heaviness.

The maidservant turned, and, seeing her awake, made deep reverence. When she stood upright, she spoke strange words, but from a speaking-box at Sharan's bedside came a translation in a stilted, synthesized voice:

"Rayati, my lady. I have the honor to bid you good morning."

"Rayati," responded Sharan. Her voice sounded far away. "Good—morning." The effort of speaking was greater than she had anticipated. She heard the translation into an alien tongue echoing from the speaker-box. She wanted to add, "I am nobody's lady. I am Paxit, as you are"; she wanted to add some form of courtesy corresponding to the fair speech she had received, but she had not the strength to form the extra words.

"Is there anything I may have the honor of doing for my lady?" asked the maidservant.

"Stay," Sharan managed to utter. She wanted to detain the girl while she found the power to speak and to think straight. The maidservant folded her hands in front of her and waited patiently.

After a time, Sharan managed to form the words, "Where is this?"

"My lady is quite safe," replied the girl.

Sharan's thoughts shifted slowly into place. When one asks a servant where one is and she replies that one is safe, it is evident that she considers a more informative reply indiscreet, and there is little point pressing the matter, especially if one finds oneself too weak for any form of insistence.

"How long have I slept?"

Again the words sounded far away. The brief pause between her speech and the mechanical echo seemed like several minutes. The girl's reply was almost inaudible and then the machine's translation seemed painfully loud, although they were in fact of much the same volume.

"Since yesterday afternoon, my lady. It is morning now."

"How did I come here?"

"It seems you had an accident, my lady. You were found and brought here."

"Recall"

"Recall, my lady?"

"Recall no accident."

"No, my lady. You are weak now. You are sleepy. You must rest again. I fear I have tired you."

"Wait. I have to———"

"You are too weak to do anything now, my lady. Very soon. Very soon."

The voice was soothing. Deft, comforting hands adjusted her pillow. Fine sheets were tucked about her shoulders. She drifted back into sleep.

CAPTAIN Antala decided that asking Her Majesty about her missing comrades would be likely to be of little use. The Lady Selvar, on the other hand, seemed to have some very useful sources of information. Her first move, however, would be to scout about the area where the ship had been and see if she could pick up any clues. She continued to enjoy the sun, the wind, and the open road. Danger to herself and to her friends was nothing new. She had no doubt whatever that she would find Her Highness and the others and extricate them from any small inconvenience into which they may have fallen.

Suddenly she became aware of a sound that penetrated even the noise of her Chandra's engine. A sound from the sky. Two fighters passed overhead. They were small craft capable of both atmospheric and aethyric flight and were moving at great speed. They turned and made another pass. Was that because they had spotted her?

Captain Antala ran off the road and headed for cover. The fighters passed again, swooping this time. A rocket flashed downwards and exploded in flames and flying debris fifty yards from the Captain. She swerved. The fighters were turning again.

There was a small wood about half a mile ahead. The Captain raced toward it. The fighters swooped in from behind and unleashed a small volley of rockets. The Captain performed her celebrated spin turn. She had always regarded it as a mere party piece. This time it saved her life as hellfire broke loose over some thirty square yards of ground that had lain directly in her path. Thick smoke rose into the air, obscuring her from the fighters. They probably thought they had gotten her. Captain Antala turned again and headed for the wood with every ounce of speed she could squeeze out of the Chandra.

She made cover. The fighters passed overhead. Had they seen her? She soon had her answer as a part of the wood a few hundred yards away went up in flames. They knew she was there and intended to burn her out.

Chapter 16

The Vikhar of Astarcheana

"Silver Vixen. Emergency override," she said to her transceiver. "Rayati, Madam Pilot. Sorry to be a bother. I have two fighters on my tail. I am holed up like a ferret in a patch of forest, and they are incinerating the landscape trying to flush me out."

"Rayati, Captain. More mascûl bad manners, I suspect. Hold on, I'm scanning."

More rockets screamed from the sky. With a deafening explosion, another section of the wood burst into flames. This one was downwind of the Captain, and choking smoke began blowing in her direction ahead of the advancing furnace. She looked for a route out of its path that avoided both breaking cover and the flames behind her.

"Of course, they may not need to flush me out. If one of those strikes gets lucky, I'll be fried where I stand."

"Don't worry, Captain. I've found the little darlings and gotten their radiation signature. In twenty seconds they'll have something bigger than you to worry about."

Captain Antala listened as engine sounds grew loud again. The fighters were coming in for another swoop. Then she heard a premature turn. Evasive maneuvers. A distant explosion. Then another.

"There they go, Captain. Nothing like a couple of Sparrowhawk seeker missiles when things are getting overheated, I always say. Anything else I can do for you?"

"No, indeed, Madam Pilot. That completes my purchases for the moment. Can I do anything for you?"

"As a matter of fact you can, Captain. I should be much obliged if you would return to the palace. They are bound to attack again if you are in the open, and I'd rather not keep using the *Vixen's* weapons systems and relocating the ship. I'd also rather not lose you at this stage in the game. Lt. Appelbeam and Cdr. Zhendel examined the site of the blondes' disappearance; I doubt you'll find much there, and you can pursue more useful investigations at the palace. I also fancy we shall want someone there. I realize I am not giving the orders, but I should appreciate your considering the suggestion."

The Captain laughed. "Same old raiChinchi! All right, I was thinking much the same myself in any case. Believe it or not, I am not raring to tangle with more sky fighters—mainly because having an enemy I can't hit personally takes all the fun out of the thing. Back to the palace. Rayati and out."

She headed back to the palace, casting a backward glance at the blazing forest behind her that had almost been her funeral pyre.

Within a few minutes of her journey back to the city, she heard the harsh clangor of motorized bells increasing in volume, and soon several military vehicles, including large engines equipped with fire-fighting equipment, passed her going in the other direction. The forest fire had clearly been reported, and the authorities were dealing with it.

As she rode into the city, several brunettes attempted to wave her down with great urgency. Since she did not know if they were police or royal officials, she thought it wisest to stop. She was, after all, a guest of the State.

As she swerved to a halt and dismounted, she found herself surrounded by a small crowd. Microphones were thrust under her nose, and cameras were directed at her.

"Rayati, honored Captain. You are Captain FiaMartia, are you not?"

"Yes——" said the Captain, taken aback.

"Could you tell us how the fire started in Shintoni Forest? Was it caused by incendiary devices, ma'am?"

"Yes. Incendiary rockets," replied the Captain.

"Fired by hostile craft?"

"They were certainly hostile to me."

"They were trying to kill you then, honored Captain?"

"Either that or they thought I looked chilly."

"Were these Kang fighters, ma'am?"

"I didn't get close enough to ask them."

"You are an off-worlder, aren't you, honored Captain?"

"Yes."

"May I ask where you are from?"

"I'm not stopping you."

"Where are you from?"

"I said you could ask. I didn't say I was going to answer."

"Is it true that you claim to be from Sai Herthe?"

"Have you heard me claiming anything?"

Several voices started clamoring at once.

"Is there an Imperial Princess with you?"

"What is your mission here?"

"Is Kang Shahtha dead?"

"What is the nature of your talks with Her Majesty?"

"Have you come as part of a Fleet?"

"How is it that you speak such fluent Astarchean?"

RaiAntala made to remount her Chandra, but there was nowhere to ride. She was hemmed in on all sides by questioning reporters, cameramaids, microphones. She felt her temper rising.

An authoritative brunette in a black uniform passed through the crowd. Even the most importunate journalists moved aside as they recognized her. She stood in front of raiAntala, and there was silence. She raised a short swagger stick in her black leather-gloved hand in a manner that was genial but brooked no argument.

"That is all, rayalini. The honored Captain has said all she wishes to say for the moment." She turned to raiAntala. "I apologize for my unmannerly countrymaidens, most honored Captain. Please come with me."

The crowd parted as raiAntala accompanied this new stranger. Her Chandra, set on 'follow', brought up the rear. RaiAntala's backward looks were enough to ensure that the curious crowd kept their hands off the machine.

The stranger looked about a hundred and twenty or thirty by Herthelan years, in what is justly termed the prime of life. She was handsome and vigorous and had a very decided air of command, coupled with the poise that comes only with hereditary rank.

"I am sorry to have met you under such trying circumstances, Captain FiaMartia. Yet I am more than honored to have met you. You will take tea with me?"

"I should be flattered to do so, but I fear you have the advantage of me."

"How very remiss of me. My name is Shunderlin. I have the honor to be Vikhar of this city."

"As have your ancestors before you," said the Captain.

"You have heard of me? I am most flattered."

"I fear I have not heard of you, madam, but I knew it by your bearing."

"I am but a humble representative of a lineage far greater than myself."

They approached a curved terrace of tall, imposing houses and mounted stone steps to the pillared front door. Raya Shunderlin pressed a brass button.

"I trust you will not mind my entertaining you here. It is a comfortable place enough and a little more secure than my suite at the palace."

An imposing maidservant opened the door. She made reverence as they entered and then took Raya Shunderlin's cloak from her shoulders. Raya Shunderlin removed her leather gloves and handed both them and her short cane to the maid.

They entered a tastefully furnished tea-room adorned with portraits of the young Queen and the former Queen and of several others whom the Captain guessed to be Shunderlin ancestors.

Fine tea was served in delicate cups that had been used for generations.

"You have certainly stirred things up, honored Captain."

"Have I?"

"Indeed. And you said just the right amount to those journalists. What they need to be telling people at present is how alien fighters have violated our atmosphere and burned our forests. It is time people learned how a nation can be treated that does not defend itself adequately. You know, you couldn't have done a better job if you'd been trying—luring those murderous pirates here. Just what the country needed."

"I hardly know what to say, madam. I am just a stranger off my course. I had no intentions of interfering with your world one way or another."

"Indeed, indeed. I understand that. But there it is. You have become involved. In the end you are likely to have to take a side, so

I can only hope that you will take the right one."

"Why should I take a side?"

"Well, of course, personally you should not. But your Princess bears with her the thamë of the Old Empire. Any decision will be hers, of course."

"Do you know where she is?"

"I do. She is at the mountain retreat of Her Majesty's honored Vizier, the Lady Telarmine."

"How does she come to be there?"

"She was taken there by members of the Vizier's private guard after being attacked by Kang warriors."

"Is she all right?"

"Both she and her companion are well——"

The door opened with what seemed like violence, and a young brunette half-entered the room. She made apologetic reverence, placing her hands together before her forehead.

"Forgive me, Raya. I did not realize you had company."

"Come in, come in, Chavran. Here is someone I think you will wish to meet. Honored Captain FiaMartia of the *Silver Vixen,* may I present my niece, Captain Chavran of the Royal Guard."

The younger brunettes made reverence to one another.

"Captain FiaMartia," exclaimed Captain Chavran. "I should say I am honored to meet you, but this is not honor, it is ecstasy. You are the warrior who blew that devil Kang Shahtha out of the aethyr, are you not? A thousand congratulations, dear Captain. I salute you. The whole Ranyam salutes you. Every gun in the city should be firing in your honor. Every drum should beat and every trumpet sound. Not only should we honor and praise you, but we should beg your pardon that we have left a foreigner to do our work for us. That mascûl dog should have been blown to Hades by us years ago. But you have come and shown us how the job should be done. I salute and honor you with all my heart, ma'am."

"I hardly know what to say," said Captain FiaMartia truthfully. "I really am not deserving of all this praise. My ship was threatened by this creature and it was necessary to defend ourselves. That is all."

"That is all, you say. And that is what you should say. That is what any sane person would say. Simple, sound common sense.

Some dog of a pirate points its guns at you, and you blast them back down its throat. What else would you do? What else would anyone do? But suppose a whole nation is attacked and affronted. Suppose a very Queen is murdered by these outland demons. Should not the retaliation be all the more swift and terrible? Should not those who dare threaten the Motherland be swept from Dea's skies? Answer me that, most noble Captain."

"That would certainly be my feeling."

"Your feeling. Yes, a sound and proper feeling. But it is not mere feeling; it is duty and loyalty, justice and truth. And, at the end of all, it is survival, for the people that will not protect itself must die and will deserve to."

"That is enough, Chavran," said Raya Shunderlin. "The honored Captain did not come here to listen to your lectures on the troubles of our world."

Captain Chavran made reverence. "Accept my apology, most honored Captain."

"Apology is unnecessary. I should feel as you if my homeland had been so threatened."

"And yet," said Raya Shunderlin, "this world is in a sense an extension of your homeland. If you are who we believe you to be, then we are your people strayed far from the Mother World, even as you are. Perhaps we are a people in error, but perhaps you are sent to correct that error."

"I am not sent at all, honored lady," replied Captain FiaMartia. "I am here as it were by accident, having lost my course."

"Are there really some things that are accidents, honored Captain? Or are not all things the weaving of the subtle threads of werdë?"

"Please forgive me," interrupted Captain Chavran, "but I have not told you what I came to say. People are saying that Shintoni Forest has been burned."

"It has indeed, Chavran. The honored Captain can tell you more about that, as she was there."

"Were you there, honored Captain?"

"I was, I fear, the unwilling cause of the conflagration. Two alien fighters were bombarding me with incendiary rockets. I took cover in the forest."

"How did you escape with your life?"

"Fortunately I was able to communicate with my Pilot, who shot down the fighters with some handy homing missiles."

"Raya!" cheered Captain Chavran. "Two more of the devils down! But they are growing bold. Invading our atmosphere. Burning our forests."

"Too bold for their own good, I fancy," said Raya Shunderlin. "Many people will be incensed by this new insult and humiliated by the fact that the violation of our atmosphere was defeated not by our own fleet but by another off-worlder. This policy of appeasement is being shown in its true colors—a policy of defenselessness and humiliation. I fancy Her Majesty will not tolerate this much longer."

"She is under the spell of that conjuress, Telarmine. She will not move without her."

"Moderate your speech, Chavran. I will not have such things said here. In any case, it may be that the wind blows in a new direction. Such a violation makes the policy of appeasement hard even for the most honored Vizier to justify; and I understand that our honored Captain has succeeded in giving Her Majesty a little instruction in the true science of Statecraft."

"Dea be praised, Captain, you are at the bottom of everything, it seems! Our holy Mother has sent you here to save us. You are no maid but an angel of protection and of victory."

"Please, please!" protested Captain FiaMartia. "This is excessive!"

"Perhaps only a little," said Raya Shunderlin. "You have helped us greatly, and it may be that we shall have further reason for gratitude toward you before this act is played out. But I hope we also may be of service to you. I am sure you will wish to communicate with your Royal Mistress."

"Indeed, you have already helped me greatly by telling me where she is."

"The Princess of the Blood Imperial?" cut in Captain Chavran. "Where is she?"

"She is at the mountain retreat of the honored Lady Vizier," said Raya Shunderlin. "The Lady Telarmine will doubtless be trying to convince her of the rightness of her cause, which I take to be no bad thing."

"No bad thing? That creature has the tongue of a golden serpent that drips venom sweetened with all the spices of the East. The revered Princess must not hear only her gilded words. She must hear our cause too."

"Let the Princess of the Blood Imperial hear the Vizier's words, and let her decide. I have all faith in the blood of Sai Rayanna. Let us not even attempt to influence her; then we shall know that her decision is hers alone."

"Do you doubt our cause then, Raya? Do you need the Princess of the Blood Imperial to confirm your own faith?"

"On the contrary, child, I have such confidence in our rightness that I have no fear of putting it to the test."

"And if the Princess of the Blood Imperial should tell us we are wrong?"

"I am certain that we are right. But if she tells us we are wrong, then we are wrong."

"How can you be certain we are right and still say that?"

"I am certain that the sun will rise tomorrow. But if it does not, I shall have been proved wrong, shall I not? I do not expect it to happen. But just as the coming of morning is the test of our faith in the sunrise, so the word of the Raihiranya is the test of any affair of State—but most particularly of this one, since the Rayannic line came to the world of touchable things precisely to fight the Dark One. She will know, and no golden tongue in this world or any other can deceive her."

"You call her Raihiranya, Raya, but she is no Raihiranya. Honored Captain, you have no Raihiranya with you. Surely I speak the truth?"

"You speak the truth, honored Captain. We have with us—or rather the Lady Telarmine has with her—a Princess of the Blood; but one many hundred paces from the Imperial Throne and far, indeed, from the throne of our own country. There are many maids in our world that hold the rank of Princess, and though she is of the Rayannic line, she would not normally be given the title of Imperial Princess, for that title belongs to the members of the immediate Imperial Family."

"I did not call her Raihiranya," said Raya Shunderlin quietly. "I said that the word of the Raihiranya is the test of any affair of State, and you must know, honored Captain, that in that sense the voice of the Raihiranya is the voice of the highest representative of the Rayannic line. And in this world—indeed, in this galaxy—your Princess is that highest representative. Therefore she speaks with the voice of the Raihiranya. Has she not changed since she was severed from the Golden Chain of the Mother World?"

"Yes, she has. How can you know that?" asked Captain FiaMartia.

"How can I know? By the same science that you have been teaching our Queen. Tell me, honored Captain, would you not trust your life to her word on any matter pertaining to her blood-borne authority?"

"Yes," said Captain FiaMartia without hesitation, "I should."

"And so should I, honored Captain. And so may many millions of people before too long a time.

"But you will doubtless wish to see your Princess."

"Indeed I do."

"I fancy the best way to do that will be to go to the Lady Vizier's mountain lodge. However, if you leave the city you are likely to encounter the sort of reception you had this morning. May I suggest that you keep your appointment with Her Majesty and pray you to continue to teach her the science of Statecraft, since you are the first that has been able to get past the Vizier's control of her education? I, in the meantime, will set about procuring a cloaking device that should allow you to make your journey undisturbed."

"Thank you so much for your help, honored Vikhar."

"We are all necessary to each other, honored Captain, and may become more so as time progresses. I shall make the necessary arrangements and may also indulge myself in watching your performance on the morning news broadcast."

"Gracious!" said Captain FiaMartia, choosing an interjection more respectable than was her wont. "I had forgotten about that."

"A fine performance. I fancy Her Majesty will have seen it by the time you reach her. She will not be pleased with this incursion into her Ranyam."

"I was a bit snerpy—that is to say, slightly enormate—with the reporters. I hope I don't come across too badly."

"You will not. They may preserve some of your more amusing quips for the entertainment of the multitude, but our broadcasters have a strong ethos of dignity and propriety. They will edit the interview to keep it in line with the magisterial tone of the Astarchean Broadcasting Companionship."

Captain FiaMartia laughed. "Some things do not change across a galaxy! It is the same at home. Broadcasters are so very concerned with form and dignity. Is it something about that square screen that makes them want to keep everything so upright and orderly?"

"The screen has nothing to do with it, honored Captain. The newspapers are the same, but since they write their news stories themselves, they are able to keep everything in the proper tone. Broadcasters must occasionally trim their material to make it fit the proper dignity of the medium. Only occasionally, of course, since most people are highly conscious of propriety when a camera is before them. It is only the occasional young tearaway that would ever dream of being less than formal under such circumstances.— And, of course, a dashing gentilmaid-of-action such as yourself after a trying encounter with the enemy."

The Vikhar of Astarcheana allowed an impish smile to flicker momentarily from beneath her composed and genial demeanor—so briefly that one might have been mistaken that it was ever there. What did she know, or suspect, about raiAntala? Well, it hardly mattered now. RaiAntala was to every conceivable purpose the Captain she pretended to be, and she and the Vikhar seemed destined to be allies.

Chapter 17

The Demon-Drug

AFTER TWO fruitless hours of searching for Sharan, talking with the local Constabel, the Priestess, and many others, Commander Zhendel, Lt. Appelbeam, raiEstrelle, and Lt. Machirta reconvened at the Red Dragon. Despite their lack of success, a sense of kinship was growing between them.

They sat wearily about their old table, and the Commander ordered cordials.

"We seem to be losing crew members at an inordinate rate," said Lt. Appelbeam.

"The enemy is at work, make no mistake," said the Commander. "So far the other side is making every move—attacking your Captain and your ship, abducting your servant, and we do not know what else."

"You feel sure Sharan was abducted?" asked raiEstrelle.

"What else can account for so complete a disappearance?" asked the Commander. "I find all this intensely frustrating. We should be taking action of our own, not merely reacting to moves from the other side."

"It is difficult to see how we might do that at present," said Lt. Appelbeam.

"I agree, but it goes against the grain to be so passive just the same."

RaiEstrelle suppressed a yawn.

"It is getting late, my honored friends," said the Commander. "I have made arrangements for you to spend the night at the inn here. Please feel free to retire whenever you feel the need."

"Thank you, honored Commander," said raiEstrelle. "I must be a little enormate and leave immediately, if you will permit it."

"Not enormate at all, dear blonde. Much sleep must be needed to maintain such great beauty."

The Commander summoned the blonde innkeeper. RaiEstrelle stood, and the brunettes stood in respect to her.

The innkeeper conducted her up the stairs. The chatter of customers faded behind them. Her hostess opened the door upon a charming little room with flowered wallpaper and a neatly made bed.

"I hope you will be comfortable here, ma'am. It is but a humble place for one such as yourself."

"Good innkeeper, this is among the most charming rooms I have ever seen."

The brunettes stayed up a little longer. The Commander bought slender scented cigars for each of them. Lt. Appelbeam managed to smoke hers without inhaling and thus felt sick only to a reasonably concealable level. They drank a rich, heady, ruby-colored drink called Quindi and made brunette jokes about the seriousness of the situation. Their making light of trouble and danger was similar to that of her own Road Angel gang—but doubtless that was a trait common to Raihira everywhere. Their manner, however, was more mature and civilized, not unlike that of her own elders at home. Or so raiEvelynn imagined. It was the first time she had been allowed into the private converse of real, grown-up brunettes. How curious that she should have had to travel so many light-years to achieve it.

Finally the Astarcheans left, and raiEvelynn asked the innkeeper to conduct her to her room. She was every bit as tired as raiEstrelle had been.

She chatted pleasantly to the blonde innkeeper, feeling extremely competent and grown-up. The provincial hostess was in awe of this far-traveller, and indeed, why should she not be?

As they reached the door of the room, the innkeeper covered her face with her hands and gave out a muffled scream.

"Good innkeeper," said Lt. Appelbeam, "what is wrong? Are you ill?"

"No," said the hostess, her face a mask of anguish, "it is my brunette child. She has been hurt."

"Hurt—when? how?"

"Now. This very moment. I can feel when she is hurt. I have always been able to feel it. She has been cut with a knife. She is in great danger."

"Do you know where she is?"

"I feel sure she is at the Hot Bean Café. That is where she always goes. She is there, I think."

"Should we call the Constabel?"

"No, no," wailed the innkeeper in a horrified undertone. "Please let no shame come upon our family."

"What is your daughter's name?" asked Lt. Appelbeam.

"Menender, honored officer, Sindeline Menender."

"Where is this café?"

"Down the road, about half a mile. It is a place by the roadside."

"Very well. I shall go there."

"Alone? But honored officer——"

"Don't worry, good madam. Everything will be all right."

RaiEvelynn wished she felt as confident as she sounded, as she raced down the stairs and out of the inn door and mounted her Chandra. She had no idea what was happening or what she might find. But what else could she do?

As her hostess had said, the Hot Bean Café was a small place on the roadside not far from the little village. It had a large garish illuminated sign in pink and blue neon, but other than that it looked rather shabby. Music pounded within, but outside stood a small group of brunettes dressed in elaborate slender-cut jackets and with eye makeup that went as far as any village girl dared go toward imitating the exotic (and, raiEvelynn privately considered, somewhat profane) temple-maiden style of their city equivalents. Most were watching, but three girls had knives in their hands. Two were close together, while the third was backing away from them toward a side wall of the café. This one was bleeding from a cut on her cheek.

Lt. Appelbeam turned her headlamp up to full and shone it on the three girls.

The girl with the cut was facing her and covered her eyes against the light. In the harsh glare her face looked white and terrified. The other two turned to see the source of the light, fearing that it might be the Constabel.

On seeing that it was not, their manner became belligerent.

"What do you want, foreigner?" one of them demanded.

"I have come for Miss Sindeline Menender," said the Lieutenant.

The other brunette laughed unpleasantly. "Well, wait around, offcomer. We might let you have what's left after we've finished with her."

The Lieutenant dismounted, leaving her beam playing on the brunettes.

"Put those weapons away," she said. "You know it is athamë to turn edged weapons in earnest against our own kind."

"Whose kind are you, freako?" shouted one of the brunettes. "You aren't Astarchean. You're some stinking alien."

RaiEvelynn was shocked. Never before had she heard such language—far less edged weapons—directed in this way by one intemorph toward another.

"Are you Miss Menender?" she called to the further brunette.

"Y-yes," she replied.

"What are you going to do, Menender?" asked one of her assailants. "Hide behind some dirty alien?"

"That's enough," said the Lieutenant, trying to act as though she were considerably older than these brunettes, when in fact at least one of them was older than she was. "Miss Menender is coming with me."

One of the two brunettes tapped the other on the shoulder. "All right. Let's do the alien."

They both moved toward the Lieutenant, knives at the ready.

"What are you doing?" cried Lt. Appelbeam. "Are you brunettes or demons?"

They said nothing and continued to advance, clearly intent on injuring her. Their faces were contorted with violent hatred—an expression unlike anything she had ever seen before. As an officer cadet, however, she had received some training in dealing with armed assault, although no one had ever imagined that such assault would come from one of her own kind.

She stepped backward and took off her jacket, swiftly wrapping it tight around her left forearm. Her assailants advanced slowly as she backed away. She plunged her right hand into her pocket, and the aggressors slowed, watching for her to produce a weapon. All that was in the uniform pocket were a few small coins. She withdrew her fist, shrugged, and then suddenly threw the coins in the face of her nearest assailant, simultaneously launching herself at her. The brunette, taken by surprise, lunged wildly with her knife. Lt. Appelbeam parried the thrust, using her protected forearm as a shield, and simultaneously delivered a hard drop kick to the knee. This would be enough to incapacitate her opponent for a few seconds. In those few seconds, she closed with the other assailant, parried a thrust to the face, pushing the attacker's knife hand high and wide, and slammed her with all her weight against the wall of the café. Before the attacker could recover her wind, the Lieutenant rammed a devastating vertical straight-arm thrust with the heel of her hand under the chin. Her assailant's head was knocked violently backward against the wall, and she collapsed to the ground.

By this time the first attacker was upon her, coming in with a lunge to the abdomen. Lt. Appelbeam let the strike proceed to the last moment and then turned aside just sufficiently to avoid it, seizing the advanced knife arm with her right hand and pulling the attacker in the direction of her own momentum. As the girl lost her balance and stumbled forward, the Lieutenant struck with the heel of her hand sharply against the base of the skull, smashing her to the ground. The crowd applauded, and to her disgust there were some cries of "Finish her!"

Miss Menender, meantime, had fled. The Lieutenant saw her leaving the road and trying to escape across country. She mounted her Chandra and was soon upon her, transfixing her in the beam of her headlamp.

"It's all right," she said, dismounting. "I am not going to hurt you."

Miss Menender turned on her, knife in hand. "Perhaps I'm going to hurt you," she said.

"Don't be an idiot," said the Lieutenant calmly. "You couldn't even take those two farm girls back there. You can't take me."

Miss Menender's face contorted with the same look of violent hatred she had seen on the faces of the other two girls.

"I can take you!" she screamed.

Miss Menender was even easier than the other two. Within seconds the Lieutenant had her in an armlock.

"You're coming with me," she said quietly. "I am taking you back to your mother."

"You're taking me no—aarrgh!"

"I can break your arm if you prefer. But after that I'll still take you back."

She mounted the Chandra, still holding the girl's wrist at a painful angle. "Get on behind me, and hold tight 'round my waist. At the speed I travel, you'll be a mess if you drop off."

In less than a minute they were back at the Red Dragon. They entered through a back door, and the innkeeper was waiting for them. So, surprisingly, was Commander Zhendel.

"Oh, thank you for bringing her back, Lieutenant," said the innkeeper. "Sindy! What has happened to you? Your face is cut. Are you all right?"

Miss Menender made reverence to her mother. "I am fine, mother—it's nothing."

"That is quite a nasty cut, actually," said the Commander. "You'd better take a look at it, honored innkeeper."

"No, really, I'm all right," protested Miss Menender, no longer in a state of fury, but still peevish.

"Just do as you're told," said the Commander. "I don't know what's been going on here, but I mean to find out."

"Please don't call in the Constabel," said the innkeeper.

"Let me talk to the honored Lieutenant, then I shall be in a better position to decide."

She took Lt. Appelbeam into the bar.

"I'm sorry you got dragged into this. The innkeeper called me to help you, but you got back seconds after I arrived. What happened?"

"They were insane—a whole crowd of them down at the café— three of them fighting with knives—that's how the girl got cut up— the rest cheering them on: encouraging them to knife each other. What's happening to these people? No intemorph uses deadly force on another unless she's mad—it's a biological imperative. I'd say these were not really girls but demons if I didn't know the child's mother."

"They aren't demons. They're just village girls. It's worse in some of the cities. Did they attack you?"

"Yes, two of them together—then this one when I tried to round her up. They all tried to knife me."

"I am so sorry. I wish I had been called earlier. Are you all right?"

"Of course I'm all right; they were just a gang of rustic juveniles with blades. But there was such hatred in their faces, such vicious madness. And they were completely out of thamë. Commander, I'm no angel, and I've knocked about with some pretty rough types, but I've never seen anything remotely like this. Something really bad was going on there. All right, they're not demons; they're just village girls. I saw that for myself. But they were possessed."

"Not possessed. But you are right that something bad is going on. It's called ophrasti."

"Ophrasti? What's that?"

"It's a drug. They burn sticks of it and sniff the smoke. In these cafés even the girls who don't buy it get somewhat affected by the smoke that hangs in the air."

"But what are its effects? Where does it come from?"

"It affects brunettes more than blondes. It gives them a sort of lift. Makes them feel powerful—invincible. In a way, you might say that it enhances their melinity—their brunetteness. It is apparently a wonderful feeling—all right, I've tried it too—it *is* a wonderful feeling. The trouble is, with continued exposure, by unseen degrees, you start to get the symptoms you have just witnessed—exaggerated aggression; the desire to hurt one's own kind badly; bloodlust; things that have never been known among intemorphic peoples."

"And yet they do bear an obvious similarity to certain other peoples."

"I know. It is rather chilling, isn't it?"

"So where does the filthy stuff come from?"

"Nobody is certain. There are pushers all over Astarche. They get it cheaply and make good money from reselling it in the cafés and dance clubs. White Rose intelligence believes it ultimately derives from Kang traders—but we don't know how. We do know that similar aggression-enhancing drugs are being pushed on schizomorphic planets and have often been associated with the spread of the Dark Cult."

"So why isn't this ophrasti stopped?"

"There is no law against it."

"But I mean, right here in Linton, there must be a District

Governess or Magistra or someone who is charged with keeping order."

"According to the doctrine of the Rule of Law, local thamelic authorities cannot take it on themselves to prohibit something against which there is no actual written law."

"Come now! I am no lawyer, but I know full well *that* isn't what the Rule of Law means. It means the maintenance of the thamë—the Golden Order. And that means anything that seriously disrupts the thamë can be prohibited by anyone in authority. What I saw tonight was the most outlandish—and I may be using the word very precisely—breach of the thamë I have ever witnessed."

"I know. That is what Rule of Law *used* to mean. But there seems to be a different interpretation lately. One more in keeping with the legalism of—certain foreign dispensations."

"So the government is tying the hands of local lawkeepers—preventing them from acting against the distribution of ophrasti?"

"Precisely."

"And I wonder who is behind this new interpretation of the Rule of Law."

"If you take a guess, you won't be wrong."

"But I still say those girls were possessed."

"But don't you see? It's ophrasti. It's a chemical thing."

"I see some peculiar thinking taking place in this Ranyam—with all respect, honored Commander."

"What do you mean, Lieutenant?"

"Do you think that chemicals *control* the mind? Do you think they create impulses that were not there in the first place? Or do you think that this animal behavior lies latent in all of us?"

"I don't think either of those things, Lieutenant."

"Then there must be another agent, must there not? Every known society has spent a lot of its time and energy warding off demons. Why do we run through the house banging drums on the Day of Sai Herthe, but to drive out the demons? We Westrennes may tend to ignore them much of the time, but they are real enough. They just need a way to get a foothold on the soul. Ophrasti provides that."

"We—uh—don't run about banging drums on the Day of Sai Herthe."

146

"You should."

"Demons are things outside ourselves, Lieutenant. They attacked the Mother World all those years ago. They were real enough, weren't they? Solid enough to kill and be killed. Demons don't float about inside us."

"They do if we let them."

"Never."

"What makes you say that?"

"Well, everything I've been taught——"

"I see."

"What do you see?"

"I see that the question of demonic possession may be a sore point historically with your people."

"Why should it be?"

"Perhaps because the thought that your whole race was led here by one possessed of a demon is one you have preferred to avoid."

"Do you think that?"

"It was just a thought."

"But it could be right. And if it is right, perhaps that is our weakness even now."

"Honored Commander, it may be so. I saw Miss Menender and the others tonight. My very stomach tells me they were possessed. There was something in Miss Menender then that is not showing itself now, but I am sure it is still there."

"What should we do, then?"

"Take her to your Priestess right now."

"Right now? At this time of night?"

"She is a servant of Dea. She will not stand upon times and places."

"Very well. We shall do as you say."

Chapter 18

The Capture of the Princess

THE PRINCESS was still manipulating the touch screen of her personal transceiver when raiCharmian returned. It had suddenly struck her that the Astarchean-translation adaption files from the *Silver Vixen's* coordinator unit would be there somewhere, and indeed they were. RairaiMela was no raiChinchi, but she had some talent in the software field. With a little work she managed to create a setting that, in theory at least, should beam a translation of spoken Astarchean direct to her earbud.

"Rayati," repeated raiCharmian.

"Rayati. Please forgive me, I was far away."

"Playing games on your transceiver?"

"Just a little housekeeping," replied rairaiMela. "What did you make of the Vizier?"

"Simply charming."

"Yes, she is, isn't she?"

"Do I detect a note of under-enthusiasm?"

"For her charm? Not at all."

"What she says makes perfect sense too, doesn't it? Intemorphic peoples must not get caught up in the endless wars and quarrels of the schizomorphs. They have been killing each other over everything and nothing ever since anyone knew about them. Astarche just can't afford to get caught up in all that."

"Very true," said the Princess. "But at the same time it is important that she should have the capability to defend herself and should not allow anyone to take advantage of her peaceable nature."

"I am sure the Vizier understands that. But there are firebrands who would go much further."

"So I hear. Ring the bell, would you? I feel it is time for a light snack."

RaiCharmian rang the bell, and almost instantly a uniformed maidservant appeared.

"What have you by way of light refreshment?" asked the Princess.

There was a pause while her words were processed, and then the mechanical voice spoke in Astarchean.

"What can you offer of the light-refreshment sort?" were the words she heard in her earbud—the Astarchean translated back into Herthelan Westrenne. It was working!

The maid spoke Astarchean, and instantly, as she spoke, the Princess heard: "We have a variety of humble offerings, madam."

And a few moments later, from the box in the room: "We have many kinds of unassuming food to offer you."

"Excellent," said the Princess. "What does the Vizier take by way of a snack?"

"She is very partial to tinling, madam, a kind of small salted fish with spiced root vegetable."

"That sounds most interesting. My friend here has not been well. Does the Vizier find that tinling improves her health?"

"I cannot say, madam. Her health is generally quite good, I think."

"Really? She seemed to be having some trouble with her leg."

"That is an old injury, madam. She has always had it."

"Always?"

"Well, not always, I suppose. But as long as I've been here."

"How long is that?"

"Nearly five years. But she had it before then."

"Really? Isn't that rather a long time for an injury to last?"

"I think she has a condition that interferes with her healing function, ma'am."

"I see. That would explain it. In any case we shall try this tinling. The Vizier is clearly a maid of taste. If she enjoys it, so, I am sure, shall we. What does she drink with it?"

"A rare tea called inchanhe."

"If it is rare we shall certainly not call upon the Vizier's supplies. A more ordinary tea, if you please."

"The Vizier wishes to extend to you her highest hospitality, madam. If it will not offend you, I shall bring inchanhe."

"Your mistress is indeed very kind."

The maid left the room with deep reverence.

"Charming girl. Charming mistress. Charming people altogether," observed the Princess.

"Yes, they are. Why were you so inquisitive about the Vizier's injury?"

"When so kind a hostess has any problem with her health, it cannot but concern one."

"You were thinking something, rairaiMela. You're up to something. What is it?"

The Princess looked pained. RaiCharmian had let her name slip —the same name they had used on the ship. If they were being listened to, her identity would now be known. What a liability raiCharmian was making of herself.

"What were you thinking about the Vizier's injury?" she persisted.

"Only what I said—that it was a long time for an injury to last. After all, if the leg had been amputated it should have grown back in a year. How could it go on being injured for so long? That was my thought. But the maid has explained it. She is suffering from an unfortunate condition that interferes with her healing function."

"A rare condition, but I have heard of such things before."

"Yes, so have I. Poor thing. I wonder if Herthelan medicine could help her."

"We have no medical personnel with us."

"I know we haven't. I was just wondering. You know—perhaps some time in the future."

"That would be nice, wouldn't it?"

"Yes, it would."

The snack arrived. Tinling turned out to be perfectly delicious, and inchanhe quite simply the finest drink either of them had ever tasted. The Vizier was indeed a maid of taste as well as a very charming individual. The Princess felt sorry for the suspicions she was harboring, but both her instinct and her sense of duty bade her proceed. The fact that the Vizier's healing function was similar to that of a schizomorphic alien only made this duty more pressing.

After their tea, the still-overwrought raiCharmian lay on a couch and chatted idly. After a while she fell silent and her breathing became heavier. The Princess made sure she was asleep.

The time had come. The Princess had already planned her exit. Outside the window was a narrow ledge running along the side of the building. It would certainly be possible to edge along it and get into one of the other windows. If she could find an empty room with an unlocked door, she would be able to explore a little and perhaps discover more about this place.

The theory was excellent, but in practice rairaiMela had always had a terror of heights, and climbing out onto that narrow ledge was a thing she found almost physically impossible. She had climbed onto the window ledge, and she could not persuade her foot to make the next step.

"You are a Princess of the Blood, Mela," she told herself. "You are the Sovereign of your people. The feelings of your private self must be as nothing. You *will* step onto the ledge, for we command it."

Rigid with tension, she obeyed her own command. She stepped slowly out onto the stone ledge and edged a little way along it, keeping her hold on the window frame. The ledge was not quite wide enough to accommodate the full length of her feet, and the drop below felt dizzying. A group of blondes and brunettes passed below, chattering. Their voices sounded distant, as if they inhabited another world. A safe world.

She found that she could edge near enough to the next window to touch its frame with her outstretched arm before fully letting go of the window she had left. This felt marginally comforting. Agonizingly slowly, she reached the new window. Perspiration was trickling coldly down her temples. She felt cautiously behind her. Her exploring fingers discovered that the window was shut firmly. Nothing for it but to try to reach the next window.

She could hear her heart pounding as she reached the second window. Once again exploring cautiously by feel, she established that this one was open. Now it really would be necessary to take a discreet look inside. The Princess tried to steel herself to the task of turning around on the ledge. This took some time, for she really could not bring herself to do it. As she was standing beside the window attempting to calm and argue herself into the necessary action, she saw a blonde walking up the path that led toward this side of the palace. She, unlike previous passers-by, was gazing upward. It would be a scant second before she spotted the figure high on the ledge. There was no time now to turn cautiously and look into the room. The Princess took a single sideways step to bring herself in front of the window and then backed quickly into it. If anyone was inside, she was almost certainly caught; but if she waited a moment longer, she was caught in any case. She thought uselessly of an absurd story about following a cat along the ledge. She could probably have carried it off, too—were it not for the fact that she could only understand Astarchean, not make herself understood.

As she stepped off the window ledge and into the room, she saw that it was blessedly empty of human inhabitants—a nicely furnished sitting room with luxurious armchairs, occasional tables, and richly decorated ornamental screens. She tried the door of the room. It was locked. She would have to get back onto the ledge and find another room in order to get out into the corridors of the palace, though it was doubtful how much use that would be or how long she could avoid being detected. She had the feeling that she was being guided in these actions. Dea had put her in this place at this time. Dea was leading her step by step toward a discovery that she had already half-made, and it was very important that she go though with it. But would Dea keep her from capture or from death? Maids had died in the service of Dea and the Motherland before now—many of them. A Raihira-maid should be ready to die if her duty called her to it. Perhaps she would come to the Jeweled Paradise. It was a comforting thought, but somehow not very comforting. She tried to remember raiAntala's nonchalant attitude to death and danger. She tried a devil-may-care sort of smile that she had used on other occasions when disaster was but a whisker away. It did not work quite so well when one was alone.

She heard the sound of a key being placed in the lock and turning. There was no time to get back to the window. She hid herself behind the nearest screen. She heard the door open and close, and then the sound of heavy footsteps and a clinking of glass. Someone was pouring herself a drink. A creaking sound indicated that the drinker was lowering herself into one of the armchairs. How annoying. She might be there for some time. RairaiMela considered various possibilities. Perhaps the occupant of the room would fall asleep and she could creep out. Perhaps she would be trapped there for hours. After a few minutes she tried very carefully getting down and trying to look under the screen. If she could see the feet she would be able to make out which chair the drinker was sitting in and which way she was facing. Unfortunately the screen came very low to the ground and she could make out little.

After a while, the occupant got up and poured another drink. There was the sound of a drawer opening and closing and a rustle of papers. Then she sat down again. She was obviously reading something. There was silence for some time, broken only by the occasional shuffle of a paper. It seemed to be a manuscript of loose pages rather than a book or newspaper—possibly some official document. Swine it! This could go on for ages.

After what seemed like a very long time, the papers were put down on a table, and the occupant spoke—presumably into a hand-transceiver. To the Princess's shock, the voice was deep and harsh, like a dog's bark. This creature was a mascûl!

She felt her heart thumping against her ribs. Calm down! There were probably personnel from off-world embassies at the palace. The Vizier and her staff probably used the palace for negotiations and the like. She forced herself to recover from the shock and pay attention to what was being said.

"Yes, I am in the private room. I have been studying the intelligence reports. Have you finished the interviews?"

There was a silence during which the other party was presumably replying, and then: "Very good. I shall see you directly then."

Did this mean the mascûl was about to leave? The Princess waited, but there was no sound of movement. She was becoming increasingly impatient, but what could one do?

Eventually the door opened again, and someone else entered the room. The mascûl stood up and said something, but this time the Princess could not understand. It was no longer speaking Astarchean. The visitor replied. She was an Astarchean, or perhaps a femîn. The voice sounded familiar; but how could it? Speaking this strange, rather guttural language, it was hard to identify, but it *did* sound familiar.

The Princess got out her transceiver. The polyvox broadcast from the pirate ship had contained streams of many languages from this galactic quadrant. Based on this, the *Silver Vixen's* coordinator could analyze any local speech and create a translation module instantly. Could her hand-transceiver do the same? She scrolled through various options. Yes, the polyvox data was present. She set up analysis mode. A progress bar appeared, beneath which scrolled several cryptic messages such as *phoneme parsing: radical stage.* Meanwhile she became a little used to the barbaric sound of the language and suddenly realized who the second speaker was. It was —unless she was very much mistaken—the High Vizier, Lady Telarmine herself.

The conversation seemed to be getting a little heated—though the tongue was so inherently harsh that it was difficult to be sure of that.

"Final pass completed: translation mode commencing," announced the transceiver screen, and at once the Princess's earbuds burst into life.

"But, darling, she could be useful," said the Lady Telarmine.

'Darling'? She was using terms of endearment to a *mascûl*? Well, this made some sense of what the Princess had already suspected.

"Uridium can be useful, but it is too dangerous to handle."

"You take me for a fool. I have alternative plans. I am just trying to keep all my options open."

"You are sure you aren't partly under the spell of this 'True Raihir' ideal?"

"Not at all. It is all nonsense. But it could be useful nonsense. Suppose we could unite all the intemorphi under one banner. We should have a tremendous power at our disposal. We shouldn't have to make terms with the Kang any more. In fact, we could eliminate them."

"What makes you think you could control a united intemorph Raihir? You have made a puppet of a young Queen. Do you really think you can do the same with this Imperial Princess?"

"She is just a girl, darling. It is possible. But if it proves impossible—well, one girl is much like another."

"Yes—I understand your thinking, but even with a true puppet in your control, what makes you think you can continue to be the puppeteer? The Esterlini are an old and cunning people. The Old

Loyalists are stubborn and resourceful. Even your own Astarchi have troublesome elements that you are hard-pressed to control. Unite the intemorphi and you are creating a giant—a giant that will change the balance of power completely—and betting everything on your ability to control it. I am sorry. The High Command will not allow that."

"I am not under the High Command, Sknetin; do not forget that."

"I do not forget it. You have been a law unto yourself. You are neither Astarchi nor Fearalyani, but a strange hybrid of both."

"Strange! You call me strange! You of all people!"

The mascûl's voice became tender—if that barking sound can ever be called tender. "Darling, I did not mean you personally. To me you are a woman and always have been—the *melin* part of your blood only makes you more intriguing and beautiful to me. You know that."

"But you called me strange. When you were angry, that is what slipped out."

"I called you strange because of your behavior, not your nature. You behave as if you owe final loyalty to no one. You are a subject of the Astarchean Queen, but you do not pay her loyalty. You seek to make her your puppet."

"You criticize me for that?"

"Not at all, my dear. We have planned together for that. But I am a citizen of the United Republics. I *do* owe loyalty to the High Command. I know you don't, but in the end—in the end one must be one thing or another."

"I *am* one thing. I am the Lady Telarmine."

A loud alarm bell began ringing throughout the building.

"What's that? A fire?" asked Sknetin.

"No. Security alert," replied the Vizier. "We've never had one before." She spoke into her transceiver. "What is happening?" she demanded.

She switched on the speaker so that Sknetin could hear. "One of our Herthelan guests has left her room, honored Vizier. She cannot be found."

"What? Was the room unguarded?"

"No, ma'am. We don't know how she got out. She vanished like a ghost. A maid went to check on them, and one was asleep, but the one we now know to be the Princess was gone."

"Have you searched for her?"

"Yes, ma'am. She is not in the nearby rooms or corridors; we haven't found her in the grounds. All security personnel are on alert, but so far there is no sign of her. We have sounded the alarm, and no one can enter or leave the building—except a ghost."

"Ghosts be burned. Find her."

"Yes, ma'am."

Sknetin raised an eyebrow. "Not so easy to control, I see."

"Stow that. Where can she be? And what is she up to?"

"Up to? She may simply have tired of being your 'guest'. No doubt she has other chims to pickle, as your people say."

"I have no people. How did she get out?"

"Why ask me?"

"You're supposed to be an 'intelligence officer'—a keyhole-stooping spy. I thought you people were good at this sort of thing."

"You *are* angry, aren't you? And for one with no people you are still full of fine Astarchean honor and contempt for 'low activities'."

"I am sorry. You angered me earlier—and now this. I don't like it. Can't you help?"

Sknetin smiled. "That is better. That is my Tela. In a way, though, it was quite interesting to see you skittered for a change."

"I was not skittered. Do put your mind to this girl."

"Well, let us assume—for the sake of argument—that she is not a ghost. She didn't leave by the door of her room, so she probably left by the window." Sknetin walked over to the window and looked out.

"There is a fine ledge here. Someone with a little nerve could make her way along it and get into one of these open windows. Even this one."

"I suppose you didn't check the room when you came in," said the Lady Telarmine.

"Why would I? Espionage is hardly a consideration in Astarche. If I had been checking, I should have moved this screen and—— look what we have here."

The Princess made a graceful bow and said, "Rayati."

"Rayati, young lady," said Sknetin and bowed in return.

"Are you a Princess or a keyhole-stooper?" demanded the Lady Telarmine, her face white.

The Princess stared at her blankly and made an apologetic gesture. She pointed at the window and spread her hands as if to say "I came in that way, but I see the game is up."

"She doesn't speak Astarchean," said the Vizier, "and certainly not Fearalyan. I shall call the guard to take her back to her room."

"Darling, if you trust me, please do exactly as I say," said Sknetin.

"Very well," said the Vizier hesitantly.

"Place your hand on the girl's shoulder in a reassuring manner. Show her we mean no harm."

The Vizier smiled and advanced toward the Princess, placing a gentle hand on her shoulder. The Princess looked up at her with a quizzical but friendly smile.

"You have the strength of a *melin*, my dear. You can snap her neck without even exerting yourself. I want you to place your other hand on her other shoulder and then kill her."

"But—"

"Please do as I say. We cannot let her live."

The Vizier moved her other hand, but before she could make contact the Princess had broken away, aiming a low kick at Lady Telarmine's shin. She made a dash for the door, but Sknetin stopped her. Lady Telarmine seized her frail blonde arms, restraining her with as little effort as it would take to hold a kitten.

"So, she speaks no Fearalyan," said Sknetin.

"Then she heard everything we said in here."

"Everything."

"What shall we do with her?"

"We? Nothing, of course. But I fancy our friends the Kang may have a use for her."

Chapter 19

The Fountainhead

"YOU MAY RISE, honored Captain," said the Queen.

Captain Antala lifted her forehead from the ground and rose to her feet with the simple grace of a fighting-fit brunette.

"You are wearing your sword in our presence as a mark of our favor," continued the Queen, "but it is a Kang sword, I perceive."

"It is, Your Majesty," replied the Captain.

"Taken in battle from a Kang warrior?"

"Indeed, Your Majesty."

"And on Astarchean soil."

"That is correct, Your Majesty."

"You were attacked on our soil by a savage outlander?"

"Yes, Your Majesty."

"You have gleaned, in your short sojourn here, a reputation for being evasive, but we do not find you so, honored Captain."

"Not with you, Your Majesty," replied the Captain, leaving unsaid: "and not since half the planet appears to know my affairs better than I do."

"You do me great honor, Captain. You have had a busy morning, I understand, being attacked by alien craft."

"That is regrettably true, Your Majesty. I appear to attract unsavory company, though I assure you it is not of my choosing."

"If they wish to come here to die, we do not object, honored Captain. They are responsible for the death of my mother and my sisters. While I do not wish to do that which my Vizier tells me may endanger my people, be assured, I do not forgive. Indeed, I wish to ask you your own thoughts on such matters."

"Any humble counsel I may give is ever at your disposal."

Her Majesty smiled and blinked and then said, with apparent irrelevance, "What think you of this garden?"

The Captain looked around the enclosed garden at the center of the palace. The fountain played ever at the garden's own center. Flowering vines climbed the walls, and from one of those walls projected a lovely balustraded balcony, no doubt belonging to the

Queen's own chamber, that she might overlook this lovely sunlit enclosure when she chose. Flowers of the season bloomed in finely fashioned earthen pots, so that they might be grown and tended away from the garden and replaced quickly when they had passed their very best. Butterflies fluttered delicately in the sunflood, attracted by certain specially chosen plants, and from the branches of small trees birdsong could always be heard. The scent of roses hung on the air by day, and scented stocks were placed to perfume the balmy evenings.

"It is very lovely," said the Captain simply.

"It was the bower of my mother and of her mother before her, and of every Queen of Astarche going back down the generations."

"Yes," said the Captain. "It has the feel of such a place."

"You disappoint me a little, Captain."

"I deeply regret that, Your Majesty. How so?"

"You see, Captain, I have been sitting here this morning thinking of many things. Thinking of my mother, of her life and her death. Thinking of the chess pieces and the things you told me about them. And thinking about this garden. And as I thought about it, I thought it to be like the chess pieces——" She trailed off into silence.

"In what way like the chess pieces, Your Majesty?" asked the Captain encouragingly.

"In that it means more than it seems to mean, honored Captain. It is not just a beautiful place, is it?"

"No, Your Majesty."

"And it is not only important for what it means, is it? It is important for what it *is*?"

"That is correct, Your Majesty."

"Well, that is why I was a little disappointed. I was expecting you to tell me about that."

"I shall tell you things, Your Majesty, for you so commanded me the last time we met. But I was curious to know what you could tell me. And I am delighted with what you have told me so far."

"Thank you, honored instructress," said the Queen, suddenly addressing raiAntala as if she had been her teacher.

The Captain smiled. "So tell me what you do think about this garden, Your Majesty. Tell me what thoughts came to you in your royal reverie."

"Royal reverie?"

"Yes. Royal reverie. You are a Queen, you know."

"And my reverie is royal?"

"Yes."

"Yes, it is, isn't it? That is one of the things I was thinking—or something rather like it. I was thinking that when I picture myself sitting here in this garden, I must picture not a girl that is orphaned and feels rather lost. I must picture the Queen. For I am the Queen even if I do not feel like the Queen."

"Yes, that is true, Your Majesty."

"And if I picture the *Queen* sitting in this garden. As my honored mother was when she was Queen. I mean Queen and not just my honored mother—if I remember how this garden used to feel before it was my garden—a sacred place, a center of all the authority in the world. And you know my mother said it was even more like that when *her* mother sate here. And I don't think that is just because no maid feels like Queen to herself. In fact, I think my grandmother did feel like Queen to herself, at least when she *was* Queen. I think it is because my mother lost a little of—of royalty, and then I lost the rest."

"You did not lose it, Your Majesty. You only lost sight of it. Tell me what you think when you look around the garden."

The Queen seemed suddenly shy. "I don't know. Won't you help me?"

"I know nothing about the history of your people," said the Captain, "but let me take a guess. Was not this palace built in a special place? A place that was special before it was a palace?"

"There were no people here before we Astarcheans came, and the palace—or its forerunner—was built in the first generation."

"Yes, I understand. But is there any story behind the choosing of this site? Often great cities grow up around ports or river crossings, but this is not such a city."

"That is right, Captain, there is a much larger city at Entreport, but that is not the capital."

"So why was Astarcheana chosen as the capital?"

"The story has it that several Priestesses came with the honored

Founders, and when they discovered the mighty river whose mouth is at Entreport, they called it the River Thamë, after the holiest river in Esterline. Then they followed the river back to its source, and at the source they founded Astarcheana———"

"And that fountain———" interrupted the Captain with a little excitement.

"Oh, you know the story?"

"Not at all. This is the first time I have heard it. But don't you see that these things follow a very definite logic?"

"So it is not just a story, or an action of eccentric Priestesses?"

"Did your grandmother think it so?"

"No, she believed it, but that was a long time ago."

"Does the truth become less true over time?"

"No, I suppose not."

"You know, Thamë is the name of the holiest river where I come from also. I think wherever our people settle they will seek out the river that is the true Thamë of that place. But tell me more about the beautiful fountain that plays before us."

"It is the very source of the Thamë. You had guessed that, hadn't you?"

"Yes, Your Majesty. Please go on."

"The water constantly flows from the spring beneath the palace, and the water plashes into the little pool that surrounds the fountain. It is drained from the pool by four underground channels that surface again outside the palace and flow north, south, east, and west through the city. Three of the streams end in the little circular waterway that surrounds the city, but the eastern stream flows away to become the River Thamë."

"And what do you understand from this, Your Majesty?"

"It all—it all has meaning, hasn't it?"

"Yes, Your Majesty. Tell me what meaning."

"The palace is the Great Citadel that houses the Source of all civilization. It nourishes the city, and the city nourishes the country. And in this garden is the source even of the palace, and I am its appointed guardian: the Guardian of the Purity of the Stream. As was my honored mother before me and her most honored mother before her."

"Yes, Your Majesty. That is exactly right. Isn't that what you were thinking before I came?"

"No, Captain. And yet, yes. I mean, I had thought nothing so clearly. I could not have told you a word of all that. But—but that is what I was *feeling*."

"That is important. You have been starved of true teaching, but your heart is the heart of a Queen."

"Thank you, Captain. But why have I been starved of true teaching?"

"That I cannot say. Perhaps your people have lost the knowledge of those things that are most important, or perhaps there are those who find it convenient that you should not know. Perhaps there are even those who feel they have an interest in the Stream's purity *not* being guarded. Even in the Stream itself becoming polluted. But know that if the Stream is tainted then the River is tainted, and if the River is tainted then the entire country is tainted. That is why the Stream has a Guardian and why that Guardian is the first power in all the land."

"That is very frightening."

"Why is it frightening?"

"Because I am not worthy. I know I am not worthy. Because I am very small and I need my mother beside me."

"Have you no one to help and advise you?"

"That is the most frightening thing of all."

"What do you mean?"

"I mean that I have always relied on the Lady Telarmine, my honored mother's Vizier and my own. Since I became Queen, she has been my trusted advisor and has directed me in all things. In a way, Captain, she has *been* the Queen in everything but name. But since you explained to me about the Queen in chess, I began to realize that was not right, and that she was not guiding me aright in that matter. And if she is not, then is she guiding me aright in others? And if not, what becomes of the purity of the Stream?"

"That is indeed the nub of our problem, I believe, Your Majesty."

"I mean, none of this—the game of chess, the meaning of the stream—it isn't just metaphor, is it? It is real. It really happens. Like —you know—like the rituals in the temple."

"Yes, of course. Didn't anyone ever tell you that?"

"My grandmother did."

"And your mother?"

"Well, she said that was what people used to believe—well, that it was true, but—well, not the way other things are true."

"What other things?"

"I am not sure—more physical things, I suppose."

"And the honored Vizier?"

"She says so many things, Captain. They turn my mind around like a snake in a maze. But all in all I feel that she believes physical things are really the only things. All other things come from our minds."

"I see, and where does that doctrine come from, Your Majesty?"

"I had not thought of it as a doctrine, Captain."

"Then I pray you, think of it now. Is there some school of thought in Astarche that espouses such a belief?"

The Queen paused, clearly searching her mind for things she had learned in her schooling. "Not that I am aware of, Captain."

"Or in Cathria, perhaps? Or Esterline?"

"I have never heard of such a school."

"Not anywhere?"

"No, not anywhere—except——"

"Except?"

"Except I have heard of the barbarians of Fearalya who believe nothing that cannot be seen with eyes and broken with hands. But that may be an hyperbole."

"It may be or it may not. But I can tell you that this is a belief that comes to certain schizomorph peoples at a particular point in their development. There is a logic in all things. The rituals we enact, whether in chess or the building of our palaces or the making of our laws, shape our destiny and our thoughts. It is said that when the schizomorphi give themselves over to their mascûli, sooner or later they will lose all contact with the things they cannot touch and will even believe themselves to be animals. It sounds like an hyperbole, I grant you, but maids who have had the opportunity to study these things declare them to be true."

"Oh, Captain—that is so interesting. You see, that is just what they say—I mean, that saying about seen with the eyes and broken with the hands—it is not about all Fearalyani, but about the ones who have made the masculi their rulers. But what has this to do with us?"

"Possibly nothing, Your Majesty, and possibly everything. But let us leave that aside for the moment, and let me tell you this. I am a maid that lives among physical things and finds them the most natural to my hand. But even I know that physical things are the least real of all things. They are what they are only because of the higher things that they reflect. If you wish to cure the spotted sickness you cannot do it by cutting off the spots. You must go to the roots of the disease. So it is with the nation—if you will cure it, you cannot begin with its physical exterior: you must begin with that fountain."

They both gazed for a little time at the small fountain playing tiny droplets into the morning sun.

"But you don't mean the water, do you, Captain?"

"Not the water that can be seen with the eye or touched with the hand."

"And if I were to take my place at the head of the fountain, should I then be alone and without counsel?"

"By no means, Your Majesty: what Queen has ever been so? But since the court seems to have lost its traditions of counsel, you will have to choose your own counsellors wisely."

"Then I choose you to counsel me on my choice of counsellors."

The Captain laughed. "Very neat. Then I counsel you to begin by summoning the Vikhar of Astarcheana."

Chapter 20

The Exorcism

COMMANDER ZHENDEL and Lt. Appelbeam returned to the blonde innkeeper, who was sitting quietly in her sitting room, stunned and silent.

The Commander spoke gently. "I am afraid we shall have to take your daughter with us, honored Miss Menender."

"Please don't, honored officer," said the innkeeper. "I have just tended her wound and put her to bed. She will sleep now. She will be all right."

"She was like a wild dog earlier. She tried to knife the honored Lieutenant. You know such things must not be."

"It was not her fault, honored officer."

"I begin to believe that. That is why we must help her."

"But not the Constabel——"

"No, not the Constabel. If all goes well, we shall have her back shortly. Show me to her room."

The two brunettes entered the bedroom.

"Get up," said the Commander quietly but firmly. "You are coming with us."

"Where to?" asked the girl. "Do you think I am afraid of the Constabel?"

"We don't care whether you are afraid or not. Just get ready. You have five minutes."

They shut the door and waited outside. Within three minutes the young brunette emerged. She was wearing a short black jacket with three-quarter length sleeves, leather gloves to mid-forearm and a flared black skirt. A quiff of raven hair fell studiedly over one heavily lined eye. She had a plaster on her cheek.

"All right. I'm ready," she said in an unconcerned voice.

"Thank you. You were very prompt. Please come with us."

The group proceeded silently to the Commander's staff car where Lt. Machirta was reading in the driver's seat. The Lieutenant got out and stood to attention, and then ushered the prisoner into the back seat beside the Commander.

The short drive was also silent until they pulled up by the little village temple.

"What are we stopping here for?" asked Miss Menender.

"Never mind," said the Commander.

"You can't take me here. Take me to the Constabel."

"Just be quiet."

Lt. Machirta let Lt. Appelbeam out of the car, saluting as if she had been a senior officer in deference to her status as a guest and a representative of the True Raihir.

Lt. Appelbeam pressed the doorbell of the little lodge beside the temple and stood in the warm night air under an alien moon, awaiting the answer. It was a longish wait as the little household had retired. A night bird called, and somehow, for a moment, the strangeness of it all overwhelmed her: the giddying sensation of being so very far from Sai Herthe and standing quietly upon the doorstep of a Priestess in the middle of the night.

Finally a hastily dressed maid in black uniform and white apron came to the door. She made reverence.

"Rayati. How may I serve you, madam?"

"Rayati. Please accept my apologies. I need to see honored Matri. It is a matter of urgency."

"Very good, madam; please follow me."

Lt. Appelbeam was conducted into a small parlor with solid, heavy furnishings. After a very short time, the Priestess appeared in a simple white robe. The Lieutenant stood and made deep reverence.

"Your forgiveness, honored Matri."

"A visitor from the True Raihir, if rumor does not run amiss. I am more than honored."

"Yes, I am from Sai Herthe, though merely a humble vikheli."

"How may I be privileged to serve you?"

"It may seem strange, Matri, that I should come so far to bring you one of your own village girls, but I do. She attacked me like a wild dog with a knife, and apparently she was under the influence of a drug called ophrasti. But I am sure a demon has entered her, honored Matri."

"You are sure, my child?"

"Honored Matri, I am but a Raihira. My belief in this matter must yield to yours. That is why I am come here."

"I have heard of these matters many times. I have asked to see these children when the frenzy is on them or soon after, but no one will bring them to me. It has taken you, coming a thousand years of light, to do it."

"Why will they not bring them to you?"

"There is an old saying, my child: 'If there is a gap the size of a mouse-hole, all the legions of the Dark One will enter through it'. There is a fear of acknowledging the influence of demons in this world, and that seems to be a gap, or weakness, among even the best of our Raihira."

"You will see her then?"

"Please bring her into the temple. I shall be there."

Making deep reverence, Lt. Appelbeam returned to the car. The Commander had succeeded in quieting Miss Menender, but when they ushered her out of the car she seemed seized with panic.

"Not the temple!" she cried. "I can't go in there! You can't make me go in there!"

Reasoning became impossible. The three brunettes had eventually to overpower her and march her into the temple by main force. All restraint left her, and she began screaming and struggling as though they were dragging her into a raging fire. Who, indeed, could tell what her eyes saw? So intense was her terror that Lt. Appelbeam almost wished to let her go. Even though the experience was a subjective one, it was clearly both real and horrifying to the poor girl. Nonetheless, they remained true to their objective and walked her, with pinioned arms, up to the Great Altar, before which the Priestess stood. Behind her was a great statue of the four-armed Daughter of Dea, serene, beautiful, and omnipotent.

The Priestess stepped forward. In herself she was gentle and frail: blonde, as many Priestesses are. Yet under the image of her holy Mistress she seemed endowed with all the authority of the cosmos: the very voice of Eternity.

The vaulted interior of the temple was an echoing cacophony of screams and of the nearest things to profanity that are known in the intemorph languages. The Priestess raised three fingers.

"In the name of the Daughter, I seal your voice," she said softly. Her words could not be heard above the screaming, but somehow all present *felt* them. Instantly silence fell.

"Please hold this child securely," said the Priestess. "She is not in control of herself. I am no conjuress. It is not within my power to still the voice of a maid. Whom I have silenced is no maid."

The body of Miss Menender struggled with superhuman strength. The three brunettes combined could hardly stop her breaking free.

"I know she is hard to hold," said the Priestess. "Pray to Dea. It is not your bodily strength alone can restrain her."

The Priestess began to chant, and the brunettes joined the chant, feeling the words of holy mantra to a depth that none of them had ever felt before.

The chant rose and fell. The Holy Names of Dea filled the vaulted interior like an audible light.

The Priestess lit candles and burned incense, all the time chanting, all the time being accompanied in the chant by her three Raihira handmaidens. Miss Menender's body struggled with a ferocity that was terrifying, but it took very little effort to restrain her. It was the light of the chant flowing through them, not bodily strength, that held her now.

Finally the Priestess made the sign of the Fora and intoned:

"In the name of the Mother

"And of the Daughter

"And of Absolute Deity,

"Dark beyond the light and Light beyond the darkness,

"I cast you hence from this mortal vessel."

There was a scream that came not from the lips of any person present, and a fourth voice was added to the Holy Chant. That of Sindeline Menender.

There was no longer any need to restrain her, but Commander Zhendel kept her hold on her, for her body now began to tremble, and after a short time she found herself supporting its full weight.

Miss Menender did not return to consciousness for some time. She was taken into the Priestess's drawing room where she was laid on a couch and covered with a light blanket. The Priestess's maid served something that was not wholly unlike hot chocolate and was even more soothing.

"Well, that rather clinches it," said the Commander.

"Clinches what?" asked the Priestess.

"We were disputing whether the condition of these young brunettes was chemically induced or was the result of possession, honored Matri."

"It is both," said the Priestess. "The chemical substance opens the door, and the dark spirit steps through it."

"Are these spirits always hovering about, honored Matri, waiting for an opening, as it were?"

"The simple answer to your question, Commander, is yes. That is the way most people have tended to see it, when they have seen it at all, and it is certainly true enough for all practical purposes."

"What is the real truth, honored Matri?"

The Priestess laughed gently. "My child, spiritual truths are not like the facts studied in elementary schools. They are not simple things to be learned from a book or a table of figures. They are not like physical things. We cannot say 'there is—or is not—a dark spirit here' in the same sense that we say 'there is—or is not—an apple in this basket'."

"You make it sound very abstruse, honored Matri, and yet there was a dark spirit in this sleeping child. We saw the evidence of that clearly enough."

"Indeed we did, Commander. Indeed we did. That is why I say that the simple truth is that these dark spirits are always with us, hovering and waiting to step in. Our forebears knew that. Why else did they paint labyrinth symbols on their doors that the spirits might become lost before they entered the house? So much of what they did was done because life was a constant battle with those dark ones."

"That was here in Astarche, honored Matri?" asked Lt. Appelbeam.

"Well, certainly in our mother world of Sai Esterline."

"Then there has not always been a fear of recognizing the dark forces—I mean, as a result of the fact that the Great Conjuress——"

The Priestess once again gave that gentle laugh that was so curious and so captivating. "I understand your reluctance, honored visitor, to become involved in our local controversies. The history of our people is long and complex, but for most of those long centuries the awareness of dark forces was very great indeed, and the precautions taken against them were at least as elaborate as in any other society. It was in more recent centuries, when our society had entered what the historians call its technical phase, that the current attitude began to set in. It had a number of causes. One was the common phenomenon of societies in this stage of their development becoming less sensitive to subtle influences. Another was the increasingly schismatic nature of the Old Loyalist movement with its claim that the Great Conjuress had done the work of the demons. For many Esterlini, this seemed like a slur upon our whole heritage, and talk of demons was often seen as distasteful for this reason. Unfortunately, the fact that they are regarded as being in poor taste does not induce demons to go away."

"And are they or are they not entities who seek to gain entrance to the human soul?" asked the Commander.

"The answer to that question is not a simple yes or no," replied the Priestess. "For that reason, it can seem unsatisfying in a technical age. But if we are to be strictly accurate we have to ask questions like 'What is an entity?' For physical beings like ourselves, it seems very simple. A human entity has a body and appears to be confined within the limits of that body. But in fact, in the lower psychic strata that lie, as it were, 'beneath' our world, things are not always so simple. Entities may rise and fall like waves in a dark sea. At one moment a wave appears to be a distinct entity, at another it seems to be simply a part of the sea. Even our own precious identities as individuals are not really as clear-cut as we like to believe, although our physical bodies—for the present—lend them a certain apparent absoluteness——

"But this is a long and complex subject upon which I am sure you did not come for a lecture. Let it suffice to say that for all practical purposes you may regard demonic forces as entities that all civilizations have been profoundly aware of, which pose a threat to both the individual and to the social order as a whole. When the integrity of either is breached, they may gain access.

"Ophrasti, by stimulating the vikhelic areas of the human mind —specifically its aggression—may open the way to the dark-vikhelic elements in the inferior psychic domain. This is a thing that has happened in some schizomorphic worlds, even without the use of ophrasti, because of the rule of the mascûli, who are dominated by the stream of vikhë and need to be counterbalanced by their femīni, who are dominated by the stream of sushuri. When the mascûli become dominant, the vikhelic strain is unbalanced."

"You mean their tendency to kill their own kind and practice torture, for example?" asked Lt. Appelbeam.

"Exactly. That is characteristic of a schizomorph society under mascûlik rule. But there, ophrasti would probably lead to even greater extremes, unleashing what I have termed the waves of the dark sea into something like a tidal wave."

"So, honored Matri, this dark sea—this inferior psychic realm— these demons—however we wish to state it—they are part of us?— or in this case part of the schizomorphi?"

"A good question, Commander. You are grasping the point. Yet still it is not quite so simple. This domain, or these beings, are not part of us, but neither are they wholly separate from us. The question 'Who am I?' has always been a fundamental spiritual exercise. When one meditates upon this question, one begins to realize that the entity we are accustomed to call 'me' is not as simple and self-evident as it commonly appears. Ultimately, there is only one 'Me' in existence, and that is Godhead Herself. Every lesser 'me' is in fact part of a shifting congeries of passions and tendencies whose exact constitution is not stable from one minute to the next. Despite the apparent boundaries drawn by the concentration of a certain group of tendencies in a particular physical body, in fact the thing we call the world soul is in a constant state of flux. In certain dreams, elements may flow freely between one level of the psychosphere and another, but even while waking, the absolute integrity of the personal 'self' is more apparent than real. It is to a large extent the rituals and norms of a given society that fix things as they are.

"But again I must apologize for my Haiela talk. Spiritual self-analysis is not what you have come to me for—though I hope one day you will each of you undertake that noble course. But you are maids of action, and you require my advice upon a subject that lies so far out upon the fringes of the world of action that it is commonly ignored in these practical times, and yet when it impinges upon the world of affairs, as it does now, it can no longer be ignored.

"So, leaving aside all deeper analysis, and treating things upon the level of individual being, we may say that the demonic forces are stirring as they have not stirred in a long time. Partly this is because the safeguards that a society normally deploys against them have for too long been neglected, and partly it is because the Dark One is stirring far away and arousing its minions wherever they may be. Partly again it is because the physical agents of the Darkness are operating not far from us and are using a variety of physical means to strengthen the hand of the Dark Realm."

"Such as ophrasti, honored Matri?"

"Indeed, Commander. The drug ophrasti has the effect of stimulating tendencies in the individual that open the way for her direct possession by dark elements. Its deployment is doubtless but one gambit in a much larger game."

"So demons and humanoids are working together as part of the same army, as it were, honored Matri?"

"Leaving aside the subtleties and complexities of the matter, Commander, the simple answer is yes. And it has always been so. Further, maidens and angels should likewise be fighting upon the same side."

"It was horrible," said a slurred voice. "What was it? I didn't know it was there. It was horrible!"

Sindeline Menender's brow was damp with perspiration. The Priestess laid a cool hand upon it.

"It is gone now, my child. Be calm. It is gone now."

"What was it, honored Matri? Will it come back?"

"It will come back if you allow it to, my child. But if you forbid it and keep yourself pure, it cannot come."

"That stuff—that dirty stuff——"

"Ophrasti, my child? Yes, it is dirty in the deepest sense of that word. You must never go near it again."

"Never, honored Matri." Miss Menender became calmer and let her eyes wander over the room. She looked at Lt. Appelbeam and became restive again.

"Honored Lieutenant—I am sorry, so sorry." She tried to get up in order to make deepest reverence with her forehead to the ground, but the gentle hand of the Priestess restrained her.

"Stay where you are," she said. "You may fully apologize to the good Lieutenant later."

"I tried to hurt her, honored Matri. Tried to cut her with a blade. I was mad, I think."

"Yes, you were demented—you were out of your mind: or rather, another mind was in you."

"Another mind. Not mine?"

"What is yours, my child, and what is not? Do not let such a mind become yours."

"Never, honored Matri. Never again." She turned her head again. "Honored Lieutenant, I owe you my thanks. I do not even know your name."

"But how remiss of me!" exclaimed Commander Zhendel. "I have introduced no one. We have been conversing without knowing who we are!" She blushed deeply. "Honored Matri, this is Lt. Appelbeam of the *Silver Vixen*. Lieutenant, I have the honor to present Matri Luculla, Priestess of the Temple of Sai Annya at Linton."

Lt. Appelbeam made deep reverence. "I am privileged to meet you, honored Matri."

"And I to meet you, vikheli of the True Raihir."

Sindeline Menender attempted to bow her head from her recumbent position. "I am honored, good Lieutenant."

The Commander quickly introduced Lt. Machirta and herself, adding, "Please, please accept my apologies."

"No apology is necessary," said the Priestess. "We were so caught up in our duty, performing each her proper function in the great Vikhail—the War of the Light—that we thought not of the forms of the daily world. And can you not see that a certain ritual was enacted by our very forgetfulness? I spoke of the shifting and uncertain nature of the self—a lesson that must be at least partially understood by those who will fight the Darkness—and while we spoke of such matters, we had, for that moment, no names. We spoke not as this person or that person, but simply as the Priestess and the Soldiers of Light. So, I feel certain, it was meant to be."

The maidservant returned with a fresh pot of the chocolate-like drink. How much seemed to have passed between one filling of the cups and another. And how true were the words of the Priestess about the ritual necessity of namelessness: for now that they each had a name in relation to the others, they seemed to have returned to their everyday selves, and they talked for half an hour about ordinary things over an ordinary hot night-time drink before the staff car delivered each of the visitors to her bed and a much-needed sleep.

Chapter 21

The Showdown

THE VIKHAR had been as good as her word. She had given raiAntala a ring with a large crystal.

"We have been using these for the last year or so in the White Roses," she had said. "You just rotate the crystal a quarter turn counterclockwise to engage the ghost field. With that engaged, you are untraceable by any of the tracking devices used on this planet and, we believe, anything the Fearalyans, and certainly the Kang, have."

Of course, it was hard to tell if it was working, unless an uneventful journey proved anything—which it probably did. She had directions to the Vizier's mountain retreat and was breaking any speed laws Astarche might have to get there.

"You there, Skips?" asked raiChinchi.

"What are you doing in my ear? I turned the transceiver to translate only."

"Sorry, Cap'n. Overrode you. You just disappeared off the scanner without a trace."

"Does it strike you that if I cut comms I probably have a good reason? I am cloaked, you g'doinker, and now you are very likely letting them pinpoint me."

"It is rather urgent, Captain, I assure you."

"It had better be."

"We traced Miss Liante and Miss Kerrice to a large complex in the mountains north of Astarcheana, apparently owned by——"

"I know all that. That is where I am headed now. That is why I am cloaked. I am going to get them out of there."

"They aren't in there. At least, Miss Liante isn't."

"What do you mean?"

"Miss Liante appears to have been taken away from the complex."

"All right, where to?"

"Off-planet—at least that looks like what they are trying for."

"Off-planet? That's crazy. Who's taking her? What are they doing?"

"We don't know. There has been no communication from her. What are your orders?"

"Follow them if you can."

"We can. We have a lock on them. We can pick you up without losing them. Do you want to be in on this?"

"Yes, pick me up and make it quick."

"Quick, Captain? Well, if you say so. I was thinking of stopping off for some coffee and a few games of pinball on the way, but shall I not?"

"All right, I'm sorry. I'm a bit on edge."

"Understandable, Captain. Decloak, if you will, and we'll be with you in a few minutes."

Within less than five minutes, the *Silver Vixen* descended softly to the ground, and the entry ramp hissed open. RaiAntala raced her Chandra into the ship before it had properly touched the ground, and it began to rise again. Within seconds the *Vixen* was fully airborne.

"Welcome aboard, Captain. Sorry we didn't have one of those little squeaky pipes," said raiClaralin.

"What's the sitch?"

"The Princess is aboard a small craft. No communication from her. We think they may have taken her transceiver. They aren't out of the atmosphere yet. Now we have you, we are on their tail. They can't outrun us. On the other hand, we can't very well shoot them down."

"Have you made wireless contact with them?"

"We've tried. They aren't answering,"

"Can we put a tractor on them?"

"We can when we get close enough, Captain. Problem is, the *Vixen's* tractors aren't exactly heavy duty. We could pull a cooperative vessel of that size with no problem, but if that thing has any serious thrust we shan't be able to hold her."

"I see you've run over this with raiChinchers already."

"I try to do my job, Captain."

"*Good* job, Commander. All right, keep on her tail. We'll see what we can do with the tractor first. I'll go talk to raiChinch."

"Glad to see you, Captain," said raiChinchi as raiAntala entered the control room.

"I am glad to see *you*, raiChinchers. How has the Commander been doing in my absence?"

"Beautifully. It really is good to have her."

"Yes indeed. The awkward times seem to be bringing out the best in everyone."

"Including you, if I may say so, honored Captain."

"Why, thank you, honored Pilot. Nothing for reforming the character like hijacking the odd starship, I always say. Pop that down in your notebook for the Royal Aethyr Command, would you?"

"Talking of awkward times, Captain, take a look at this."

RaiAntala watched the monitor tracking the target ship and the rapidly changing figures on its HUD. "They're pretty fast, aren't they?"

"They are. They're entering the upper atmosphere and nearing escape velocity rather sooner than I expected. I don't think our tractor is going to hold that ship."

"Keep on their tail. Whatever we do, we mustn't lose them. Wherever they go, we follow. We'll run them down one way or another."

"Chalwë, Skipper."

"And let's not have any more bad news."

"Certainly not. Bad news is banned from here on in."

"Have we any idea who took rairaiMela, or how, or why?"

"Not really. She seems to have been taken to that place in the mountains owned by the Vizier. She hasn't spoken to us, but she sent regular 'all-serene' blips until a few hours ago. We are assuming she either lost consciousness or lost control of her transceiver."

"All right, Captain—I need you and the Commander to sit down and use a safety strap: we are leaving the atmosphere."

RaiAntala left the control room. "Buckle up, Commander," she said to raiClaralin. "We are heading into aethyr."

"That's not good."

"Not especially, no. We'll keep on their track until we find a way to stop them. How are the others?"

"RaiCharmian is still at the Vizier's cozy lodge. Lt. Appelbeam is in a little village with raiEstrelle and some new friends—members of the

White Rose Sisterhood. She has had some rather alarming adventures of her own, and I have to say you were right as usual, Captain."

"Right in what?"

"Do you remember about a year ago, I said Evelynn Appelbeam would never make a Road Angel, and you said she had the right stuff in her? Well, you were right—she is really coming into her own now."

"I'm glad to——"

"Captain, come here! This is an emergency!" raiChinchi's voice shrilled from the speakers.

The Captain unbuckled and bounded into the control room.

RaiChinchi pointed at one of the monitors. It indicated three ships moving in toward the planet.

"What do you make of those?"

"Very odd assortment. They don't look as if they come from the same planet, and they are all black."

"Like the *Black Boar*."

"Yes—pirate ships, you think?"

"Kang ships or I'm a chenkireet; and armed to the teeth."

"That's nice."

"And the Princess's ship is on course for the biggest one."

"I thought you said you weren't going to give me any more bad news."

"How about double no-bad-news tomorrow?"

The Captain shouted into the mic, "Commander to the control room. Take the secondary beam cannon."

"Incoming, Captain," said raiChinchi.

"All right, I'll try to intercept. Reply with missiles. Concentrate fire on the big one. Commander, intercept incoming."

Four out of five missiles were intercepted by the Captain and the Commander. The ship shook like a tower in an earthquake as the fifth one hit the force shields.

"We can't take many like that," said raiChinchi.

"How are our missiles doing?"

"Two hits, but they are well shielded, and the Princess's ship is docking with the big one."

"Wonderful. All right, try to take out the other two."

A hail of missiles came in. Frantically the Captain and

178

Commander intercepted, but two more hits racked the ship.

"Captain, I hate to say this, but I think the game's up," said raiChinchi. "We can't take any more, and look at that." She indicated the monitor. Three more black ships were emerging from deep aethyr: one was still a speck in the distance, but the other two were quickly enlarging and taking shape.

A mascûl voice boomed from the *Vixen's* speakers:

"This is Kang Avankh, son of Kang Shahtha, Captain of the Black Python *and head of the Kang. Silver Vixen, we have you outnumbered and outgunned. We can destroy you."*

"This is Antala Fiamartia, Captain of the *Silver Vixen*. Acknowledged you can destroy us. We will take at least the *Black Python* with us. We are nearing you on a collision course and will detonate fission weapons."

"The pod carrying your Princess has just docked with the *Black Python*. We have her," said Kang Avankh. "But I do not want your Princess, and I do not want to destroy your ship. I want only one thing, Captain FiaMartia. I want you—my father's slayer."

"You want to kill me?"

"Of course I want to kill you. But I am a warrior, not a murderer. I want you to dock with the *Python* and come aboard. I want to fight you man to—melin. If you slay me, you, your Princess, and your ship go free. If I slay you, your Princess and your ship still go free. All I want is to slay you in fair combat. What say you?"

"I will consult with my crew."

"Of course. You have five minutes."

"Shut the comms, Madam Pilot."

"Shut. Do you trust them?"

"Like a fox in a chicken run."

"What will you do?"

"I can't see any alternative to boarding. Kang may be honest. If not, we all die, which is what happens anyway."

"They may try to nullify us when we dock, but I can fix that. Let me say a few words to the snake-mascûl."

"Certainly."

RaiChinchi spent two minutes furiously setting parameters on one of the ship's consoles and then reconnected the comms system.

"*Black Python*, this is Reteliyanhe Chirenchihara, Pilot of the *Silver Vixen*. We are preparing to dock with you. Please be aware that I have primed a matter-antimatter fission device to detonate immediately. It is being held in check by a force shield that isolates the elements. If the *Silver Vixen* were to lose power for any reason, the shield would drop, and the device would detonate instantly."

The mascûl voice laughed. "You do not trust my word. I am hurt. I have told you that I want nothing but fair combat with your Captain. Please dock forthwith."

"One more thing, honored Captain," said Captain FiaMartia.

"What is that? My patience grows short."

"Don't try mine. I wish to speak with the Princess to be sure she is with you and alive."

"As you please. Ardash! Bring the chelan! She is on the line, honored Captain. Speak to her."

"Your Highness," asked the Captain, "is that you?"

"Captain, this is your Princess. I am safe and well." It was rairaiMela's voice.

"What sort of cat am I?"

"The toughest in town. It is me all right. What is going on? I haven't been able to understand a word they are saying."

"They want me to fight their leader, which is dinky-doo by me. I'll be dropping in to get you out of there in a few minutes."

"You think they'll let us out if you win?"

"Well, they said so."

"I want you to come wearing the Captain's sword. That is an order."

"Chalwë, Your Highness."

"Are you satisfied, Captain FiaMartia?"

"Perfectly satisfied, Captain Kang. We shall be docked with you in minutes. Close comms, Madam Pilot."

Commander Carshalton was already bearing a long shape wrapped in red silk edged with spun-gold thread. She knelt before the Captain, holding it up to her in her outstretched hands.

Silently the Captain took the sword and unwrapped it. The sacred steel seemed to cast a light over the whole control room: not a physical light but a light of the Spirit. In old times it was said that

Sai Vikhë, the Angel of Battle, resided in a True Blade in all her winged glory, and not one of the three maids in that room at that moment, for all their life among the brash hoverbike riders of Doriston, could have conceived of disputing it.

Reverently, the Captain buckled on the holy blade. It was a moment that raiAntala realized she had been subconsciously looking forward to—one that should have been glorious.

The Captain was every inch an officer and a noblemaid. The uniform had always had the effect of transforming her into something a light-year from her Road Angel persona, but the sword, while its visual impact was small, did something more. It changed her entirely and gave her an aura. Something more than the visual was at work here: something that might be called a chemistry between the soul of raiAntala and the soul of the sacred blade.

"Prepare for docking!" said raiChinchi, who was monitoring the ship's autopilot from her transceiver. "They have us in a light tractor, and we dock in three."

"Well, kiddies," said raiAntala, "time to say goodbye. I don't know if we'll meet again in this universe. Probably not, I fear. I just want to tell you—well—I'm sorry. Sorry I dragged you into all this. I didn't know it would end this way. None of us did. But it was my fault. I don't know what to say now except goodbye, and—I'm sorry."

"Sorry for what?" asked raiClaralin. "We could have died any day back home on any chicken run. If we'd been so concerned about our lives we'd never have been Road Angels in the first place. This is a much more spectacular way to go than being spattered over the pavement in Doriston. I think this is a rather jolly way to go."

"The truth about all of us," said raiChinchi, "is that we are warriors born in a time of peace. Our hearts are made for war. We are children of Sai Vikhë. Yes, me too, though you probably think you dragged along a hapless Haielin. We were built for the Defense of the Light, and we were born in a time that had no real need of us. So we made our own dangers. And then we went off by ourselves to find a real war where a people like our own really needed defending. Or did we go by ourselves? I often wonder about that."

"I wonder if we did them any good—our noble hostesses," said the Captain. "I suppose we shan't know the answer to either question now."

"War is like that," replied raiChinchi. "We fight. We do what we must. Many of us die without ever knowing the results of our actions. But we have served the Light. We have defended the Golden Order. That is what is asked of us, and that is what we have done. And you, Captain, if I may say so, have never flinched in the face of danger, never failed to smite the enemy. I want to say that I am proud to have served under you."

"And I," said raiClaralin. "Proud to have served under you and happy to die with you. Apologize for nothing, honored Captain. You have led us to a more worthwhile life and a more meaningful death than we ever had at home. It has been all too brief—but that is war. I have no regrets for myself and nothing for you but thanks."

"Thank you, both of you," said the Captain. "Haya Vikhë!"

"Haya Vikhë!" echoed the two officers.

"All right, comms on. Let's move," ordered the Captain.

RaiChinchi took the main controls. Instructions were barked over the speakers. The docking procedure was fast and smooth. The *Silver Vixen's* portal hissed open, and the ramp led into an enclosed docking area. Several Kang guards were already flanking the exit. They saluted as Captain FiaMartia appeared at the top of the ramp.

The Captain returned their salute and descended the ramp. The portal hissed up, sealing off the *Silver Vixen* again.

Silently, the Captain accompanied her Kang escort along steel corridors. The Kang were not uniformed but were dressed in variants of the leather semi-armor raiAntala had encountered in Astarche. Some of them had various ornaments and items of jewelry, presumably looted from their various victims. The ship itself still bore the defaced insignia of some merchant fleet from which it had been taken. Presumably its light armaments and shields had been replaced with the serious battle array it now boasted.

They arrived at what looked like a main concourse area. A large group of Kang pirates were gathered. Lashed with heavy ropes to a steel pillar stood the Princess. Her mouth was taped over with some kind of adhesive material. RaiAntala bowed to her, and she nodded her head with regal courtesy.

One of the Kang stepped forward: a huge creature with golden beads attached to the braided strands of its facial fur and gold chains across its heavy leather breastplate. It saluted, and its dog-like voice, somewhat distorted by a rather rudimentary translation speaker, boomed forth: "Captain FiaMartia, we meet at last. Such a pleasure. I am Kang Avankh."

"Captain Kang," replied raiAntala, returning salute, "the pleasure is mine, I assure you."

"To fight a warrior such as yourself is an honor. You have slain my father, so I have no option but to slay you. I believed your destruction of the *Black Boar* was perhaps mere luck. I sent out emissaries to kill you, which seemed a simple matter. They did not return alive. You are more than you appear, Captain FiaMartia. A personal duel becomes necessary."

"You flatter me, Captain Kang. I am but a humble vikheli in the service of my country."

"And you are ready to die?"

"I have been ready to die since the day I was born, Captain. And you?"

"I do not think the matter arises, Captain."

"Perhaps. Though if you have gods, a small prayer might not be out of place."

"Our gods are the gods of war, Captain FiaMartia. We make our prayers with our swords."

The Kang drew its great war sword and motioned to one of its crew, who came forward with a heavy, three-foot wooden beam some thirty square inches in cross-section. It presented between its outstretched hands. The Kang, with a fierce but elegant motion, swung its ferocious blade, chopping the beam cleanly in two across the grain. The two parts fell to the steel floor with a heavy thud.

"This is the sword you are facing, Captain."

Captain FiaMartia drew, for the first time, the gleaming sword she had taken for her own today. She felt the blade was a part of her soul, she felt she knew it as she knew her own limbs, and she knew that this was no common steel. She withdrew from her sleeve a fine lace kerchief, used on formal occasions by ships' officers, and raising it above her head she flicked it lightly into the air. As it fluttered downward, she made a pass with her sword almost too fast for the eye to follow, and the kerchief floated to the ground in two separate halves.

She raised the sword to her forehead in salute. "And this, Captain, is the sword you are facing."

"No more talk," barked the Kang. "My sword grows thirsty."

It stepped forward with a down cut calculated to smash through any defense and kill in the first moment of combat. RaiAntala barely managed to step aside but simultaneously made a thrust to the undefended body of her opponent. The Kang, with agility that belied its great bulk, avoided it with a last-minute twist.

They circled each other slowly, each realizing that her opponent was more skilled than anything she had faced hitherto. Probing thrusts and cuts were made and parried or dodged. Each was now looking for a way into the other's defenses. Studying movements, studying faces. Each was keeping her own intentions masked and seeking a clue to the other's.

"What are you playing? Finish her!" shouted one of the pirates.

Without turning, the Kang flicked its great sword in a backward movement, smashing the rib cage of the one who had yelled the taunt and quickly recovering to full defense. Blood dribbled from the pirate's mouth as it fell to the ground.

RaiAntala's eyes strayed briefly to the ugly spectacle, and in that instant the Kang struck, nearly penetrating her defense. She leapt backward out of sword range. The Kang pursued her. She leapt onto a steel table, and one of the pirates who was standing by it moved to pull it out from under her. She slashed at the pirate's head, and it scurried for cover. Kang Avankh, believing her momentarily distracted, came in for the kill, but the slash aimed at the pirate's head had never been intended for it—raiAntala had calculated upon its evading the stroke and carried the sword around in a full circle to bite hard into Kang Avankh's shoulder. The Kang roared and made a clumsy strike. In a contest like that, one clumsy strike is fatal. RaiAntala drove her sword through its chest, and it fell silently to the ground.

She had not been unaware of two burly pirates tracking her throughout the fight. She had guessed that their job was to dispatch her if she won.

The first, sword drawn, closed silently from behind. Half-turning at the last moment, raiAntala cut it down. The second drew back a little, but the sound of two dozen swords being drawn now filled the air. RaiAntala found herself in a ring of steel: ugly grinning pirates ahead of her, flanking her, behind her. There was a brief standoff. None really wanted to be the first to be cut down by raiAntala's blade. But they were not cowards, and they could not appear cowards before each other.

A harsh voice barked out, "All of us at once. NOW."

The next move would have been the inrush of heavy steel, but something else came first. A bone-jarring impact shook the ship, sending several of the pirates sprawling. Then another, and another.

"We're under bombardment," roared a voice over the ship's speakers. "Battle stations, battle stations. Man the guns."

In the panic that ensued, raiAntala got to the Princess and cut her bonds. A new voice came over the speakers—a human voice this time.

"This is Admiral Perentella of the Royal Astarchean Navy. We have you outnumbered and outgunned. You have one chance to surrender before we blow you out of the aethyr."

"Surrender?" barked the reply. "We'll see you in hell first."

Massive impacts continued to rack the ship. The lights went out.

RaiAntala heard barking voices amid the chaos:

"But Telarmine said we wouldn't be attacked however close we came."

"So the half-breed betrayed us—is that so strange?"

"Pour it on, boys. No surrender. We'll go down fighting!"

"Rayati, Captain, having fun yet?" RaiChinchi's voice spoke in raiAntala's earbud.

"Laugh a minute. These creatures may be ugly, but they sure know how to throw a party."

"All right, listen. I've scanned the ship. There are several Wasp-type small craft docked below. You've got the Princess, haven't you?"

"Yes, she's with me."

185

"Good. I've got you on my tracking screen. Just follow my directions. But hurry—that ship will be going up in smoke any minute."

"Yes, I gained that impression myself."

Chapter 22

Diaspora

RAIRAIMELA felt giddy and a little nauseous. She had been close to paralyzed with fear for hours. Shock had followed shock. First being bound painfully tightly by that foul Vizier and her pet mascûl, then being handed over to other mascûli who made the pet look relatively civilized.

She had seen Kang up close before, of course, but it had been quick, her adrenaline had been rushing, and she had killed them. Now she was bound and helpless as a huge, swaggering creature with little braids in its black face-fur led her like a captured animal to a small craft that had landed in the grounds of the Vizier's palace.

She had no idea what these creatures might do to her. When they came close their scent was rank and heavy like that of some beast of prey, and they exuded violence with every movement and sound.

Actually, other than leaving her bound, they had treated her with what appeared to be a reasonable degree of respect. Presumably, as a high-value captive, she was off-limits for any rough treatment by inferiors, though she had no idea how she might be treated by those with the authority to do as they wished with her.

The journey in the little craft swam and swirled in her head. She wondered whether she had somehow been drugged or whether she was in some kind of shock. She was aware of the craft docking and of being led along metallic corridors, aware of huge fur-faced Kang staring at her, and finally she was introduced to their Captain and leader, Kang Avankh. She could not understand a word spoken by any of them. Her captors had hardly spoken to her in any case, but Kang Avankh now addressed her. Its manner seemed respectful, and it reproachfully ordered its minions to loose her bonds. It even seemed to bow to her.

Whether this behavior was ironic, she had no idea. Certainly she was a prisoner, and she had no doubt that she might be killed or mistreated at any moment. Her captors were slavers and killers of a particularly ruthless kind; so much she knew of them, and their appearance and bearing confirmed it. Nevertheless, their leader affected an air of barbarous civility, at least for the moment.

She had been confined to a small metallic room but had been provided with fine food and drink and even, oddly, a gold bracelet and a necklace of gold and precious stones. Her jailer had given her these with a short speech of which she understood nothing, but supposed it was saying that they were a gift from Kang Avankh and presumably giving a reason. She had looked at the delicate, well-wrought jewelry and wondered from whose body it had been taken and whether it was dead or alive at the time. She did not wear it.

After what had seemed an age in her little metal cabin, she was brought out, and a heavy alien transceiver was thrust into her hand. She heard the most welcome sound imaginable—raiAntala's voice. The chances of the Kang actually letting either of them go seemed remote, but the thought of dying suddenly seemed less horrific if raiAntala were to be by her side. For a moment she had been about to tell her not to come into what was surely a death trap, but she knew that the Captain's first and overriding duty was to attempt to save her Sovereign, however remote the possibility.

She was bound to a pillar and her mouth taped over. This was done in a manner that seemed paradoxically respectful, and she, in her turn, had attempted, to the best of her ability, to bear herself with regal dignity.

From the point of raiAntala's arrival, events had moved with confusing speed and violence. She concentrated hard on maintaining her royal bearing while feeling weak and sick with terror. Within minutes Kang Avankh was dead, the ship rocked by volleys of missile fire, and the crew in panic action. She was cut loose and led by the arm through metallic corridors. Pirates, intent on saving the ship, mostly ignored them, but if any made a move toward them they were cut down instantly by the Captain's sword.

They came near to a docking bay where numerous Wasp-like fighters were stationed. Their forward momentum came to a stop, and raiAntala pulled her backward into a crouching position in one of the metal corridors. With a single fast motion, she pulled the tape off rairaiMela's mouth. It hurt. RairaiMela wanted to make some quip about her having left it on so long, but she felt sick and could think of nothing.

"Those ships are our way out," said raiAntala, "but we've hit a problem."

Two large pirates rushed past them brandishing blasters. They had no interest in the two intemorphs crouching by the corner but made for one of the ships. They were cut down by a hail of blaster fire. They tried to defend themselves with their own blasters, but they were hopelessly overmatched by fire from heavy-grade combat weapons fired by guards in strategically placed watchposts.

"Why are they killing their own people?" asked rairaiMela.

"Those guards are there to stop deserters in time of crisis," said raiAntala, "but they'd be just as happy to kill us, I imagine."

"I'm guessing they are our problem."

"You're guessing right." RaiAntala drew a hand-blaster of her own.

"You aren't planning to get past them with that?" asked rairaiMela.

"Yep. But not quite in the way you're thinking."

She stood up facing the way they had come, and within a minute another pirate came running down the corridor. She leveled her blaster at it.

"Halt," she said in a steady, commanding tone.

The pirate went for its weapon, but raiAntala shook her head. Its hand froze midway to the blaster.

"Smart move," said raiAntala. "Look, you're still alive!" She moved forward and relieved the pirate of its weapon, throwing it into a waste chute.

A horrible boom and rending of metal nearly deafened them as the ship shuddered convulsively beneath another terrible impact.

"This crate's going down," said the pirate desperately. "In a couple minutes none of us is going to be alive. I've got to get to the lifeships."

"That's right," agreed raiAntala. "And you will."

Two more Kang rushed past, ignoring them. They rounded the corner, and then the sound of heavy blaster fire and screams filled the air.

"You want to end like those two?" asked raiAntala. "Or will you do what I say and get off this bucket free and clear?"

"What do you want me to do?"

"Take my blaster. You're going to take the Princess and myself to one of the lifeships. We'll have our hands behind our heads. You'll tell the guards you have orders to take us off the ship."

"They'll wireless for confirmation."

"Their comms are down."

"How do you know?"

"I have my sources. Do you want to do it my way, or try rushing a ship and get hacked to shreds?"

"Give me the blaster."

RaiAntala handed over the weapon, butt first. "And don't get any ideas just because you're holding the gun. I'm in charge here. I'm always in charge."

The pirate smiled, thinking that raiAntala was blissfully unaware of the old mascûl saying that all authority derives from the snout of a blaster.

RaiAntala's plan went perfectly. The Princess and her Captain rounded the corner slowly, in attitudes of obvious surrender. They were followed by their captor, who stopped and explained its mission. After a short pause, it was given permission to continue, and marched the prisoners into the best available lifeship.

"Now wasn't that nicer than being one of those pools of blood and bones we stepped over to get here?" asked raiAntala.

"You're a real genius," said the pirate.

"Stick with me and you'll go places," said raiAntala, taking the ship's controls.

"All right, they're away," said raiChinchi. "Permission to disengage, Commander?"

"Chalwë, Madam Pilot. Get us clear before the whole shebang goes up."

The *Silver Vixen* pulled elegantly away from its dock with the *Black Python*, and once again stood clear and proud in aethyr.

"Where now, Commander?"

"The *Vixen* is still badly damaged. I think we should——"

"The idiots!" shouted raiChinchi. "The Astarcheans have fired a missile at the Princess's escape craft."

"Can you deflect it?"

"I'm trying."

There was a flare on the monitor.

"What happened?" asked the Commander tensely.

"It was programmed to blow on proximity. I managed to deflect it at the last moment—but I don't know if it was far enough."

"There they are," said the Commander, as the flash-disruption cleared. "They're still in one piece at any rate."

"Yes. I think they must have taken a hit though," said raiChinchi.

"Can you wireless the Astarcheans?" asked the Commander.

"And tell the Kang who's in that craft? Their internal comms are down, but they are still monitoring external signals from the bridge."

"We can't risk another hit from the Astarcheans—they must think this is a Kang maneuver."

"Wait. They've stopped firing," said raiChinchi.

"You think they've somehow found out who is in the craft?"

"No, I mean they've stopped firing altogether. All the Astarchean ships have stopped attacking the pirates."

"What's going on?"

"I don't know. They seem to be withdrawing."

"That's insane," said the Commander. "They've nearly pegged the Kang mothership."

"It may be insane, but it's happening. They are definitely withdrawing from battle."

"What in the name of the Eagle is going on?"

"If you're in the market for a guess," replied raiChinchi, "I'd suggest that the Vizier has somehow managed to regain control."

"That sounds all too disgustingly likely."

"The surviving pirate ships are withdrawing too. They're scattering. There goes the *Black Python*. They are taking the opportunity to escape."

"All right—get after the *Python*."

"Are you serious, Commander? The *Vixen* is half-crippled."

"And the *Python* is nine-tenths crippled. I don't care what the Astarchies do—those devils aren't getting away. Not on my watch."

"Their thrust is still good, Commander. They are making speed into deep aethyr. I don't know how quickly I can get the *Vixen* up to full speed. I don't even know if I can."

"I don't care. Just keep them in track and keep on their tail. We'll follow them to the edge of the galaxy if need be. They're going down."

"Chalwë, Commander."

"WHAT is the most disrespectful phrase in your language?" asked Commander Zhendel. She had been listening to a voice over her transceiver for some minutes, her expression growing darker and darker.

"There are several, and I hardly like to mention them," said Lt. Appelbeam. "They often have to do with imputations of animal parentage."

"Well, you can use them all as freely as you like," said the Commander. "It seems the attack on the Kang incursion has been called off."

"But why? It has only just been called on."

"Why indeed? It seems your Princess has exerted her authority as the senior royal personage in this world to protect the Kang from our navy."

"That is nonsense. Forgive me, but she would never do that."

"It appears that she has been a semi-voluntary guest of our honored Vizier for some time. I can assure you that the Lady Telarmine is a very subtle and highly persuasive person. She can convince one that the sky is green and the grass blue given enough time."

"Not our Princess. She has the Sun Blood in her veins. She just *knows* where matters of Polity are concerned."

"I am sorry, but the facts are before us."

"No. There is something wrong somewhere. Believe me, there is something amiss here."

"Suppose you are right—and somehow I feel inclined to believe you—if we go to the palace, perhaps you can get to the root of the problem."

"There is a chance I could."

"Machirta, get the car," ordered the Commander. "We're driving to Astarcheana." As her Lieutenant went for the car, she said, "There is one piece of good news."

"I am glad to hear that," said Lt. Appelbeam. "What is it?"

"The *Black Python* was badly hit and made its escape as soon as our attack was called off. But your ship has gone after it in hot pursuit."

"The *Silver Vixen*?"

"Yes, and I must say there isn't a ship in our navy I'd rather see on the tail of those demons—Machirta! What are you doing back here without the car?"

Lt. Machirta had indeed returned on foot in the company of another uniformed officer. It took another fraction of a second to notice that the two of them were in fact joined by a pair of handcuffs; a fraction more to see that uniformed officers were stationed at the doors and windows.

One officer in a more elaborate uniform than the others strode up to the Commander and saluted.

"Rayati, honored Commander Zhendel," she said. "It is my unfortunate duty to arrest you and your associates on suspicion of belonging to a treasonable organization by the name of the Sisterhood of the White Rose."

THE Wasp shook horribly as a missile exploded not a hundred yards from impact.

"That was the g'doinking Astarche Navy," said raiAntala.

"Friendly fire?" sneered their recent captor.

"Not all that friendly. They meant to blast us to the nether regions. Thank Dea raiChinchi and the Commander were on the job."

"What do we do now?" asked rairaiMela.

"I am going to try to put us down on Astarche before they blow us to smithereens."

For tense minutes raiAntala concentrated on the small ship's controls, coaxing the damaged vessel into a downward orbit of the planet.

"What's happening now?" asked rairaiMela. "The Astarcheans have stopped firing. They seem to be pulling back."

"They are," said the Captain. "What in the name of the Eagle are they up to?"

She turned her attention back to the control console. The ship was becoming increasingly hard to control.

Suddenly the Kang raised the blaster raiAntala had given it and pointed it directly at her.

"Step away from that console," it commanded.

"I don't think you understand," said raiAntala. "This ship is in pretty poor shape. We've got to get her down."

"We're not landing in Astarche," said the Kang. "We're no longer under fire. That changes everything. The Princess here is the most valuable captive in the quadrant, and I have her."

"Don't be an idiot," said raiAntala.

"Oh no," sneered the Kang. "Be assured I won't be an idiot. You were the idiot when you gave me this blaster. You'd probably fetch a fair price yourself, but I've seen what you can do. You have to die right now." It ratcheted up the setting of the blaster all the way—several notches beyond "Lethal".

"You'll be making a big mistake if you pull that trigger," said raiAntala.

"I'll be making a bigger mistake if I don't," responded the Kang. Its lip curled in a determined leer, and there was a harsh crackling sound followed by the acrid stench of charred flesh. The Kang screamed and fell lifeless to the floor.

RaiAntala shrugged. "I told it it was making a mistake."

"What happened?" asked rairaiMela.

"RaiChinchers made a little modification to the blaster. We felt I shouldn't be without a firearm, but we were aware that it could easily be turned against me, so she reversed the polarity of the blast. It kills the person who fires it. I can reset the program from my transceiver—but obviously I wasn't going to give that dog a weapon it could use on me."

"Thank Dea for that. So we are finally in the clear?"

"Not quite. This tub is—if you'll excuse the expression—shot. I think I can get us down in one piece, but it's going to be touch and go."

"We can't follow them much further, Commander," said raiChinchi. "We're almost out of juice. I haven't enough power to launch a torpedo."

"Wait, they're slowing down," said Commander Carshalton. "Maybe they're out of juice too."

"Or maybe they're appalled at how far we've followed them and want to deal with us before they *are* out of juice. They must be carrying a lot more than we are."

"They need a lot more too, and——"

The *Silver Vixen* lurched violently, but not the way it had before, when it had been hit. It felt almost like a 'sucking' impact.

"What was that?" asked the Commander.

"They're grappling us," said raiChinchi. "They have us in a tractor beam. If they can pull us into the docking area, they can rip open this ship like a sardine can and board us. At that point I respectfully suggest suicide before they reach us."

"Can we resist?"

"We're resisting now, and still slipping toward the *Black Python* at a disgusting rate, but I can't pull us back at all much longer. We've nothing left to pull with."

"Do you know what?" said the Commander. "I don't think they've made a very smart move here. You said you can't launch a torpedo—but can't you just release something down the chute?"

"You mean——?"

"Exactly. Let them pull it to themselves."

"It is dangerous. Are you giving the order?"

"Certainly, madam Pilot. Destroy the Outlander."

"Permission to try something that may blow us to the Blessed Isles or save our lives?"

"Well, we're pretty much dead anyway, so why not?"

"All right. Here goes."

There was a few seconds' tense pause, and then the forescreens were suffused in glare as the *Black Python* exploded in silence.

"Well, if we do die at least we nailed the *Python*," said the Commander with satisfaction. "Greenies, where are you taking us?"

All screens were now glaring lividly, and warning bleeps were sounding. A digitized voice that sounded like a brunette librarian kept repeating:

"*Area unsafe, please withdraw—Area unsafe, please withdraw——*" until raiChinchi shut her off.

"Into the conflagration," she replied.

"The conflagration?"

"Yes. The torpedo I used is often vulgarly termed a disintegrator, but what it actually is, is a combustor."

"But you can't have combustion in the aethyr."

"Well, you can't have actual Fire, that is true, because she is sister to the element of Air and can't burn without her. But what combustion really is, is the reduction of tangible matter to its energy form. That is what we've done to the *Python*. We've killed her, and now we are trying to eat her."

"Eat her!"

"Yes, in a manner of speaking. We really have no energy left, so I am trying to harvest the combustion. Of course, the *Python* only produces a fraction of the energy of a sun, but she was a far bigger vessel than the *Vixen,* and I have us right in the heart of her combustion with all receptors open. Most of the energy is dispersing, but I am trying to harvest whatever we can and hoping we don't become part of the chain reaction."

"Could we?"

"Very easily. But that will be quicker and nicer than dying of cold and asphyxiation, which is what will happen if we run out of juice."

The monitors were already returning to normal. RaiChinchi switched the alert system back on.

"*Radiation decreasing—approaching safety level——*" intoned the digitized librarian.

"Good news, I take it," said the Commander.

"Yes, we aren't going to combust. Less-good news though: we didn't glean as much energy as I was hoping for, though to be honest we are lucky to have gotten any at all. I wanted to make for that sun and charge up properly, but we haven't enough to get there."

"What now?"

"Well, you're the Commander. The only recommendation I can give you is to put down on that planet." She indicated a very close body on the starboard monitor.

"Do you know what it is?"

"Yes, the *Python* was clearly making for it. I think they intended a landing. That's why they started grappling us. Atmospheric entry is a pretty vulnerable operation, and they couldn't risk us taking pot shots at them while they were engaged in it."

"But what g'doinking world is it?"

RaiChinchi flashed an apologetic grin. "I'm afraid it is Fearalya."

"That's good. A schizzie world and a dead ship by the time we get there, I suppose."

"Yes, ma'am. I can cloak the *Vixen* during approach and entry —which we really need to do—and I *think* I can slow our descent enough to stop us burning up from atmospheric friction. With a bit of luck, I can make a half-decent landing or at least a splashdown. But after that—well, the lights may be working or they may not. Any hope of take-off—even for short-distance planetside transit—is highly remote."

"Would it be pushing our luck too far to charge my blaster?"

"Under the circs, I think it's a risk worth taking."

"HAVE we made it?" asked rairaiMela.

"I think we can be cautiously optimistic, Your Highness," said the Captain. "We have come through the atmosphere without burning up: now all we have to do is get down onto *terra firma*."

"Where are we?"

"I have absolutely no idea. Only about half the instruments are working. There is land up ahead—big land. Looks like a continent to me. I am guessing it is probably a few hundred miles away. We are higher than it seems."

Suddenly the ship fell silent. Screens blanked. Needles flicked back to zero. And total darkness fell. RairaiMela stared into the darkness.

"What was that?"

"Power cut?" said the Captain.

"Are we out of juice?"

"No. I think that continent must be Cathria Maya."

"You mean—like the East in our own world?"

"Yes, exactly like that. Technics just don't work there."

"But the law of gravity does, I suppose."

"I am afraid so. We've really bought it this time. There's nothing more I can do." The Captain knelt in the darkness. "Rayati, my Princess. Hail to the sun in thee."

"Rayati, my Captain. May Dea bless and keep thee. May——" Her speech was cut short by an agonized scream. The Princess put her hands over her head, shrieking in sudden pain.

"RairaiMela—what is it?"

"My hair! It feels as if it's being pulled out by the roots!"

There was a lurch as if the ship's fall had stopped and it was bouncing upward. Both occupants were thrown about the cabin as the ship seemed to bounce again and again.

"Hold onto something!" ordered the Captain.

They were relatively gentle bounces and getting gentler, as if the ship were hitting something yielding, something that sloped downward and was letting the ship descend in ever decreasing bounces. But each time it bounced, the Princess clasped her head again and yelped in pain.

The monitors were dead, so it was impossible to see what was actually happening, but somehow, as in a dream, raiAntala could 'see', in the manner of hypnogogic images in the darkness, the ship bouncing down tightly stretched silver beams or wires.

Finally they seemed to hit something more solid, and with that last jarring impact the ship was still, and rairaiMela stopped clasping her head convulsively, but lay where she had last been thrown, unconscious.

The Captain struggled with the mechanical override to open the hatch. It gave, and her eyes were dazzled by strong sunlight.

"Rayati," said a strong but high-pitched voice. "Good afternoon to you."

"Rayati," replied the Captain, shielding her eyes with her hand and trying to see who or what it was that must be standing just outside the ship.

"Is the Princess all right?" asked the voice.

RaiAntala was cautious. Was this some kind of trick to discover if the Princess were aboard? "Princess?" she asked, a little vaguely.

"Yes, the Princess," said the voice. "That landing must have been a bit hard on her. I am sorry about that. It was the only way I could get you down safely."

"It was a bit bumpy," said raiAntala, taking the opportunity not to confirm any Princess.

"I don't mean that," said the voice. "I mean her hair. I had to use her hair to bring the ship down. Didn't you see?"

"Yes, yes—I did see. But what do you mean?"

"What do you think I mean? The hair of any maid symbolizes the rays of the Supernal Sun, but the hair of a Princess Imperial of the Solar Rayannic line—that is one of the strongest things in the universe."

"Not her physical hair?" said the Captain. This time her vagueness was genuine.

"Of course not her physical hair," said the voice a little impatiently. "Any more than that sun in the sky is the Supernal Sun Herself. But they are connected, naturally. Her royal and physical head must have felt it."

"The lady is asleep," said the Captain. "I think she needs to rest a little."

"Lady!" shouted the voice, screeching with laughter. "That was no lady, that was the Princess. How else could I have brought that metal boat down on her hair? No need to be coy with me. I am a friend, thank Dea. You could have fallen into very different hands, if you had not died."

"I thank you, ma'am."

"No need to 'ma'am' me, though you're welcome if you want to."

"I am sorry. My eyes are growing accustomed to the sudden light, but I fear I still cannot see you."

"Oh, I am sorry. I forgot about Westrennes." The place where the voice was coming from had seemed to the Captain no more than a sort of shimmering in the sunflood, but now that shimmer solidified and took on the shape of a small brunette in a yellow dress with matching gloves and shoes and a circlet about her head.

"Is that better?" she asked.

"Yes, I can see you now."

"Not too *chibi* for you? I could look grander if you like."

"No, no, please appear just as you are."

"Well, how I am is a mixture of my essence and your perception, I suppose. We can adjust either if we want to."

"It doesn't matter. Thank you so much for saving us."

"Oh, you are more than welcome. In any case, there was a touch of self-interest in it."

"Why so?"

"I don't want the dark ones to win. Nasty brutes. We are for the maidens. Life is much nicer with the maidens."

"Then you aren't a maiden?"

"Do I look like a maiden? Oh—I suppose I do rather. But that is because you do. I can look pretty much how you like."

"Captain——" The voice was weak, and it was the Princess's.

"RairaiMela!" The Captain rushed back into the ship.

"We're alive! What happened?"

"You saved the ship, Great Highness. My name is Aeriel, by the bye. I should have introduced myself before." A yellow fairy seemed to hover before the Princess.

"I dreamed I let the ship down gently with my hair."

"You did so, Your Highness; bless you. And I helped a little; bless me."

"Then I didn't dream it?"

"Oh yes—you dreamed it. Is 'dream' not your word for seeing without eyes?"

"Dreams usually are not real," said the Princess faintly.

"Is all you see with eyes true, and all you see without eyes untrue?"

"Not all, I suppose——"

"But perhaps you are better practised seeing with eyes—like the hen that has wings but prefers to walk?"

"Perhaps so, but in any case, thank you for rescuing us."

"Oh, but you did that, Great Highness. I only pointed the way a little."

"And we are in Cathria Maya, Aeriel-chei?"

"In the far-flung outreaches of the Pure Empire, ma'am. Far-flung and I fear but poor-defended."

"And no ships of the air like this will fly here?"

"No, indeed, ma'am, nor any like workings work their ways."

"Then I wonder how my translator can render your words to me and mine to you."

"It cannot, for a surety, ma'am, but we speak not with lips, though you move your lips, 'tis true, and make a sound between them--and a beguiling pretty sound it is, I dare observe—as is the custom of your kind. But for all, it is not by that sound, nor yet by any sound that comes, or seems to come, from you or me, that we understand each other."

"Seems like we're going to understand the other humans around here just fine," said the Captain.

"Hahee! When you say 'fine', you mean 'not fine'. Your speech is strange, but I understand it, and I can take you to a maiden who can help with understanding of the other maidens. She will give you food and shelter too. You do require food as maids do hereabouts?"

"From time to time, yes," replied the Captain. "But is this place far for my Princess to walk?"

"But half a mile, good Captain. I can walk it myself, and shall to bear you company, though I am not often one to tread feet upon the soil."

And so they walked in the sun-filled afternoon among tall trees and luxuriant undergrowth. They passed a cottage, burnt out and deserted, and a little way on, another in like condition, yet there seemed no sign of fire elsewhere among the woods.

"What has happened to these homes?" asked the Princess.

"The dark ones burned them out," replied Aeriel. "Though whether them that made their lives within fled first or were slain, I do not know. I do not know because I choose not. If you were to listen close you would hear what passed, I fancy; but I do not recommend it."

And taking this hint the Princess asked no more, and in deference to her sensibilities, neither did the Captain. And so they walked on amid sunshine and verdancy and jewel-bright flowers and death.

Soon they came to what had once been a village or a very small town. Some buildings still stood as burnt-out shells; others had been razed to the ground. Wells were filled in with boulders. Oddly, on the air floated the sound of a delicate wind chime. Aeriel led them toward the sound until they saw the glass ornament hanging from the charred lintel of what had once been a quaint little house. Or was it still? One saw the charred and empty lintel, and yet one also saw a sturdy oaken door in it. One saw the empty lot, and yet one also saw the house that had been there—a very odd house— like a small, round tower.

Aeriel knocked at the door that was or wasn't there and then stood aside for her companions to go in. She did not follow them.

Inside there was no ambiguity at all. They were in a round room with parchment-colored walls. Solid walls that cut out the light of the sun except where it streamed in through high-arched mullioned windows.

There were scrolls stacked in various places, some maps, and a large many-armed statue that cast her gentle gaze upon the room. Before her burned incense, and at the other side of the room was a low table with legs no more than six inches high and silken pillows set out around it. Upon it was a finely painted teapot and three small cups without handles made from eggshell china.

By the table, cross-legged and saffron-robed, sat an elderly maiden with her eyes closed. She seemed at first so deep in meditation that no sound they made could reach her outer ears. But then, though they were silent, she addressed them without opening her eyes.

"Welcome to my unworthy home. Will you do me the great honor of taking tea?"

The Princess made deep reverence, though the gesture was presumably outwardly unseen. "The honor is mine, gracious lady."

She approached the table and knelt upon a pillow, beckoning raiAntala to follow, which, making deep reverence, she did.

"The most honored Imperial Princess," said the elderly maiden, and, turning her head in raiAntala's direction, "the most noble Imperial Captain."

RaiAntala (perhaps for the first time since rairaiMela had known her) felt abashed, and said, "Well, honored lady, not exactly in my case."

"Did not your Princess appoint you, Captain?"

"Yes, ma'am."

"Then exactly."

"Thank you, ma'am."

"Don't thank me. You've nothing to thank me for. You may well be sorry you ever met me before too long. I am not being kind to you in accepting your captaincy. Indeed, it is not for me to accept or deny it. I am simply introducing a little clarity. There must be absolute clarity from now forward. The time wherein you indulged in ambiguity is passed. You saw this town?"

The Princess and the Captain touched their fingers to their foreheads and then to their chests.

"We saw it, ma'am," said the Princess.

"They fled, most of them, the townsmaidens, before the dark ones came. They burned the temple themselves so it might not be desecrated. They filled the wells and burned what crops they could not carry. And when they came, the dark ones burned the rest."

"And what of you, ma'am?"

"I stayed here. The dark ones can't see this place. I heard their noise and their vile words. It is all one to me."

"But how do you eat and drink, ma'am?"

"My needs are small, and Aeriel supplies them. But I am forgetting myself." She clapped her frail-looking hands. "Aeriel, tea for our guests, if you would be so good."

A figure who looked somewhat like a small girl in a white robe —like, perhaps, a very young temple-maiden—appeared and knelt to pour tea into the small, delicate cups. Her hands were translucent; one could see the teapot's painted cherry branches through them.

"We met a sprite called Aeriel," said the Princess. "She brought us to you."

"They are all Aeriel. They are not individuals like you, or you—or even me. Which reminds me. I haven't told you my name. They call me Elestre hereabouts. Or did, when there was anyone hereabouts."

"I am glad to meet you, Raya Elestre," said the Princess, making seated reverence. "I am Shuratil Liante Melenhe."

"Thank you, I know. And this is Captain FiaMartia Antala."

"Did Aeriel tell you about us?"

"No, I told them."

The tea was delicate and finely scented. The Princess wondered if Raya Elestre had such excellent tea every day among the ruins. As if she had spoken the question, Raya Elestre answered:

"It is the last of the excellent crop from Rahilla. I was saving it for you."

"You knew we were coming."

"Of course. I know she who sent you."

"With respect, ma'am," said the Captain, "no one sent us. I have tried to explain that to the Astarcheans."

"I did not say *you* knew she who sent you. I said I did."

"We stole the *Silver Vixen* of our own free will. We put out to aethyr by our own choice."

"As it was foreordained you should."

"Every authority on Sai Herthe would have stopped us from leaving, and it was our own intention to return."

"But you did not. Instead you traversed half a galaxy."

"The reasons for that, ma'am, were purely accidental."

"They were not. You saw a ship. A ship that was not there. And rather than surrender, you parted the curtain of the unknown——"

"A ship that was not there. What do you know of that, ma'am?"

"It is of no importance. You parted the curtain of the unknown. Had you not been the hero who knows not what fear is, you would have turned back to Sai Herthe."

"'The hero who knows not what fear is'. You make me sound like something from a fairy tale."

"The pure Forms those tales recount of: are they not here among us every day? Yet how many dare embody her Form in all its purity? You do, honored Captain. That is why more mundane people have found you so difficult. The string that is tuned to perfection sounds discordant to the strings that are tuned more loosely."

"You are kind, ma'am, but I am far from perfect."

"As are we all, or else we should not be here. A clock may be broken and begrimed yet still tell perfect time, when other clocks are a moment slow or fast. And so you parted the curtain and set forth across immeasurable space, like the maid who sought the well at the world's end, or the ship that would sail west of the sunset.

"You fought the great boar that guarded the way, and you came with your crew to Ranyam Astarche. And now your crew is scattered. One part remains in Astarche, where a new falsehood has arisen. One part has slain the python that was mother of the boar, and will arrive at the land of the Barbarian. And you have come to this place, which, although, in vulgar terms, it lies on the same world as Astarche, is, counted in the true leagues that no stick can measure, further from Astarche than is your own Ranyam."

"Then all my children are alive?" said the Princess.

"All live, Highness, and all are in mortal danger," said Raya Elestre. "A battle is upon you now that is greater than Astarche or Cathria, greater than Fearalya or the false but golden empire of Esterline."

"But if the *Python* is destroyed, ma'am, then the Kang are all but defeated."

"The Kang are no more than pawns upon this board. Your Captain, I think, knows whereof I speak. The battle is with darkness itself, even as the battle of Noonday Night."

The Princess blanched at the mention of that terrible day, which, although more than three millennia ago, is branded on every Herthelan heart as the most terrible day in history.

"Is—is even Sai Herthe at risk?" she asked, hardly daring to listen to the answer.

"If the evil is not defeated, there is nothing it will not encompass."

"Tell us what to do, and we'll do it," said raiAntala.

"The first thing to do, honored Captain, is to sleep."

"We are strong and we are ready. This is no time for sleeping."

"After that tea, dear Captain, you will sleep, I assure you, and sleep long. And in your sleep you will regain all your strength, and also I will teach you.

"For every fragment of that strength, and of that teaching, you will need for the trials that lie ahead."

END OF THE FIRST BOOK

Cast of Characters

List of significant characters in *The Flight of the Silver Vixen*

SILVER VIXEN PERSONNEL

Princess Melenhe Celestina Viktorya li'Caerepurh Liante (Princess Mela, rairaiMela, blonde, Estrenne): The highest-ranking of the *Silver Vixen's* crew, being a Princess of the Blood Imperial.

Antala Fiamartia (raiAntala, brunette, Estrenne): Leader of the Road Angels; Captain of the *Silver Vixen.*

(Cdr.) Claralin Carshalton (raiClaralin, brunette, Westrenne): Second-in-command of the Road Angels; raiAntala's rival for leadership.

Chirenchihara Reteliyanhe (raiChinchi, brunette Estrenne): RaiAntala's best friend; Pilot of the *Silver Vixen,* and technical genius.

(Lt.) Evelynn Appelbeam (raiEvelynn, brunette, Westrenne): The youngest of the *Silver Vixen* brunettes.

Charmian Kerrice (raiCharmian, blonde, mixed ethnicity, Estrenne/Westrenne): School friend of the Princess.

Estrelle Moorland (raiEstrelle, blonde, Westrenne): The youngest of the *Silver Vixen* blondes.

Sharan (blonde, Westrenne): Senior maidservant/waitress aboard the *Silver Vixen.*

Sulannie ('Lannie, blonde, Westrenne): Junior maidservant/waitress aboard the *Silver Vixen.*

OTHER HERTHELANS

Fs. Anna Candret (brunette, Estrenne): Fleetsoldier on guard duty at Ushasti Fleet-Base.

Fs. Velenthe (brunette, Westrenne): Fleetsoldier on guard duty at Ushasti Fleet-Base.

Ray' Shuratil Liante (brunette, Estrenne): Hereditary Aethyr-Vikhar (Naval Space Commander) for the Ushasti region; the brunette-mother of Princess Melenhe.

Alinda Maxentia (brunette, Westrenne): Probationary member of the Road Angel gang.

ASTARCHEANS

Queen Ephranaria (deceased, brunette): Former Queen of Astarche, killed along with her court and elder daughters.

Queen Ashhevala III (blonde): The youngest and only surviving daughter of Queen Ephranaria; current Queen of Astarche.

Lady Telarmine (brunette): Vizier to Queen Ephranaria and Queen Ashhevala.

Commander Zhendel (brunette): Naval intelligence officer stationed in the Linton district.

Lt. Machirta (brunette): Cdr. Zhendel's aide.

Lady Deranyin (blonde): Highest-ranking blonde of Linton Village.

Miss Menender (blonde): Innkeeper of the Red Dragon at Linton.

Sindeline Menender (brunette): Daughter of Miss Menender.

Matri Luculla (blonde): Priestess of the Temple at Linton.

Raya Shunderlin (brunette): The Vikhar (military area-commander) for the Astarchean capital, Astarcheana.

Capt. Chavran (brunette): Member of the Royal Guard; niece of Raya Shunderlin.

Lihashte Chavran, Schionte Tennara, Tivrate Ariet: Three brunette schoolgirls encountered by Capt. Antala.

ALIENS
(Schizomorphs from male/female races)

Kang Shahtha (mascûl): Captain of the *Black Boar;* leader of the Kang pirates.

Kang Avankh (mascûl): Captain of the *Black Python;* successor to Kang Shahtha.

Lady Entresne Selvar (femīn): Ambassadress of the Chenri Confederation (Fearalya).

Thirin (mascûl): Aide to Lady Selvar.

Sknetin (mascûl): Secret Service agent of the United Republics (Fearalya).

CATHRIANS

Raya Elestre (blonde): An anchoress and mystic.

Ariel: A/several air spirit/s.

Glossary
Of words and linguistic usages

Aethyr: The fifth, immaterial, element, from which the four material elements are derived. Wherever in cosmic manifestation no material element is manifested, the immaterial element must exist. Hence the term "aethyr" is also used for what Tellurians term "space", since empty space cannot exist.

Athamë: The state of being out of **thamë**; ritually impure.

Capitalization: In this book we capitalize words more freely than is currently the custom in English. This is a way of indicating in English the higher linguistic honor given to ranks, titles, functions, and other elements of Form in both **Herthelan Westrenne** and Astarchean.

Chalwë: Military term of salutation, also used for the acknowledgement of orders.

Chandra: A hoverbike made by Chandra-Alarente of Esterquelle, Novarya.

Chei: As suffix to a first name or surname, the normative honorific (like Miss/Mr), much more formal than the **rai** prefix but not deeply honorific like -chenya. "Miss" is used in the book to indicate Westrenne (as opposed to Estrenne) usage.

Chelan: The child-bearing **intemorphic** sex, colloquially called "blonde" because light hair is a secondary sexual characteristic.

Chenkireet: Rabbit-like creature with hands and rudimentary powers of imitative speech.

Ehr chalwë: A more ceremonial form of **chalwë**.

Enormate: Literally, outside the Norm, or proper ordering of things, but not as extreme as **athamë**. Usually roughly equivalent to "rude".

Femīn: Female creature of a **schizomorphic** species, including, but not limited to, women.

Femīnil: Of the rule, or dominance, of the feminine principle and/or female beings in a **schizomorphic** society; "matriarchal".

Fora: An equal-armed cross imposed upon a circle with the arms extending beyond the circle, an ancient religious symbol.

G'doinker/G'doinking: This is not a curse word (which do not exist in the Tellurian manner among **intemorphic** peoples). A loose translation might be "fool/foolish". G'doink is actually onomatopoeic of a harsh and clumsy noise, but implying gracelessness, discordance, and social disruption (cf. the Tellurian expression "to drop a clanger"). It is considered quite rough and is more taboo than it sounds to Western Tellurian sensibilities because it implies a rupture of the sacred social harmony (**thamë**).

Gnati: Know, or understand. An archaic and literary term, but also used as slang.

Haiela: The First—priestly and intellectual—Estate, or a member of that Estate.

Haya: Originally this was a ritual word of considerable spiritual significance. Today it survives mainly in the battle invocation "Haya Vikhë"—and, by extension, is used as an encouraging cheer in combat and other sports. Cf. **Raya**.

Herthe, Sai: 1. The Angel of home and hearth-fire, whose day is celebrated in midwinter. 2. The homeworld of the Caeren Empire.

Herthelan: Belonging to the planet Sai **Herthe**.

Herthelan Westrenne: Language of many Western nations of Sai **Herthe**, spoken by the *Silver Vixen's* crew.

Human: The term human is used in the book to mean what it means in everyday English speech, i.e., "one of our species", "a normative sentient being". The main characters of the book are not human in the more technical sense of being Tellurian *homo sapiens*. The **schizomorphic** beings, whom the main characters regard as non-human, are actually closer to being human in the Tellurian sense.

Intemorphic: Of a humanoid species having two feminine sexes.

Khindi: Child, the melinic form; the chelanic form would be khinda.

Mascûl: A male creature of a **schizomorphic** species including, but not limited to, men.

Masculik: Of the rule, or dominance, of the masculine principle and/or male beings in a **schizomorphic** society; "patriarchy".

Melin: The non-child-bearing **intemorphic** sex, colloquially called "brunette" because dark hair is a secondary sexual characteristic.

Paccia: [pron. paxia] The Fourth Estate, servants.

Paxit: [pron. paxt] A member of the Fourth Estate, a servant.

Quirridip: Slang term meaning a fun-loving, frivolous, and light-headed person from the nation of Quirinelle.

Rai: [pron. rye] As a prefix to a first name, this is a very informal honorific. Using the first name alone with no honorific at all would sound infantile, so young, informal groups tend to use informal honorifics. Doubling intensifies it, so Princess Melenhe is called rairaiMela—probably about the least formal way a Princess could be addressed.

Raihir: Empire.

Raihira: The Second—aristocratic and warrior—Estate, or a member of that Estate.

Raihiranya: Empress in the line of Sai Rayanna.

Raihiralan: An adjective with many meanings, but as used in this book refers to a knightly, or warrior, ethos comparable to European chivalry or Japanese bushido. Also used more loosely for the modern "upper class" and its characteristic manner.

Ranyam: Realm, Queendom.

Raya: Lady in the "lord" sense. Also the Angel of the Sun. As an interjection, it is a cheer word, like "yay!"

Rayalini: Literally "ladies of noble rank". A polite form of address to a group of people.

Rayati: Salutation meaning "Hail to the Sun (within you)". Idiomatically, one "gives", rather than "says", rayati.

Rayati Raihiranya: Salutation meaning "Hail to the Empress, the Sun incarnate".

Rayin: Queen.

Schizomorphic: Of a humanoid species having a male and a female sex.

Sushuri: The Angel of Love. Without capitalization, the cosmic principle of love.

Thamë: The Golden Order or fundamental Divine Harmony of Being, believed to be the foundation of both human law and the laws of nature, and to rule everything from a blade of grass to the movement of the galaxies. Humans are the only beings with the free will to act out of thamë, and have a special responsibility to maintain the Golden Order.

Vaht'he: Insane, lacking in ordinary caution or common sense. Originally meaning possessed by a divine Intelligence or Inspiration whose wisdom is folly to this world.

Vikhë: The Angel of Battle. Without capitalization, the cosmic principle of valor or combat.

Vikhail: The eternal war of light against darkness.

Vikheli: 1. A member of any armed Service. 2. A **vikhelic** art or discipline.

Vikhelic: Pertaining to the battle Angel, Sai Vikhë; martial.

Werdë: Personal fate, karma.

Yerthing: Avatar (in the original Sanskrit sense of an earthly incarnation of a spiritual being).

CPSIA information can be obtained
at www.ICGtesting.com
Printed in the USA
FSHW011559020821
83752FS

9 780615 464794